PURO ARTE

POSTMILLENNIAL POP

General Editors: Karen Tongson and Henry Jenkins

Spreadable Media: Creating Value and Meaning in a Networked Culture
Henry Jenkins, Sam Ford, and Joshua Green

Puro Arte: Filipinos on the Stages of Empire
Lucy Mae San Pablo Burns

Puro Arte

Filipinos on the Stages of Empire

Lucy Mae San Pablo Burns

NEW YORK UNIVERSITY PRESS
New York and London

NEW YORK UNIVERSITY PRESS
New York and London
www.nyupress.org

References to Internet Websites (URLs) were accurate at the time of writing.
Neither the author nor New York University Press is responsible for URLs that
may have expired or changed since the manuscript was prepared.

LIBRARY OF CONGRESS CATALOGING-IN-PUBLICATION DATA
San Pablo Burns, Lucy Mae.
Puro arte : Filipinos on the stages of empire / Lucy Mae San Pablo Burns.
p. cm. — (Postmillennial pop)
Includes bibliographical references and index.
ISBN 978-0-8147-4443-7 (cloth : alk. paper)
ISBN 978-0-8147-2545-0 (pbk. : alk. paper)
ISBN 978-0-8147-0813-2 (ebook)
ISBN 978-0-8147-4449-9 (ebook)
1. Filipino Americans—Ethnic identity. 2. Ethnicity—Political aspects—Philippines.
3. Performing arts—Political aspects—Philippines. 4. Performing arts—Political
aspects—United States. 5. Popular culture—Political aspects—Philippines. 6. Popular
culture—Political aspects—United States. 7. Nationalism—Social aspects—Philippines.
8. Imperialism—Social aspects—Philippines. 9. Philippines—Relations—United States.
10. United States—Relations—Philippines. I. Title.
E184.F4S29 2012
305.89'921073—dc23   2012024950

New York University Press books are printed on acid-free paper,
and their binding materials are chosen for strength and durability.
We strive to use environmentally responsible suppliers and materials
to the greatest extent possible in publishing our books.

Manufactured in the United States of America
c 10 9 8 7 6 5 4 3 2 1
p 10 9 8 7 6 5 4 3 2 1

CONTENTS

ACKNOWLEDGMENTS

I must begin by expressing my profound gratitude to the artists, cultural workers, performers, and many others who occupy the multiple stages of this book. Your labor has given me much to think about and engage with. I remain plagued by the limits of my own analysis but hopeful that what I begin here will be enough to generate further thoughts on, and surely much more complex readings of, Filipino/a performance. I thank Alleluia Panis, joel b tan, Christine Bacareza Balance, and Olivia Malabuyo for allowing me to run with *puro arte.*

My interest in Filipino performance was first galvanized by the social protest theater of Sining Bayan. I thank Ermena Vinluan, Abe Toribio, and the late Helen Toribio for their generosity and kindness. Their years of political work marked by disappearances, loss, and death did not taint their willingness to share their KDP stories and materials. My work with Roberta Uno, New WORLD Theater, and the Uno Archive Collection of Plays by Asian American Women started me on the pursuit of Sining Bayan. Where it got me may be quite different from where I started, but they have all made a lasting impact on my writing. Roberta provided opportunities and was the first to recognize the potential in my work. I am grateful to have been a part of her vision of a new world. I must also thank my Filipina faculty mentor and friend at the University of Massachusetts, Sally Habana-Hafner; her work with local immigrant and refugee communities in Amherst, Massachusetts, made such a difference to many of us. I have enjoyed seeing where Sunaina Maira, Cathy Schlund-Vials, and Anita Mannur, collaborators in building Asian American Studies in the Five Colleges, have taken the field of Asian American Studies.

I began this project when I was a University of California President's Postdoctoral Fellow at UC–Santa Cruz. My two years at UCSC were hugely formative. The Feminist Studies Department was welcoming and encouraging, beginning with Bettina Aptheker. Judy Yung kindly agreed to be my faculty mentor during the first year of the fellowship. During my time at UCSC, I experienced the support of a robust and vibrant feminist presence, with colleagues such as Gina Dent, Angela Davis, and Carla Freccero. The few people whom I could have a conversation with about Filipino Studies and Asian American performance included Felicity Schaeffer-Grabiel, Karen Yamashita, and Neferti Tadiar. Neferti is and continues to be an inspirational mentor in every way.

At UCLA, I am thankful to be a part of the Department of Asian American Studies. Colleagues such as Purnima Mankekar, Victor Bascara, Grace Hong, Thu-huong Nguyen, and Keith Camacho keep my commitment to Asian American Studies aspirational. I look forward to our continued collaboration. Min Zhou, Don Nakanishi, Cindy Fan, Jinqi Ling, King-kok Cheung, and Lane Hirabayashi kindly guided me through my status as junior faculty. In World Arts and Cultures, I enjoyed the support of Susan Foster, David Rousseve, and Cheng-Chieh Yu. I particularly appreciated David Rousseve's leadership and his strong support at a time of transition for the department. Kathleen McHugh was a source of sage advice. I must also thank the Department of Women's Studies for their enthusiastic welcome of me as a "0 percenter."

Barbara Gaerlan, Eloisa Borah, Meg Thornton, and Melany de la Cruz encourage me with their tireless dedication to Filipino American Studies. Don Nakanishi and David Yoo of the Asian American Studies Center and Barbara Gaerlan of the Center for Southeast Asian Studies provide crucial support to Filipino Studies at UCLA. The inspired teachings of Michael Salman, Victor Bascara, Nenita Domingo, and Damon Woods create a community for/of Critical Filipino Studies at UCLA. Ever-so-energetic students keep alive the Campaign for Filipino Studies at UCLA and give meaning to the everyday labor at the university.

I am equally fortunate to have met Tracy Buenavista, Joanna Poblete, Denise Cruz, Lorena Alvarado, P. J. Nadal, Paul Ocampo, Jolie Chea, Vivian Wu, Michael Atienza, April Joy Limayo, Diana Aquino, and Stephanie Santos at UCLA. They embody the academy as a place of transformation. I want to thank Lorena Alvarado, Liza Anulao, and Sarah Gonzaga for their research assistance.

The UC President's Postdoctoral Fellowship and the Woodrow Wilson/Andrew Mellon Career Enhancement Fellowship for Junior Faculty provided me with much-needed time off to complete this book. Alicia Arrizon was a terrific faculty mentor for the Junior Faculty Fellowship, and I am honored that she continues to provide counsel. Other sources of funding include UCLA Faculty COR Grants, UCLA Senate Research Enabling Grants, a Center for the Study of Women's Faculty Development Grant, and UCLA Asian American Studies Center Faculty Research Support Grants. Portions of this work received valuable feedback through workshop settings. I thank the following colleagues who took time out of their own work to share their observations: Grace Hong, Purnima Mankekar, Sondra Hale, Lisa Lowe, Thu-huong Nguyen, Deb Vargas, Paul Ocampo, Preeti Sharma, Lorena Alvarado, Kathleen McHugh, Laura Kang, Keith Camacho, Setsu Shigematsu, Tammy Ho, Caroline Tushabe, Jody Kim, Mariam Lam, Felicity Schaeffer, Christine Balance, Joanna Poblete, and Mel Wong. Extended feedback from Rachel Lee, Victor Bascara, and Martin Manalansan helped shape the direction of this manuscript. I also want to thank Catherine Ceniza Choy and the Critical Filipino Studies Collective at UC–Berkeley for inviting me to give a talk very early into the reworkings of the chapter on *Miss Saigon*. I appreciate Adria Imada and Priya Srinivasan for graciously including me on a panel at the 2008 American Studies conference where I presented an early version of my introduction. Mariam Lam gave smart, useful comments on chapter 4. Under the recommendation of David Román and Kathleen McHugh, I was invited to participate in the USC-UCLA joint junior faculty workshop. My presentation, which became chapter 2, benefited from an elegant response from Viet Nguyen, and generative comments and questions posed by David Roman and Karen Tongson. Portions of this chapter are published in *Dance Research Journal* 40.2 (Winter 2008): 23-40. Thank you to Laura Kang, Jeanne Scheper, and the Department of Women Studies at UC Irvine for inviting me to be a part of their Keywords Interdisciplinary Conversations. It was fun to play with the word "movement" through Sining Bayan.

This work was enriched by several gatherings on Asian American Theater and Performance Studies: "Asian/Asian American Performance and the Body: A Symposium," organized by Josephine Lee, Ananya Chatterjea, and Maija Brown at the University of Minnesota; "Bodies of Spectacle," organized by Esther Kim Lee and Yutian Wong at the University of Illinois–Urbana Champaign; and "Transnational Imaginaries in Asian and Asian American Performance: A Symposium in Shanghai," organized by Priya Srinivasan, with the support of University of California Riverside's Department of Dance Studies, held in Shanghai, China. Josephine Lee and Karen Shimakawa have been the most giving of senior colleagues. Over the years, Esther Kim Lee, Sean Metzger, Sansan Kwan, Priya Srinivasan, and Yutian Wong have been constant in their commitment to Asian American performance. Our interactions have enriched me.

A cadre of Filipino/Filipino American Studies scholars across the Pacific engage the field with dynamism: Robyn Rodriguez, Allan Isaac, Neferti Tadiar, Rick Bonus, Christine Balance, Robert G. Diaz, Peter Chua, Rowena

X   << ACKNOWLEDGMENTS

Tomaneng, Maria Josephine Barrios LeBlanc, Dylan Rodriquez, Linda Maram, Joan Rondilla, Gladys Nubla, Augusto Espiritu, Eric Reyes, Sunny Vergara, Francisco Benitez, Pearlie Baluyut, Nerissa Balce, Fidelito Cortes, Jeffrey Santa Ana, Richard Chu, Jody Blanco, Sarita See, Theo Gonzalves, Vernadette Gonzales, Tracy Buenavista, and Theresa Suarez. I enjoyed "Philippine Palimpsests: Contemporary Scholarship on Filipino and Filipino Diasporic Studies," organized by Martin Manalansan and Augusto Espiritu. They created an exciting gathering where we learned more about each other's wonderful research on Philippine-related topics. Having Robyn Rodriguez on my side emboldens me. Martin Manalansan and Allan Isaac exemplify grace rare in this line of work; their support over the years has sustained me. To them I am much obliged.

I have learned much from Oscar Campomanes's writings, which have been formative to the direction of contemporary Filipino American Studies. He has kindly introduced me to a vibrant group of scholars. Manila is now a place of return thanks to friends like Roland Tolentino, John Jack G. Wigley, Gary Devilles, Ferdie Lopez, Jay Robillos, and Delan Robillos, who renewed my relationship to going back home. Nicanor Tiongson, Preachy Legasto, Jing Hidalgo, Bien Lumbera, Virgilio Almario, Jina Umali, and Dean Alegado generously met with me on different occasions and always provided helpful information. I look forward to seeing my friend Jennifer Hagedorn, who makes visits to Manila meaningful.

The works of Christine Balance, Theo Gonzalves, Sarita See, and Martin Manalansan affirm critical approaches to Filipino diasporic performance. My dearest of all the *kasamas*, Maria Josephine Barrios Le Blanc, stands firm in the political necessity of Filipino performance, those who create it, and write about it—*sama ako sa rebolusyon mo Ate Joi*.

I am grateful to collaborators who expand my potential with their trust and openness to create and make art together: Alleluia Panis of KulArts, Inc., Leilani Chan of TeAda Productions, Kelly Tsai, R. Z. Linmark, David Rousseve, and Cíndy García. The following individuals and arts organizations have also provided opportunities for this scholarly research to take on other forms and reach diverse audiences: Dipankar Mukerjhee and Meena Natarajan of Pangea World Theater in Minneapolis, Jilly Canizares of FilAm Arts in Los Angeles, Bobby Garcia of Atlantis Production in Manila, East West Players in Los Angeles, Theater Ma-yi in New York, Kuusela Hilo of Bayan USA, Bev Tang and Terrie Cervas of SiGAW, Melissa Roxas and Apollo Victoria of Habi Arts, Jon Lawrence Rivera of Playwrights Arena, Mia Katigbak of the National Asian American Theater Company, Ralph Peña and Jorge Ortol of the Mayi Theater Ensemble, Antoine Diel, Leilani Chan, Ova Saopeng,

Laurence Padua, Reme Grefalda, Gina Osterloh, Jennifer Wofford, joel b. tan, and Jason Magabo Perez. They and their work are sources of information and inspiration.

Claudia Castañeda's editorial support came at a crucial time in the writing of this book. With Anne Pelligrini's help, my manuscript came to NYU Press's attention. Eric Zinner found a place for this book alongside other Filipino Studies–related works. Ciara McLaughlin was reassuring with her replies to my many queries. They found the smartest anonymous reviewers. My manuscript took the shape of a more coherent book because of the invaluable feedback from two anonymous readers. Being in Karen Tongson's and Henry Jenkin's Postmillenial Pop Series pushes this book's promise. Despina P. Gimbel and the team of editors at NYU Press deserve much thanks for the care they put into copyediting this book.

Maraming salamat to Alleluia Panis, who shared materials on early POMO Festivals. Thank you to Lea Salonga, to Monique Wilson, and most especially to Aura Deva for sharing their experiences of *Miss Saigon*. Bobby Garcia and Dong Alegre gave crucial history to how Filipinos got to *Miss Saigon*. Jon Rivera, Joan Almedilla, Jennifer Paz, and Jenni Selma and their collaborative piece *Road to Saigon* imparted new insights to chapter 4. Helpful staff from various archival sources paved the way for a pleasant research experience: Uno Collection of Plays by Asian American Women at the W. E. B. Du Bois Library at the University of Massachusetts at Amherst, the Performing Arts Library in the New York Public Library System, and the East West Players archive at UC Santa Barbara.

I wish to acknowledge those who have helped secure images used in this book: Rukshana Singh and Abe Ferrer at Visual Communications, Jennifer Cartwright of Cameron Mackintosh Ltd., Bobby Garcia of the Atlantis Productions, Harry Wong III of Kumu Kahua Theater, Cheyne Gallarde, Jessica Hagedorn, and R. Z. Linmark. I would like to thank the following for granting permission to reprint the figures in this book: for figures 1.1 and 1.2, Duke University Rare Book, Manuscript, and Special Collections Library; for figure 1.3, Alleluia Panis, Kul Arts Inc.; for figure 2.1, the Missouri History Museum, St. Louis; for figure 2.2, Visual Communications Photographic Collections; for figures 3.1, 3.2, and 3.3, Atlantis Productions; for figures 4.1 and 4.2, Cameron Mackintosh Ltd.; and for figures C.1 and C.2, Kumu Kahua Productions.

Jessica Hagedorn and R. Z. Linmark share so much, show me the path, inspire whole new worlds, giggles and all along the way. I am in awe of their creativity and their generosity.

Zack and Allan have done so much to help me make sense of Manila during several research trips. In doing so, they may, indeed, have accomplished a little bit of the impossible. On these trips, during shared meals, Harry Potter movies, Lovie Poe, MRT rides, and as we crossed footbridge crossings for our lives, their remarkable musings informed this work.

I am ever so lucky to benefit from Laura Kang, Gina Dent, and Geeta Patel—from their sharp minds, expansive intellect, and committed feminist politics. Even at times unbeknownst to them—in between points at the tennis court, consultations about which yoga pose for which ailment, and what green tea for shifting taste buds—their critical voices always provoke.

Years of friendship and "time pass" with Karen Yamashita, David Rousseve, Conor McTeague, Karima Robinson, Iris Schmeisser, Keith Camacho, Bishnupriya Ghosh, Bhaskar Sarkar, Anindyo Roy, Jon Beller, Raka Ray, Saba Mahmood, Chaumtoli Huq, and Kath Weston are years of pleasure in being in a community of thinkers. Writing days with Laurence Padua distracted me from the pain of producing pages. He kindly engaged with my insignificant wonderings. Echoes of his attentive listening are in these pages.

Christine Balance Bacareza brings openness and much thought to everything she encounters. Her support gives courage to this work. I have gained so much from Sansan Kwan's careful and insightful readings. My writing group with Sansan and Priya Srinivasan nourished my critical thinking and assured my writing. With them, this book finds its confidence.

Many times in the process of completing this project, and other works, I have had to turn to Priya Srinivasan and Cindy García to give me reasons to keep going. They helped me make sense of my own thoughts. If this book is a long walk, each word is a step that Cindy took with me. Priya applied her not-so-secret super powers of honing in on what this book is about; she has also kept me honest about why we do what we do. In sharing our writing, especially in its most raw form, they have shown me the depths of friendship.

Salamats to my family for their unconditional love. My parents, William Burns and Purificacion San Pablo Burns, allowed my pursuit of higher education. I think about their brave choices, made long ago, every day. Glenn, Ana Liza, and Mary Grace Burns make me feel lucky and always with company; they are the coolest siblings. They have also helped me directly by providing housing and food at different stages of this research work. I am most excited at the possibility that one of these days, my nieces and nephews—Logan, Brooke, Ethan, Tavis, Amihan, and Tala—might read this book. I look forward to their questions and their own thoughts about the world. Auntie Kavita Arondekar and Uncle Ramakant Arondekar give me so much love, making Bandra and Bombay a home I look forward to returning to every year. In Los Angeles, Thomas Holden, Priya Jaikumar, and Meha Holden transformed the way we spend our Sundays.

Each thought that made it into a sentence, upon which a paragraph was crafted, that became pages upon pages following this acknowledgment, received careful attention from Anjali Arondekar. Anjali provided critical feedback, close readings, meals, and other forms of love. I am thankful for her patience sitting through countless shows and as I wobbled through to the end of this book. Our every day for the past twelve years has been a shared life of *puro arte, desipina* version.

Putting on a Show

"*Puro arte lang iyan*" ("She's just putting on a show"). This is a phrase I heard often as a child growing up in Olongapo City. I can still hear my aunt's dismissive tone as she brushes aside my complaint as mere exaggeration. My protestation—she has cut my hair too short—is read as theatrical, superficial, and hyperbolic. To be called out for being *puro arte* is to be questioned about one's veracity and authenticity. Another variation is "*O tingnan mo, puro arte talaga*" ("Just look at her put on a show"). This version highlights the attention-seeking element of *puro arte*, directing notice to the performing body, already perceived to be overacting. What compels the speaker's admonition is the body's performative extravagance, a spectacle making that must be disciplined, reined in. To be called out for being *puro arte* at once exposes the performing subject's propensity for histrionics and puts her in her place for showing off. It is a complex construction that foregrounds the overdramatics of performance precisely to make light of it.

Yet, to be *puro arte* is to strategically refuse unmediated or clear-cut expression. The invocation of *puro arte* also carries an acknowledgment, almost an admirable recognition, of the theatrics at play. Putting on a show calls for an awareness of the labor of artful expression, of the creative efforts required to make something out of nothing. Furthermore, *puro arte* expresses an appreciation of the gall, the guts, and the sheer effort needed to put on such a display. Such a dual structure of *puro arte* is at work, for example, in playwright/writer Glecy Atienza's description of Filipinas who are routinely read as *maarte* (fussy, particular, demanding); she writes, "*Kaya pala mukhang maarte ay dahil may mga di masabi* [She is overacting precisely because there are things she cannot say]" (xii). For Atienza, Filipinas deploy *puro arte* as a mode of self-presentation to exceed their erasure as subjects. Through their exaggerated flair and ostentation, they appear as difficult subjects who press against the accepted norms of gender and performance.

Puro arte, translated from Spanish into English, means "pure art." However, in Filipino, as mentioned above, *puro arte* performs a much more ironic function, gesturing rather to the labor of overacting, histrionics, playfulness, and purely over-the-top dramatics. In this book, *puro arte* functions as an episteme, as a way of approaching the Filipino/a performing body at key moments in U.S.-Philippine imperial relations. I am inspired here by the creative "flippin'" of poet/performance artist joel b. tan in his poem "ignacio—in 2 parts": "seguro in spanish means surely. / seguro in tagalog means probably" (15).[1] Like tan, I perform an appropriative act that considers and highlights the playful and productive possibilities of *puro arte* as an embodiment of the Philippines' multiple colonial histories. The many uses of the term point to its complex and at times seemingly contradictory referentiality: *puro arte* is superficial and overstated as it is creative and risky. In turning to *puro arte* as an epistemology for the Filipino/a performing body, I have no desire to discipline or question the term's authenticity. Rather, my partiality is toward *puro arte*'s recognition of the effort to be performative, of the creative labor devoted to making a spectacle. *Puro arte*'s emphasis on the labor of theatricality is mined here for its potentialities in alternative forms of political and cultural expression. *Puro arte*'s ironic workings are brilliantly illustrated in a play such as Jessica Hagedorn's *Dogeaters*, as well as in the political aspirations of Sining Bayan's social protest theater. In both locations, *puro arte*'s valuing of indirect expression, of laboring to articulate politics in ways that may not be familiar, shines. To be *puro arte* is to take risks in forms of political and artistic participation. As the imaginary curtain parts on this book, several questions become central: When it comes to Filipinos and performance, what is all the drama about? What are the various sites/stages on which Filipinos perform, and what politics do they engender? And last but not least, what is the "world creating power" of the Filipino/a performing body?[2]

This book situates Filipino/a performing bodies within the contexts of nation building and community formation, and highlights the imbrication of Filipino/a racialization with histories of colonialism and imperialism. More broadly, the present work tracks the emergence of the Filipino/a performing body as it negotiates key historical events: the U.S. acquisition of the Philippines as a colony in the late nineteenth century; the dawn of Philippine independence (1920s-1930s); the tumultuous years of the Martial Law (1972-1981); and the closure of U.S. military bases in the Philippines at the end of the twentieth century. I trace the Filipino/a performing body across various sites, which include the 1904 St. Louis World's Fair, early American plays about the Philippines, the Filipino patron in the U.S. taxi dance halls, theatrical performances about the Martial Law, and the phenomenon of Filipino/a actors in *Miss Saigon*. In so doing, my project conjoins and centers the history of the Philippines with U.S.-based race relations and discourses of globalization. Throughout the book, the Filipino/a performing body appears equally as a sign/object and as a laboring body, produced and producing within an uneven global cultural and economic system. The very term "Filipino/a performing body" is mobilized as an indicator of both embodied representations of "Filipinos" and of Filipino/a performance practices on various theatrical and political stages.

Within these varied sites of performance—the World's Fair of 1904, early-twentieth-century American theater, U.S. taxi dance halls, anti–Martial Law protest performances and plays, and global productions of *Miss Saigon*—the Filipino/a performing body exhibits the "twin effects of bodily display and disappearance" (Pollock 3). It is both spectacularly visible and invisible, cast as it is within the triangulations of U.S.-Philippine relations, Filipino nationalisms, and globalization. Michel Foucault's notion of emergence, "the moment of arising," is most appropriate to invoke here. "Emergence," writes Foucault, "is always produced in a particular state of forces," in a "relationship of forces" (376). To mark the Filipino/a performing body's emergence, its "eruption, [its] leap from the wings to center stage" is not to fix its origins within specific sites of display. Instead, *Puro Arte*'s concerns are genealogical, working more with the conditions of profit *and* pleasure that make possible the production and circulation of the Filipino/a performing body.

One serious challenge to situating the Filipino/a performing body within such narratives of colonialism and imperialism has been the charge of a return to "negative histories." That is, approaching the Filipino/a performing body through the figuration of *puro arte* merely reproduces pathologizing colonial characterizations of Filipinos as unoriginal, excessive, and devoid of distinct cultural traits. Or worse, such an analytic makes visible a Filipino/a

performing body shaped primarily by and through multiple colonial genealogies. How does one then study the emergence of the Filipino/a performing body without reifying its colonial forms? What is gained by recourse to
the fraught concept of *puro arte* for an analysis of an already fraught object?
Rather than accede to such privileged readings of pathos and erasure, this
book examines the epistemological possibilities afforded by a turn to *puro
arte*. To call upon *puro arte* as an episteme is to interrogate how the Filipino/a
performing body is made visible in its multiple colonial contexts and what
the affective and material politics of that presence entail. To be clear here,
this book is not interested in attenuating the lived brutalities and legacies
of colonialism(s); it is interested more in the differentiated exposure of the
Filipino/a performing body on various stages of imperial contestation, at
interstitial sites of racial and cultural violence.

I: Filipino/a Racialization

"Invisible," "forgotten," "unrecognizable": these words have defined U.S.-Phil-
ippine relations and Filipino American racial identity in the United States. I
come at these descriptors of Filipino/a (racial) imperceptibility by turning to
chosen moments and sites in the last century when the Filipino/a is visible,
acknowledged, at the precise moment that s/he is misrecognized and erased.
In so doing, I am interested in the effects of such historical performances
of visibility and misrecognition and the kinds of communities and identity
formations these performances facilitate. My engagement destabilizes the
authority of colonial misrepresentations. These concerns are not meant to
reify recognition and visibility as desirable correctives to the problem of
Filipino/a representation. Rather, I wish to complicate, as feminist studies
scholar Laura Kang puts it, the natural linkage among "voice, visibility, and
liberation" (17).
    Any genealogy of Filipino American representation for scholars such as
Allan Isaac must first be mediated through an understanding of its affective
attachments to the dominant logic of the U.S. nation-state. More specifically,
Filipinos' seemingly desperate search for national belonging in the United
States, their desire to be part of "any national story as a *sensation*," as Isaac
deftly puts it, is symptomatic of a long history of spectacular imperialism
(xix). His observation that Filipinos "desire and pleasure to be a visible part
of the national story as a *sensation*" (xix) foregrounds a process of racialization constituted by and through the trope of sensationalism.[3] Working
within and through Isaac's, or rather Filipinos', "fondness for the sensational,"
for *puro arte*, this book mines established representations of the Philippines,

Filipinos, and Filipino Americans, to account for the "particular state of forces" that produce the emergence of the Filipino/a performing body (Foucault 376).

For full dramatic effect, allow me to narrate briefly the story of Filipino/a invisibility. For decades, as Oscar Campomanes eloquently argues, U.S. imperial pursuits were euphemistically cast in the language of globalism, internationalism, and protectionism. U.S. control of the Philippines and other unincorporated territories was rarely described as aggressive international occupation; instead, the United States was hailed as a forceful new nation, benevolent in its foreign relations. The United States, or so the story goes, could not be characterized as a colonizing force because colonizers, like Spain, were throwbacks to the dark ages; they tortured, killed, and enslaved captives. As a nation born out of democratic desires, rule by the people, of the people, for the people, the United States did not at all resemble aging colonial empires whose reigns involved excessive coercion and brutality. Rather, U.S. involvement in global affairs was heralded as the beginning of a new and modern age of international relations. Within such a whitewashed colonial narrative, Filipinos/as remain unintelligible, erased by the systematic denial of U.S. imperial history and ambitions.

Such a narrative of U.S. imperial amnesia (whose by-product is the myth of U.S. exceptionalism) has had a corresponding arc in the field of Asian American Studies. As Campomanes pointedly asks vis-à-vis the history of Filipinos and Filipino Americans, "Who is doing the forgetting? What is being forgotten? How much has been forgotten? Why the need to continue forgetting?" ("Filipinos in the United States," 164). Such questions not only are directed at the sanctioned amnesia of historians and scholars of American Studies and at the larger logic of American collective memory but also equally implicate the field-formation of Asian American Studies. Histories of colonialism, Campomanes argues in another essay, have posed a profound challenge to Asian American Studies, whose critical orbit has routinely circled around what he calls the "domesticity axis" ("New Formations," 527). "Domesticity axis" characterizes the hegemony of post-1960s identity politics and cultural nationalism as a driving agenda within the field. While such an agenda generated significant foci, such as comparative ethnic and racial formations, the dominant one nation/U.S. nation orientation allowed much to fall away.

More specifically, the field's approach to immigration, unhinged from the history of U.S. imperialism, contributed to Filipino Americans' invisibility and, to use Rick Bonus's description, to an "unsettling" condition within Asian American Studies (166). As the field continues to expand, we see more of a critique of early Asian American Studies' embeddedness in the one nation/U.S. nation paradigm. Filipino Americans are now granted a founding exceptionalism, as we learn more about how the story of Filipinos in the United States exceeds the field's dominant attachment to the U.S. nation. It is thus no coincidence that newer scholarship in the field now exhibits Asian American Studies' engagement with extranational subjects such as transnationalism, diaspora, and migration. Bonus's use of "unsettling" as an epithet for the status of Filipino Americans is also apt for highlighting Asian Americans' settler status on other island nations (such as Guam and Hawaii) that have been and continue to be under U.S. occupation.

Debates around the geopolitics of Asian American Studies have also significantly opened up the scholarship on Asian American performance. The "domesticity axis" within Asian American theater is characterized by Josephine Lee as a dialectic "between hyphenation and immigration." For Lee, the problem lies in the very staged distinctions made between theater by "'hyphenated' Americans" (later generations of Asian Americans) and "immigrant theater" ("most usually only in terms of nineteenth or early-twentieth century performances of traditional Chinese opera, or perhaps Japanese Noh or Kabuki") ("Between Immigration and Hyphenation," 45, 50). There is a telos implied, as Lee argues, even imposed upon these works, such that "immigrant theater" is expected to evolve into the kind of theater produced by "hyphenated Americans." What I propose here redirects these debates around the "domesticity axis" toward a set of concerns that differently cast the drama of Filipino/a invisibility. In addition to situating the practice of theater and performance within the epistemologies of imperialism, I look to the genre's own analytical offerings, or what performance values, to consider the problem of theorizing the Filipino/a performing body. This book places the Filipino performing body not just within debates on U.S. imperialism, Philippine nation building, immigrant belonging, and the press of globalization on a racialized performing body. I have also chosen Filipino performances that critically intervene in debates about theater, race, and performance on American, Filipino, and global stages.

For now, I want to address the particular structure and politics of invisibility within the practices and genres of performance, in particular of American theater. On the one hand, theater is a cultural practice that privileges transformation, the disappearance of one body into another. That is, if a performer is evaluated through her ability to suspend disbelief, to transform perceptions of her body, then invisibility could mean the (desired) disappearing of oneself to create another life-world. Yet, such a process of transformation falls short when juxtaposed with questions of racial labor. In other words, the emphasis on transformation works unevenly as it facilitates more exclusionary and discriminatory practices that routinely favor white bodies. Within hegemonic theories of performance, such a transformation is primarily available to unmarked (read: white) bodies, as phrased by Peggy Phelan. Unmarked bodies are the ones perceived as open to change and possibility. Thus, when Filipino/a migrant subjects fraternize U.S. taxi dance halls and out-perform their white counterparts, their spectacular (or what I will later call "splendid") dancing marks them more as visible than as invisible bodies. As Filipinos transform their bodies through the stylizations of American popular dance, they become instead troublesome, overly visible, exceeding, as it were, the assigned script of Filipinos as docile U.S. colonial subjects. The unintelligibility of their status as "nationals" hovers between the languages of "hyphenation and immigration," producing further anxiety and concern. In what follows, I engage theories of Filipino/a performance and theories of racialized performing bodies to attend precisely to such moments of historical hypervisibility and misrecognition within and against histories of U.S.-Philippine imperial relations and globalization.

II: *Palabas*, *Gaya*, and Theorizing the Filipino Performing Body

Diana Taylor's playful opening paragraph in *The Archive and the Repertoire* engages the idea of performance as interpreted by various artists from Latin America. Through a string of anecdotes, approximations, and translations of "performance" in several languages, Taylor recenters geopolitics in the field of Performance Studies. Instead of offering a fixed theory of performance, she deliberates more on the limits and possibilities of "performance" both as "an object of analysis" and as "the methodological lens that enables scholars to analyze events as performance" (3). Taylor's interventions directly address the field's linkages to colonialism exemplified in the Orientalist genealogies of the term "performance" itself and its shortcomings in adequately accounting for non-Western expressive practices. Ultimately she commits to "performance" "as a term simultaneously connoting a process, a praxis, an episteme, a mode of transmission, an accomplishment, and a means of intervening in the world" (15). As for the lament over "performance" as an overarching term that may be reenacting the violence of colonialism, Taylor maintains that a mere word substitution does not undo "our shared history of power relations and cultural domination" (15). In many ways, this book stands in solidarity with Taylor, not only in foregrounding the ongoing, "shared history of power relations and cultural domination" but also in celebrating the acts of survival and imagination that undergird such histories. I have chosen to name my study of the Filipino/a performing body *Puro Arte* precisely to recall and celebrate such histrionics and geopolitics of performance.

Puro Arte owes a debt to a long tradition of theoretical concepts through which Filipino/a performance has been analyzed. One key concept is *palabas*, literally meaning "show" or "theater." *Palabas*, developed on the battlegrounds of an emergent Filipino nationalism, grants the Filipino/a performing body its resistive possibilities. Such a rendering of *palabas* is most evident in Doreen Fernandez's eponymous collection of essays on Philippine theater history. While Fernandez translates "*palabas*" as "performance, show, entertainment, and fun" (viii), she also reads it as "people-based and community-oriented," where acts of "performing . . . [become] part of living" (viii). The opening essay roots Philippine theater in mimetic rituals organized around representations of daily life. Fernandez argues that indigenous cultural expressions were unrecognized and unacknowledged by colonial scholars who dismissed Filipinos as not having structured theatrical practices. In turn, she reroutes drama's definition from prepared text to "various imitations of life" based on Aristotle's drama as mimesis (4). As the essays in the collection move from the precolonial to the Spanish, from the American occupation to Martial Law and Philippine drama in the late twentieth century, Fernandez returns to the potential, realized and unrealized, of *palabas* as a shared and dynamic performative practice. For Fernandez, there is "no division between audience and performer" within *palabas* as its communal structure presumes the needs and purpose it serves. Her understanding of *palabas* equally privileges locality; in other words, the performance event happens within a specific context, enacted by and for an informed audience. In valuing context, Fernandez builds a critique of appropriation and performance directed toward an unknowing, outsider audience. Within such formulations, *palabas* provides a vernacular and material contrast to colonial understandings of performance as exotic cultural practices produced by colonized bodies for consumption by the colonizer. These practices become exotic precisely because they are performed for (and later even by) outsiders, in contexts where they are regarded as alien, strange. Such a process of exoticization reinforces racial and cultural forms of otherness that justify colonial violence in the form of territorial occupation and denial of self-rule. Refusing such colonial genealogies of exoticized performance, Fernandez's work on *palabas* instead constructs Philippine drama and its sensibilities against the backdrop of a vibrant Philippine history straining against the incursions of colonial rule and foreign occupation.

In conceptualizing *puro arte*, I am informed by *palabas*'s attachment to the performing body as a locality, as a mediated and contested space of performance. That is, if the performing body itself is a locality, what is the relationship between *labas* (the outside/exterior) and *loob* (the inside/interior)? Such a question is of great import to scholars (such as myself) who envisage theater and/or performance as an artistic expression and a perception of actions in everyday life. In the case of *palabas*, the exterior becomes a space of resistance and ambiguity, equally reflecting *and* deflecting the landscape of the interior. Akin to *palabas*, my turn to *puro arte* too complicates performances dismissed as entertaining, mundane, quotidian, diversionary, obvious, vulgar, or simply superficial. *Puro arte* wrestles with the creative labor behind the historical spectacle of failed and/or exaggerated Filipino/a performances.

Rey Ileto's *Pasyon and Revolution*, a book on the history of Philippine revolutionary movements, provides further insight on the link between *labas* and *loob*. In his discussion of the way revolutionaries perceived the meaning of their actions and the revolt itself, Ileto regards exteriority and interiority as intimately connected. He argues that the revolutionaries' participation in Holy Week rituals, in particular their performances of the *pasyon* (a verse narrative of the life and suffering of Jesus Christ), crucially influenced "the style of peasant brotherhoods and uprising during the Spanish and early American colonial periods" (11). Ileto deviates from previous analyses of the *pasyon* as a colonial disciplinary apparatus that instilled "loyalty to Spain and the Church" and focused on the "preoccupation with morality and the afterlife rather than with conditions in this world" (12). Instead, Ileto reads the performativity of *pasyon*—repetition with a difference and mimicry as intervention—arguing for an understanding of *pasyon* as a vibrant and disruptive folk tradition for those in lowland Philippine society. The ritual of *pasyon*, argues Ileto, provided "language for articulating its [lowland Philippine society's] own values, ideals, and even hopes of liberation" (12).

Palabas, in Fernandez's and Ileto's works, interprets and stages the Filipino/a performing body as an embodiment and/or a vehicle of nationalism. It highlights the potentiality of the Filipino/a performing body as a resistant subject, clearly identifying the site and practice of performance as oppositional. Nationalism unavoidably surfaces in any analysis of *palabas* as the concept emerges against the press of the cultures of imperialism. Yet the limits of nationalism, which include its hegemonic position as *the* resistant political ideology and its own demand for homogeneity, are equally visible within cultural projects that closely identify with nationalism. As a cultural agenda, nationalism's restrictive tendencies surface within the phenomena of diaspora and migration. For example, when Ma-yi Theater Ensemble in New York started as a company in the early 1990s, they staged plays about

Filipino/a life and contemporary conditions in the Philippines. Soon the company realized that the plays they were producing were an ocean removed from their audience members, mostly immigrant, diasporic Filipinos whose primary and daily life was in the United States. Their Philippine-focused repertoire inadvertently passed over Filipino/a lives in the United States, privileging instead nationalist episodes of collectivity and memory. Eventually, Ma-yi even widened their mission statement to include the term "Asian American" so as to move towards a more multi- and interracial agenda in their programming. Theater Ma-yi's move toward a racially expansive representational agenda was directly influenced by their location in New York, in the United States, in the diaspora. My own emphasis in this book too is less on recovering the nation (in the guise either of the Philippines and/or of the United States) than on dialoguing with the creative and critical legacies proffered by concepts such as *palabas*.

A second critical concept that makes an appearance in this book is the well-rehearsed concept of mimicry. In particular, *puro arte* enfolds the complex of mimicry as embodied in the labor of Filipino/a performing bodies. Mimicry/imitation is a familiar trope of colonial/postcolonial studies and performance studies, particularly as it engages with the struggles of minoritized subjects (such as women, queers, and people of color, to name a select few). I am drawn here by the historical and material processes that make the trope of mimicry such a literal and metaphorical space of performance. My interest in imitation/mimicry does not seek to valorize and romanticize postcolonial appropriations of "Western" cultural practices, or to simply narrate these practices as always already oppositional. Rather, the complex of mimicry (in all its fraught and celebratory forms), I want to suggest, is crucial to understanding the emergence of the Filipino/a performing body. The stages of Filipino/a mimicry I examine are marked by the labors of imitation, producing a body of performance riven by the historical stress of its own emergence.

One noteworthy example linking Filipinos and mimicry in colonial discourses is Arthur Stanley Riggs's introduction to *Filipino Drama*, the 1906 collection of seditious play scripts. Riggs declares Filipino theater as a prime example of "the deficiencies and limitations of the people" (2). He characterizes Filipino literature as "singularly adulterated by foreign influences" (1). Expert anthropologist Albert Ernest Jenks, who reports that Filipino creativity "lacks inventiveness," substantiates such observations (4). For Riggs and Jenks, Filipino drama's absence of inventiveness reflects the naïve childlikeness of Filipinos, and their absence of culture. Two decades later, an article printed in the *New York Times* supplements such early readings as it explains how colonial subjects made up for their "lack of inventiveness" and what they could do with "foreign influences":

> Stage stars soon will be coming here from the Philippines, according to F. S. Churchill, a theatrical producer of Manila. . . . "For the past twenty years American vaudeville has been exceedingly popular in the Philippines," said Mr. Churchill, "but the distance we are from the United States has made it an expensive proposition for us to offer Occidental amusement. Therefore, of necessity, we have had to train the local talent and I must say they have proved able entertainers. They are most apt in singing and dancing acts. Each year they grow more clever and American and European stages will be invaded by the Philippine artists before long." ("Filipinos Apt on Stage," 15)

This news article predicts, or rather warns, of the impending face-off between the colonizers and their colonial subjects. The touted invasion of Philippine artists into the metropole speaks directly to the specter of colonial panic. As Theater Studies scholar Joseph Roach writes, "performances propose possible candidates for succession" whereby "the anxiety generated by the process of substitution justifies the complicity of memory and forgetting" (6). Roach's meditation on the linkages among mimicry, performance, and colonialism is helpful in understanding the trepidation toward the colonial subjects who have proven themselves to be "able entertainers."

An older colonial text, however, provides a different recognition and possibility for the Filipinos' knack for imitation. Jean Mallat, a French colonial figure who penned *The Philippines: History, Geography, Customs of the Spanish Colonies in Oceania*, speaks directly to the Filipino "talent" for "imitation":

> It is mainly by the talent for imitation that these people [Indios] distinguish themselves, and this does not exclude, up to a certain point, genius and invention; to imitate well a thing often seen only once, one must know how to create, if not the thing itself, at least, the means to be used for executing it, now it is enough to tell the Indios to make such and such a thing, and they conceive on the spot the way of proceeding to do it. (458)

I am intrigued by Mallat's observation here, which recurs in various parts of his text. Mallat does not foreclose originality or uniqueness despite his conclusion that mimicry is *the* distinguishing ability of the Indios/Filipinos. He acknowledges the skills and labor involved in "imitation," beyond characterizing this "distinguishing talent" as a symptom of the Indios' lack of originality (hence dooming them from entering modernity) (458). There is an almost grudging admiration of the mimicking skills of Filipinos, offering a shift in tone in what is otherwise a dismissal of "imitation" in colonizers' records of the natives.

Many critics interested in imitation as a complicated and recursive practice within Filipino culture have expressed concern about the dangers of forgetting the centrality of the concept in Filipino/a performance. Rather than treating imitation as a cheap trick or mindless aping, it has been regarded as an act that can be deliberate, an experiential method of learning, and a way of knowing the world. While I do turn to well-recognized performance sites such as the mainstream global stage and popular spaces of entertainment such as taxi dance halls, my analysis extends to more marginalized sites of study—everyday, quotidian forms of mimicry, by gay, working-class, and other minoritized subjects. Mallat's nuanced rendering of the "Filipino indio's distinguishing talent for/of imitation" provides inspiration as it underscores the dynamic labor of imitation. Phenomena such as Filipino/a participation in *Miss Saigon* productions provide a rethinking of "imitation" beyond a sedimented form of labor to a consideration of it as a more exacting and creative labor.

Roland Tolentino's work on transvestites in Filipino cinema during the Martial Law era mobilizes the concept of *gaya* (mimic, imitate) to underscore the richness of imitation as creative process. For Tolentino, *gaya* "foregrounds the transvestite's operation of mediating and transforming high and low" ("Transvestites and Transgressions," 334). Building on Judith Butler's generative revisioning of repetition in performance (and cautious of Homi Bhabha's concept of mimicry in colonial discourse for its "homogenization of the signifying field"), Tolentino offers "gaya" as "an idiom to articulate and historicize the liminality of transvestism in the national culture" (336). He emphasizes the possibility of "imitation" as challenging the repressive regime of the Marcoses. Similarly, Fenella Cannell's work on Bicolano culture, and specifically on gay mimicry, reads imitation beyond mere derivativeness. For Cannell, "imitation of content can constitute a self-transformative process" (224). She concludes that taking part in performances "which use idioms thought of as American. . . . is both to move towards the pleasures of empowerment which come with 'knowing the words' of a text and making it one's own, and also to move towards a transformation in which what is distant, powerful, and oppressive is brought closer and made more equal" (255). Mimicry, as Cannell implies here, requires self-knowledge, an intimacy with the object that one is mimicking. Such a knowledge toys with intimate proximity to overturn the equation of who mimics and who is mimicked. Lastly, for Martin Manalansan, Filipino gay transmigrants' performative practices, such as cross-dressing in gay Santacruzans, suggest more than "a parody of the real" (138). Decentering "parody" as the hegemonic, politicized intent of (white) drag, Manalansan reads the potential to "transform mimicry from mere simulacrum to a strategy that questions colonial and postcolonial power" in gay Santacruzans (140). This Filipino ritual appropriated in queer performance highlights the function of rituals in community formation and its performances as practices of reinvention toward a collective political voice.

Tolentino, Cannell, and Manalansan focus in particular on gay practices of imitation to produce a generative theory of Filipino/a mimicry, one that goes beyond mere "lack of inventiveness" and depleted cultural traits. They argue for the productive possibilities of the practice of imitation—from self-transformation to a subversive critique of an authoritarian regime that accounts for postcolonial and queer difference. With *puro arte*, I shift the site of inquiry to an interrogation of imitation as colonial context, process, and narrative. *Puro arte* interrupts the original/copy dichotomy and proffers a more supplementary form of analyzing acts of, and at times those read as, imitation.

III: At Rise: A Century of Filipino Acts

Theater scholar John Rouse writes, "No body ever simply appears on stage. Bodies are, rather, made to appear in performance, rendered visible as the encoded tissues interwoven by systems of ideological representation that mediate the anxieties and interests at play in specific historical moments" (iv). In the following four chapters I tease out the "anxieties and interests" of specific historical moments in U.S.-Philippine relations. Each chapter locates the Filipino/a performing body at key moments in U.S.-Philippine relations in varying sites. These moments are as follows: U.S. acquisition of the Philippines as a colony in the late nineteenth century; the dawn of Philippine independence (1920s-1930s); the tumultuous years of the Martial Law (1972-1981); and the closure of U.S. military bases in the Philippines at the end of the twentieth century. Even as the chapters in this book can be described as chronological, each chapter carefully preserves a dialectical relationship between the past and the present. The copresence of the past and the present allows for the complex consideration of the performative not as an uncritical site of visibility, resistance, or agency but as a relationship constituted through a shifting struggle and relationship of forces.[4] To that end, the temporal order of the book situates the colonial histories of the Philippines within U.S.-based race relations and discourses of globalization, moving back and forth, as it were, between the imperialisms of the past and the hegemonies of the present.

The sign of "history" equally assumes multiple roles in this study on the Filipino/a performing body. On the one hand, history can be understood here as chronological and/or linear. Key dates and events provide an organizing logic to the narration of the drama of the Filipino/a performing body in the century-long "special relations" between the United States and the Philippines. I purposely capitalize on this conventional take on history not to reify these events as stable markers of Filipino/a emergence. Rather, in rerouting these histories through performance, I am interested in the mundane and transformative acts that make such histories possible and even desirable. More crucially, I interpret these historical spots of time as temporalities of Filipino/a racialization. In other words, these defining times in U.S.-Philippine relations become scripts of emergence, of a (mis)recognition of the Filipino/a as a racialized body. What appears as "historical" in this book is not simply history *qua* history; it also assumes various aliases, forms, and meanings: moments, instances, scenes, and occurrences. As I look at the Filipino/a performing body *during* these periods and in performances *about* these periods, I share Davíd Román's interest in "a critical temporality [what he defines as contemporary] that engages the past without being held captive to it and that instantiates the present without defining a future" (*Performance in America*, 1). By engaging the Filipino/a performing body on diverse arenas at different temporal moments, I theorize Filipino American theater and performance as a practice that is dynamic and in the making. In other words, the production and circulation of the Filipino/a performing body is a matter of doing, a process of relation, not simply reified nor a given.

While I make use of history to locate how and where the Filipino performing body finds itself during these historical moments, I also pay attention to these performative acts as self- and community-expressions of, interpretations of, and interventions in these historical events. At times, I follow the lead of the performances and their points of reference. In doing so, I have created unexpected temporal reorderings, defying what may be obvious affiliations and pairings. For example, in chapter 1, a more predictable juxtaposition of early-twentieth-century imperial stage acts might have set the Philippine seditious plays against the contemporaneous World's Fair. These "seditious plays," performed mostly in Tagalog and staged in greater Manila, Bulacan, and Ilocos Norte, were banned for inciting anti-American sentiments and provoking riots. Recuperated in Philippine theater scholarship as the ultimate theater of Filipino nationalism, the seditious plays' anti–U.S. colonialism and enactments of Filipinos' aspiration for free nationhood become an easy read against colonialist display of Filipinos in the Philippine Reservation of the St. Louis World's Fair. Vince Rafael has argued that these nationalist dramas "resignify the vernacular so as to reclaim the capacity of people to nominate themselves as agents in and interpreters of their experience" (46). In this book, these plays are noted as a crucial citational presence in a discussion of Sining Bayan's anti-imperial transnational politics. In researching Sining Bayan's social protest theater against Marcos' Martial Law, I came to a renewed understanding of these seditious plays beyond their reified place in imaginings of nationhood. I have argued elsewhere that the recuperation of seditious plays in Filipino American progressive organizing signals a decolonization of the stage that distinctly departs from a reconstitution of "native," as proffered by Christopher Balme, and moves more toward a recognition of the impossibility of such a project.[5]

The stages on which I locate the Filipino/a performing body shuttle between the nation and the diaspora. These locations are treated as fluid and contained, separate but connected. Here, the Filipino performing body appears in display, in protest, in and as a disguise, as an impersonation, and more. While I consider the forces of and with which Filipino American theater and performance emerge, I return over and over again to the imaginative world(s) these performing bodies create for themselves and for those who experience their performance.

IV: Stages of *Puro Arte*

In the following chapters, I interrogate moments of Filipinos' visibility, their audibility, their "splendid dancing," and their dramatic abilities. These occasions, at times, have been celebrated as forms of accomplishment, of inclusion, of overcoming racism, of rising above institutional and personal barriers. Following the language of *puro arte*, I examine instead how these spectacular accomplishments tend to blind us, serving often to mystify rather than open up historical conditions. I work against treating these moments simply as temporalities of Filipino corporeal, vocal, and emotional exceptionality; they are more opportunities to interrogate the complex interplay of corporeality and history. Of concern here is the politics of what enables emergence—whether it be in the form of sound, movement, or visuality.[6]

The first chapter, "Which Way to the Philippines? The United Stages of Empire," examines dramatizations of U.S.-Philippine contact during the years leading up to, during, and immediately after the Spanish-American

War. In the early years of the American empire, the Filipino/a performing body appears in piecemeal form on diverse U.S. stages, including the 1904 St. Louis World's Fair, as part of chautauqua circuits, and on theater venues in major American cities such as New York and Chicago. I turn to two of these sites, the Philippine Reservation at the 1904 St. Louis World's Fair and the musical comedy *Shoo-Fly Regiment* by the African American creative team of Bob Cole, J. Rosamond, and James Weldon Johnson. I approach these various performing stages as "contact zones," as complex terrains of interaction among American patrons, Filipino/a performers, and the Philippines (Pratt 7). In this chapter, I also ask how this early contact between the United States and the Philippines is present in contemporary Filipino Americans' self-imagination. The centennial celebrations, between 1996 and 2006, provide a glimpse into theatrical explorations of this query.

The world's fair and musical theater productions participate in and extend U.S. imperialism, performing, as it were, the complex and often contradictory sentiments of a newly burgeoning and increasingly racialized empire. In these early years of empire building, the Philippines is assigned a prominent role. More specific to my focus is how the Filipino/a performing body, and performances *of* Filipinos/as, as in the case of *The Shoo-Fly Regiment*, become part of national debates and anxieties consuming the nation as it grapples with its new identity. Expanding existing scholarly works on the significance of the 1904 St. Louis World's Fair to the United States' bid for a seat among nations of empire, I emphasize the crucial role played by the Philippines and the Filipino/a performing body within American women's and African American men's struggle for suffrage. I end with a reflection on how such early scenes of Filipino/a visibility are represented in contemporary Filipino American artistic practices such as the POMO Festival in San Francisco. Initiated as part of the Philippine Independence Centennial celebrations, the POMO Festival wrestles with the visibility of Filipinos gained through these early portrayals and performance stages.

Nearly two decades after the Philippines became a U.S. acquisition, the "Philippine Question" gripped the U.S. nation once again, this time in the guise of a threat posed by Filipino male migrants. Chapter 2, "Splendid Dancing: Of Filipinos and Taxi Dance Halls," traces the popular mobilizations of taxi dance halls as an American urban phenomenon, and thinks through the Filipino performing body within such a social formation. The taxi dance halls were at peak popularity in the United States during the 1920s and 1930s, when male patrons of various kinds eagerly came to pay to dance with (mostly white) women. Significantly, Filipino male patrons, who were students and migrant laborers, constituted a quarter of the patrons of the taxi dance halls, a demographic that can be attributed partially to the influx of imperial/colonial subjects into the metropole. This was an era rife with anti-Filipino sentiments, which soon became the basis for the Filipino Exclusion Act. I read the dance hall as a complex and prominent physical and cultural space of exchange between the native and immigrant communities.

Taxi dance halls facilitated one of the few spaces of social interaction between Americans and the new Filipino subjects of American imperialism. Within spaces such as the taxi dance halls, the spectacle of the Filipino dancing body emerges as a vibrant and potentially violating instantiation of the effects of U.S. imperialism. This "brown menace's" "splendid dancing" is a corporeal testament to one of the key anxieties of American men. Filipinos competed for jobs in a rapidly shrinking American labor market, even as American men warily regarded Filipinos and their appeal to white women as *the problem* of the decade. Unlike "other Orientals," whose masculinity was defined as asexual, the Filipinos' supposed hypersexuality fueled the very fire that ignited their eventual exclusion. Part of my contention here is that the persistent reading of Filipino corporeality (as splendid dancers and passionate lovers of white women) through the lens of "exceptionality" equally circulates and corrupts the very languages of U.S. imperialism.

Chapter 3, "Coup de Théâtre: The Drama of Martial Law," interrogates the mobilizations of Martial Law under Ferdinand Marcos (1972-1981) in contemporary Filipino American theatrical works. I am interested in the spectral intersection of the past and present within the history of Filipino American performance as staged in the juxtaposition of Sining Bayan and productions of Jessica Hagedorn's *Dogeaters*. My concerns in this chapter are twofold. First, I map the use of theater during the anti–Martial Law activism in the United States, representing the Filipino/a performing body in protest. I focus on the work of Sining Bayan (translated as "Theater of the People"), the cultural arm to the radical Filipino American anti–Martial Law/anti-Marcos political group Katipunan ng mga Demokratikong Pilipino/KDP. From 1972 to 1981, Sining Bayan staged plays about the struggle of Filipino people in the Philippines and in the United States. During these years, Sining Bayan was an artistic and public voice for the radical politics of the KDP in the United States. In many ways, engaging the multiple histories of Sining Bayan was one of the most challenging narrative tasks of this book. Laura Briggs, in her essay "Notes on Activism and Epistemologies," calls for an acknowledgment of the intellectual work of activist movements. She opens her essay by providing a scene of camaraderie by narrating a story about an event at an activist reunion/conference, where she found herself participating in a sing-along of "Solidarity Forever." I was struck by the various ways Briggs articulated how she felt about this scene—she found it fun, funny, and also a little bit embarrassing. This opening scenario provides Briggs the launching point for her discussion of ascribing ideas to political movements. In the essay, her prepositions vary—"speak for," "speak from," "speak of"—as she talks about the political movements. Prepositions establish, name, articulate relations to movement. Reading Briggs's essay, I ask myself, What preposition do I use to articulate my relationship to this movement that I write about? This prepositional quandary is also compounded by the fact that the language by which I came to know the world has one preposition—"*Sa*." As noted in Paraluman Aspillera's *Basic Tagalog for Foreigners and Non-Tagalogs,* "The universal use of *sa* in Tagalog and other Philippine languages could be the reason why Filipinos find it difficult to learn the different meanings of and the various uses of English prepositions" (116). The predicament I found myself in informed the way I have crafted words, yet it is also crucial to how I relate, in this instance, to Sining Bayan's political movement that I write on, of, about, or around, in this chapter.

The chapter shifts the discussion to focus on the way Martial Law is dramatized in Jessica Hagedorn's *Dogeaters: The Play.* Encouraged and pursued by the highly acclaimed American theater director Michael Greif, Hagedorn embarked on a multiyear process to adapt her novel into a play. In the latter half of the chapter, my motivating concern as I discuss *Dogeaters: The Play* is to make visible the palpable force and persistence of Martial Law in the Filipino/a and Filipino American theatrical imaginary. The referentiality of Martial Law mandates a paradoxical structure of both forgetting and remembering, a model of memory that returns to life, only in its dark and vivid hauntings—to echo Filipino American director Jon Rivera—that are lodged deep in the body politics of nation.

Chapter 4, "How in the Light of One Night Did We Come So Far? Working *Miss Saigon,*" extends the discussion of the Filipino/a performing body on the contemporary global stage through a focus on the casting phenomenon of Filipinos/as in the musical *Miss Saigon.* The continuing worldwide productions of one of the most famous and indeed controversial musicals in contemporary musical history clearly demands further scrutiny. On this performing stage, the Filipino/a body becomes an icon of intersecting colonial histories—the United States in the Philippines, France in Vietnam, the United States in Vietnam. In this chapter, I shift the conversation that *Miss Saigon* has so famously generated about American theater's fraught history of yellowfacing and racist labor practices to attend to the ways in which labor, being, self, and affect are collapsed in the phenomenon of Filipinas in this musical industry. I am compelled by the question of where the body of the performer ends and that of the character begins, as framed by African American theater scholars Harry Elam and Alice Rayner in their discussion of a production of Suzi Lori-Parks's play *Venus*. This question, of course, carries higher stakes for feminized and racialized performers who are called upon to both represent and exceed the scripts of their characters. As I argue in this chapter, Filipino/a performers in global productions of *Miss Saigon* bear the weight of their own successes, and the interpretations of, expectations of, and impositions of their global audiences, the Philippine nation, the Filipino people, and each other. Broadly speaking, this final chapter fittingly gestures to the world-making possibilities of performance and considers what forms of being in the world the space of performance can and must provide.

1

"Which Way to the Philippines?"

United Stages of Empire

The fame of the Philippine exposition has captured the World's Fair city, and the most constant question which the Jefferson Guards have to answer is, "Which way to the Philippines?"
—*New York Times*, 1904

In the early decades of the twentieth century, the Filipino/a performing body appears in piecemeal form on diverse U.S. stages, including the 1904 Louisiana Purchase Exposition, also known as the St. Louis World's Fair, and touring assemblies called "chautauquas" that featured music, lectures, speeches, and other acts combining education and entertainment. Some choice (and well-known) representations included Filipinos as buxom "Visayan girls, noted for their beauty" or as savage "dog-eating and head-hunting Igorots" ("Which Way to the Phillipines?"). Filipinos were also objects of mimicry in theater productions, by both white and black Americans, in venues across major American cities such as New York and Chicago. On the one hand, the sheer number of such reproductions of the Filipino/a performing body speaks to its formulaic, and often numbingly savage presence on the stages of U.S. empire. On the other hand, the familiarity and portability of the Filipino/a performing body occludes the very material and affective attachments that found its visibility. In this chapter, I track this recurring appearance of the Filipino/a as an imaginative and embodied consolidation of the institutions of empire, and as a corruptive presence on the stages of empire: Filipino/a bodies are consumed for profit even as they are appropriated for pleasures that exceed the workings of empire.

I turn to two prominent performance sites, the St. Louis World's Fair and the genre of American musical theater, to consider what role Filipinos played within the larger imaginary of U.S. empire. These various performing stages function, in many ways, as a "contact zone," a complex terrain of interaction between American patrons and Filipino/a performers, and so also between the United States and the Philippines. In her well-known formulation, Mary Louise Pratt defines "contact zones" as "social spaces where disparate cultures meet, clash, and grapple with each other such as colonialism, slavery, or their aftermaths as they are lived out in many parts of the world today" (7). Pratt offers the concept of "contact zones" to shift away from the overdetermined expansionist expression of "colonial frontier" and "diffusionist accounts of conquest and domination" (7). The term "contact zones" stresses the "interactive, improvisational dimensions of imperial encounters, emphasizing how subjects get constituted in and by their relations to each other" (8). This semantic shift, from "colonial frontier" to "contact zones," extends our readings of imperial encounters to include multiple viewpoints, decentering the hegemonic perspective of conquest and domination. "Interaction," "copresence," and "interlocking understanding and practices" undo the totalizing script of colonialism to emphasize a relational process. The mutually constitutive character of the "contact zone," as Rafael Perez-Torres argues, is not a "simple mélange or passive mixture but a volatile, contested, contestatory, and endlessly innovative dynamic" (33). The concept of "contact zone," as interactive and improvisational, I suggest, forges affinity with the analytic of performance.[1] The lens of performance foregrounds a structure of hermeneutics that leaves open the possibility of interpreting the colonial script. Through spectacular acts of performance, through *puro arte,* Filipino/a bodies instantiate and exceed the totalizing script of colonialism, inviting forms of critical engagement that emphasize more the incompleteness of and the possibilities of inherited histories. Here, the concept of "contact zones" frames the various stages upon which U.S.-Philippine history are re/enacted, insisting on the uneven relations of power that undergird these exchanges and events.

Ambivalence marks the early years of U.S. imperial rule, as colonial fantasies collided with the spiraling dreams of Philippine nationhood. Sites such as the St. Louis World's Fair, chautauquas, and theater productions convey the extent to which popular entertainment participated in the consolidating of U.S. imperial culture.[2] They had a shared interest in developing the pedagogical dimension of popular entertainment as a vehicle of empire. These cultural sites performed the necessary labor of imagining the "unknown" of imperial contact, of literalizing the kinds of relations it would produce. The St. Louis World's Fair, more so than other sites, sought to demonstrate the United States' emergence as an industrialized nation at the forefront of technological explorations. The all–African American musical theater production *The Shoo-Fly Regiment*, which toured in numerous states, including New York, Ohio, Pennsylvania, Texas, and Arkansas, was among a repertoire of plays and musicals that also dramatized the vagaries of U.S.-Philippine conflict. Together, these two seemingly diverse cultural sites, the World's Fair and American musical theater, compel, I will suggest, complex brownface performances of the U.S.-Philippine contact zones.

Let me first qualify the two forms of brownface performances at work here. First is the Filipino/a body at the St. Louis World's Fair, staged as a spectacular exemplar of racial difference. The U.S. government, in collaboration with Filipino state officials, brought Filipinos to St. Louis as anthropological/ethnographic displays. People from different parts of the Philippines were exhibited in their native garb, and made to perform their daily life for the fairgoers. A distinct area of the fairground was designated as the Philippine Reservation, also known as the Philippine Village, to approximate the spatial and material origins of its savage inhabitants. The Philippine Reservation and its activities were designed, in short, to route the Filipino/a body into a discourse of civilization. The exposure of the Filipino/a body in this instance is a brownface performance orchestrated for and by an imperialist agenda.

The second form of brownface performance I wish to demarcate is the portrayal of the Filipino/a and the Philippines by non-Filipinos, enacted to service the narrative of a benevolent U.S. empire. While the St. Louis World's Fair has been the subject of numerous scholarly works in Filipino Studies, *The Shoo-Fly Regiment* has yet to be interrogated for its staging of the Philippines and the Filipino/a body. The brownface performance of the Philippines and the Filipino/a body in this musical accentuates the radical malleability of the black performing body. In an attempt to depart from the dominance of minstrelsy as the only recognizable form for the expression of the black performing body, this staging of the exotic Filipino/a provided an avenue for black performers to transgress constrictions imposed by the white-black binary of the U.S. racial hierarchy. At a time when Jim Crow laws brutally restricted African American freedoms, such brownface performances vividly demonstrated the transformative powers of the performing black body. By focusing on an all black-musical theater production that sought to advance African American citizenship, we can explore instead a more robust "minor" view of the contact zone, and of the Filipino/a performing body. "Minor," as invoked here, draws its analytical force from Francois Lionet's and Shumei Shih's theory of "minor transnationalism," which emphasizes lateral relationships among minoritized groups (2).

There is of course no doubt that in both instances brownface performances of the Filipino/a body were largely Orientalist productions for consumption by the American public. My interest in these early brownface performances considers the crucial affective and material role of cultural production in the emergence of a U.S. imperial imaginary.[3] As Daphne Brooks and Angela Pao have variously argued, such enactments of racial otherness are crucial to understanding the genealogy of the racialized performing body (whether it be blackface or yellowface), which at times functions to defamiliarize the spectacle and/or technologies of otherness.[4] What is of import here is the necessary engagement of the contemporary Filipino/a performing body with such early and decidedly fraught brownface performances. After all, these performances (in all their variegated racial forms) constitute the ways in which Filipinos existed in the larger U.S. imperialist imaginary.[5] Indeed, this book regards the Filipino/a performing body in different sites and genres of performance as a laboring body that is racialized, gendered, and sexualized, precisely as it negotiates critical moments in U.S.-Philippine imperial relations. These enactments of Filipinos on U.S. colonial sites and by African Americans impersonating Filipinos challenge attachments to the fixity and object status of the Filipino/a performing body. To read the Filipino/a body through performances of brownface is to consider a genealogy of the Filipino/a performing body beyond the celebratory essentialisms of historical recuperation. In turning to such a model of historical genealogy, I echo the cautions of Coco Fusco's formative essay, "The Other History of Intercultural Performance." Through her collaborative performance with Guillermo Gomez-Peña, A Couple in a Cage, Fusco reminds us of racialized performance's own entanglements with the very imperial ideologies and practices it seeks to exceed. I follow the lead of contemporary Filipino American performance projects and artists, such as KulArts, Inc.'s POMO Festival of Pilipino American Modern Art, Gigi Otalvaro-Hormillosa, Julie Tolentino, and Pearl Ubungen, who similarly confront colonial representations of Filipino/a performing bodies alongside the desires and ambitions of contemporary Filipino/a American performance.

I: The World's Fair on My Mind: Dogeating,
G-Strings, and Bare Breasts

The significance of the 1904 St. Louis Worlds' Fair is most vividly captured in
the film *Meet Me in St. Louis*. As the Smith family gazes in awe at the mag-
nificent lights and awesome structure of the fair, Esther Smith breathlessly
exclaims, "And it's all right here in St. Louis. Right here where we live." *Meet
Me in St. Louis*, Sally Benson's memoir-turned-film-remade-for-television-
twice-turned-play, is set in 1903, a year before the opening of the "greatest fair
on earth." The book records the Benson's family life from the point of view
of a young woman (Sally), capturing a local view, if you will, of a powerful
nation on the verge of imperial conglomeration. Though *Meet Me in St. Louis*
is a story of the United States at the turn of the twentieth century, both the
memoir and the film were released in the midst of World War II. The movie's
closing words, "right here," focus on the local comfort of a small city, held up
as equally promising against the big city. As the war among nations brings
uncertainty to the world, Esther's utterance of "right here, in our own city"
is a reassurance of the safety of American lives within U.S. borders. Within
such a volatile historical context, the staging of the World's Fair emerges as
a stabilizing symbol and a reaffirmation of U.S. international involvement.[6]
"Right here in St. Louis" declares the arrival of the world in the United States
and of U.S. presence in the world.

We know now that the St. Louis World's Fair's most popular stop was the
Philippine Village and that the Filipino/a performing body was *the* spectacle
to behold. David R. Francis, head exposition director, noted, "ninety-nine out
of a hundred fairgoers visited the reservation" (qtd. in Rydell 170).[7] Though
Filipinos were present in earlier world expositions in the United States,
the heightened focus on them in the St. Louis World's Fair is the subject of
many writings on Filipinos in nineteenth-century world expositions. At the
Philippine Village, approximately twelve hundred Filipinos were exhibited,
including Igorots (from Bontoc, Suyoc, and other regions), Manobos, Moros,
Visayans, and Negritos, as well as the Philippine Scouts and Constabulary. So
grand was the Philippine portion of the exhibition, and so expensive, that it
has been referred to as the fair within a fair (Fermin 63).

"The fame of the Philippine exposition has captured the World's Fair city,
and the most constant question which the Jefferson Guards have to answer is,
'Which way to the Philippines?'" ("Which Way to the Philippines?"). What
are we to make of fairgoers' enthusiastic response to the Philippine exhibit?
What solicited their reaction? How did fairgoers react to what they were seeing? Recorded accounts, specifically in newspapers, drew attention to the

Igorot dog-eating rituals, various Filipino peoples' manner of (un)dress, the beautiful Visayan maidens, and the Philippine Scouts and Constabulary. References to "dog-eating and head-hunting Igorots," to Filipinos as "savage," and to the Negrito as "the missing link" were made with ease, naturalizing Filipinos/as as savage and barbaric.[8] The Philippine Village was designed to display different people from the Philippines in their "natural environment" ("Which Way to the Philippines?"), thereby collapsing everyday life with a decontextualized display of the exotic. Scenes such as the Igorots' dog-feast, "dwarf Negritos . . . shooting with their bows and poisoned arrows, light[ing] fires with the friction of bamboo sticks," the "Visayan girls, noted for their beauty, . . . weaving bamboo hats and basket work," and "the little naked Moro boys tumbl[ing] in and out of their small dugout canoes" beneath the bridge of Arrowhead Lake were presented as depictions of typical life in the newly acquired tropical colony ("Which Way to the Philippines?"). These activities may well have been daily routines to the peoples of the Luzon mountain provinces and women of the Visayan region. On the platform of the World's Fair, however, the display of everyday activities subscribed to a racist imperial ideology that characterized Filipinos as the "missing link" in human evolution (Fermin 107).[9]

During the seven months of the Filipino exhibit at the World's Fair, the spectacular and the mundane intertwined in some strange and comforting twists: elders died, couples wed, and children were born.[10] One of the children born on the fairgrounds was named after the city of St. Louis and the fair's presiding officer, David Francis. While Americans set up colonial shop in the Philippines, by way of governance, education, and other forms of repressive and ideological state apparatuses, the St. Louis World's Fair paved consent for the U.S. imperial project in the metropole. It was, par excellence, a pedagogical exercise, teaching not just about the outside world but also about how they—as Americans—inhabited the world.

Recorded responses of the patrons demonstrated that Filipino dog eating and the Filipino manner of dress drew much heated commentary. A fairgoer expressed strong response to the consumption of dog as food, writing the following to his wife: "I went up to the Philippine Village to-day and saw the wild, barbaric Igorots, who eat dogs, and are so vicious that they are fenced in and guarded by a special constabulary. . . . They are the lowest type of civilization I ever saw and thirst for blood" (qtd. in Vostral 19).[11] This dietary and culinary practice caused a lengthy debate, involving the Humane Society. For each response of disgust among the American public came offers such as the following from another American, printed in the *Missouri Republic* under the title "Letter Offering Dogs."

Dexter, Mo., April 12, 1904.—

Governor Hunt, Manager Igorrote Tribe:

I have been noticing that for some time your charges, the Igorrotes, have been complaining about their not receiving any dogs for eating, as is their custom. I am desirous of furnishing them dogs for this purpose.

I put in many a weary day in their own country and many a day while there I have yearned earnestly for a few bites of those dishes which I left back in the good old State of Missouri. This has won my sympathy for the poor, disconsolate wretches, separated from the rations which they were reared upon.

Now, the Humane Society has no jurisdiction over the dogs of Southeast Missouri and I will send you as many dogs as you can use, up to the number of 200. I seek no remuneration whatever except that you pay the freight. Hoping for an early reply, I remain, yours truly

MORTIMER T. JEFFERS.

Offers to send dogs by the hundreds flooded the fair's administration.[12] These expressions of support for the dog-feast are a mix of cultural relativity, cultural sensitivity, patronage, and Orientalist fetishism. American responses to Igorots' dietary choices reiterate Karen Shimakawa's notion of "national abjection." Linking feminist psychoanalytic theorist Julia Kristeva's work on "abjection" to national identity formation and racism, Shimakawa emphasizes the mutually constitutive process between seemingly different or even opposite locations. As abjects within the U.S. racial hierarchy, racial others are regarded as repulsive. Fervent attention to dog-eating Igorots illustrates the persistence of perverse curiosity and desire directed toward racial others, despite and precisely because of their grotesqueness. The curious performance of the exoticized and "barbaric" Filipinos and their strange eating habits becomes a histrionic part of American identity formation during this period of empire building. The exchange over this dog-eating spectacle highlights that which is "occupying the seemingly contradictory, yet functionally essential, position of consistent element and radical other" (3).

The clothing of the Filipino/a performing body also drew sensationalized attention. Igorot and Negrito men in *bahag* and the women with exposed breasts caused quite a stir among some of the fair's patrons.[13] As 1904 was an election year, debates on whether these Filipinos should cover their bareness extended to the White House. Warring parties exuberantly discussed the "Philippine problem," with anti-imperialist Democrats casting doubt on the benevolence of the U.S. role in the islands. For anti-imperialists who were against annexation for racist reasons, the bareness of the Igorots and the Negritos consolidated their bigoted perception of barbarism and savageness.[14] Such representations provided ample fodder for the interrogation of the very narrative of progress, uplift, and civilization undergirding the annexation project. Additionally, Missouri was a key state in the 1904 election, and the local media's lurid coverage of the Igorot and Negrito men and women threatened the incumbent Roosevelt's pro-annexation stance.[15] Fearing that the "scantily clad" Filipinos would expose the loopholes in the U.S. civilizing project, Roosevelt attempted to manage this crisis with the help of Governor Taft. Initially, the response to concerns about decency was to provide additional clothing for the Filipinos: "short trunks would be enough for the men, but for the Negrito women there ought to be shirts or chemises of some sort" (Taft, qtd. in Rydell 172).[16] Yet, akin to the responses to dog eating, there was a diversity of views on the proposed men's vestments. In his chapter on the St. Louis World's Fair, Rydell summarizes the dilemma: "Putting on pants raises [their] 'nativeness' as an issue and intervenes in the ethnological/education process. Yet their bareness puts into question their capacity to be lifted in progress" (174-75). In many ways, the debates around the appropriate (or inappropriate) bareness of the Filipino/a body converged with the earlier debates about their consumption of dogs as food. In both cases, the space of the World's Fair allowed for scenes of contestation and desire, hitherto disclosed only in the ideological imaginary of the imperial state. The conundrum of whether a naked or clothed Filipino/a body best performed the script of empire became, as it were, the very theater of U.S. national identification.

The St. Louis World's Fair's evolutionary schema presented Visayans and the Philippine Constabulary and Scouts as exemplars of the Filipino's potential for progress and civilization. Mary Talusan's study on the popularity of the Philippine Constabulary Band documents the enthusiastic responses to Filipinos' musicianship and showmanship. The band's pleasing drill performances received high praise that even earned an invitation to the White House from President Roosevelt himself. For Roosevelt, the success of the band served as a rousing endorsement of U.S. imperial policy and the positive effects of its presence in the Philippines.[17] Talusan points out that the band members were specifically celebrated for their ability to perform U.S. battle hymns and to do so without interruption under extraordinary circumstances such as a power failure. This recognition of Filipino musicianship is attributed to good pedagogy; they are, after all, performing what they have been taught, in front of their teacher, the U.S. audience, and the American president. Such a convenient erasure of the long history of brass instrument playing in the Philippines dating back to the sixteenth century, Talusan argues, is an erasure necessary to the justification of colonial presence in the Philippines. Recognition of the Constabulary Band becomes a supreme performance of American self-aggrandizement, a high compliment to the tenacity of U.S. tutelage.

II: Philippine Village: A Stop on the Way to Women's Suffrage

While newspaper accounts recorded responses, particularly those of male government officials, the fair's history and experience were "preserved" through related objects such as guidebooks.[18] One such guidebook is entitled *An Evening Trip to the St. Louis Fair*, "personally conducted by Mrs. Coonley Ward." Mrs. Lydia Avery Coonley Ward, a member of upper-class society, was active in various aspects of the women's movement, and known to have been an acquaintance of suffragette Susan B. Anthony (Harper 750).[19] At the Columbian Exposition of 1893, where she hosted social functions as a member of the Women's Committee, Ward met her husband-to-be, Henry Ward, of Ward's Natural Science (McKelvey 9).[20] American women actively shaped the culture of U.S. imperialism in their various roles as teachers, entrepreneurs, and medical professionals. The fairgrounds were one of the few public spaces that afforded American women a rare chance to establish "contact" and engage with cultural references beyond the horizon of their nation-state. The exposition, with its combined atmosphere of education and entertainment, seemed like a wholesome social space where American women could express their latent cosmopolitan aspirations. In the case of Ward, and the nuanced relations in the "contact zone" of the St. Louis World's Fair, empathy was a powerful tool utilized by women in their fight for equality.[21]

Ward's tour-guide booklet is one prime example of how American women were active in the "contact zone" of the World's Fair. *An Evening Trip* takes the form of a guided tour conducted by Ward herself. Her role as a tour guide is influential as her comments shaped and mediated the experiences of patrons, and, perhaps, even familiarized the American public with the structures of U.S. empire. Ward commences the tour with an introduction about the origins of the fair, its commemorative goals, its construction, and last but not least, its emergence into the fairgrounds. She makes her first intervention by pointing out the deliberate design of the Philippine Village as she introduces her listeners/readers to the fairgrounds. She conveys that the "disadvantage" of the evolutionary logic of the village layout "results in many visitors carrying away the impression that the primitive tribe is the typical Filipino and that the evidences of intelligence and education are largely due to the American schools. This is far from true, although much has been done, as the Filipinos gladly acknowledge" (92). Falling short of saying that such scenes were merely staged for the justification of U.S. presence in the Philippines, Ward carefully navigates the relationship between Filipino/a primitiveness and America's civilizing role. Empathetic statements pepper her entry about the village and her reactions to encountering members of the Bagobo tribe from the southern Philippines: "It is difficult to realize that these people are humans as ourselves and that these clothes and this kind of life seem as natural to them as ours do to us. Certainly our ways must be incomprehensible to such people as the Bagobo couple" (94-95). Ward attempts to demystify "these people" through her efforts to establish an equal playing field of mis/comprehension. How might we read this empathy in the context of the contact zone? Saidiya Hartman's notion of the black slave's body as fungible is helpful here. Hartman posits that even in the empathetic sentiment of white abolitionists, the black slave's body still services whiteness, captured as it is within the white liberal gaze. In this context, the Filipino/a tribal body becomes a "fungible body" through which a white woman's empathetic faculties are realized and mobilized.

The 1904 World's Fair brought the world to Americans, without the risk of traveling to a foreign land. The fair aimed to expand Americans' access to and ideas of the world while at the comfort of being (close to) home. Elizabeth and Sarah Metcalf, two American women from Worcester, Massachusetts, attest to how the World's Fair expanded the American imagination. The fair piqued their curiosity about what lay beyond the borders of the nation. It provided a glimpse of what was in store for the expansion of the United States. The Metcalf sisters were not satisfied with the staged wonder they encountered at the St. Louis fairgrounds. Despite the hyperbolic claim that the Philippine Village alone provided a "broader knowledge of the Philippine Islands than could be gained by a trip of months' duration," the sisters traveled to the Philippines and lived in various parts of the country. They set up a business in Manila, and eventually died there, decades after they pursued an extended relationship with the Bagobo men and women they befriended in St. Louis ("Which Way to the Philippines?"). They are noted to have amassed "one of the best collections of Bagobo textile and dress in the United States" (Quizon 530). In the case of the Metcalf sisters, whose amateur and academic interests depart from those of other American women who were in the Philippines at this time, Cherubim Quizon argues that their "middle class cachet (or at least their well deployed savings, investments, and inheritance) . . . allowed them to be less of outsiders to the powers-that-be in the colonial social space, despite their very contrarian political views, and to be critical participants in the American colonial hierarchy in the Philippines" (539). As bodies came into contact in the World's Fair, empathy was an affective response that sanctioned the U.S. imperial project. Filipino/a bodies in performance serviced American women's empowerment during a crucial period in the history of U.S. women's emancipation.

III: *Nikimaliká*: Filipinos Experience the World's Fair

While the idea of the "contact zone" opens up the possibility of an intersectionality that moves beyond mere exchange, it also emphasizes the literally uneven terrain of the "interactive, improvisational dimensions of imperial encounters," including crashes, collisions, and even hit-and-runs (Pratt 8). Hundreds of objects—newspaper reports, photographs, letters, diaries, memoirs—account for American impressions of the World's Fair and the Filipinos in it. The very design of the World's Fair had a built-in structure for recording its place in history; in other words, the World's Fair was already declaring its impact on U.S. history through its meticulous self-archiving process. The asymmetrical production of records from the point of view of those exhibited at the fair underscores the unevenness of imperial relations. As Eric Breitbart notes in the introduction to his book of photographs from the World's Fair,

> most of the "native peoples" photographed on the Pike and in the anthropology exhibits at the St. Louis Fair are anonymous. In almost every case, they were brought to St. Louis not as individuals, with names and personal histories, but as "types," representing a particular tribe, race, or culture. . . . [T]hey lived on the fairgrounds as subjects for scientific study by ethnologists and anthropologists, and as objects of curiosity and amusement for visitors to the fair. (12)

While the majority of available representations follow this pattern, some accounts of specific Filipinos' reactions to the World's Fair are, however, available in public records. Most accessible are statements by the U.S.-convened Honorary Board of Filipino Commissioners, made up of Filipinos from various regions and of varying occupational and class statuses.[22] The members were predominantly men, although wives and other kin accompanied some of them. The commission used their travel to discuss Filipino self-rule; taking advantage of the heightened publicity around their visit, the upcoming presidential election, and the spectacle of the World's Fair, members of this commission strategically addressed the possibility of Filipino self-governance. As reported in the *New York Times*,

> Dr. T. H. Pardo Tavera [board president], as spokesman of the visiting Filipinos, said yesterday that they would ask President Roosevelt at once for a general election of a popular native government under the act of Congress of June 30, 1902, providing that when, after a period of two years of peaceful conditions and good government, the natives, excepting the Moros and pagans, should vote for native delegates to a lower house, the upper one to be the United States Commission, they should have their will. In addition it had been provided that two representatives should be elected to Washington. ("Filipinos Say It's Time for Native Government")

The commission's call for self-government is framed in gratitude to the United States, playing up to the U.S. ideal of self-government as the ultimate form of democracy. It is unclear whether their call for self-rule was different from national independence, or whether their dismissal of "Moros and pagans" as ineligible to vote was sustained in future discussions. Nonetheless, of interest here is that the Filipino Commission mobilized the spectacle of the World's Fair to advocate for Filipino self-rule.

Another primary source of Filipino responses to the World's Fair can be found in the scattered accounts provided by the descendants of the Filipinos who labored and were exhibited in the fair. A new set of perspectives emerges, disturbing the fair's staged panopticon. Though they appear in piecemeal form, these accounts unsettle issues such as consent: Were Filipinos at the World's Fair recruited, did they willingly agree to leave, and did they freely accept a job to "exhibit themselves" in the United States?[23] While some admitted to being tricked, lured, or lied to, others explained their presence as a response to military orders (from organizations such as the Philippine Scouts and Constabulary). More interesting, one Filipino confessed to pretending to be an Igorot in order to come to the United States, while others, such as the Samal Moros, initially refused. As Jose Fermin writes in his *1904 World's Fair: The Filipino Experience*, "the chiefs were unwilling to exhibit themselves to the Americans and to perform in accordance with the wishes of the showmen, until Datu Facundo [one of the Moro chiefs] consented to accompany them" (60). Patricia Afable and Cherubim Quizon, in a special issue of *Philippine Studies* on the St. Louis World's Fair, further challenge the totality of domination that constructs Filipinos as mute and victimized. Re-collecting the experiences of the Filipino/a performers/workers at the fair, they emphasize reactions and impressions about the journey to the

United States and life on the Philippine Village. Afable and Quizon introduce the term "*nikimaliká*," a term referencing "those who went to America/Maliká" within the Bontoc community. "Maliká," the editors add, "conjured a faraway, almost mythical, time and place that only the oldest of the travelers knew about" (441). The personal stories they present break down an all-encompassing imperial master narrative that silences the colonial subject. Antonio Buangan's essay similarly brings to life the subjects of the photographs of "types" to which Breitbart refers. Afable, Quizon, Buangan, and others offer a view of the Filipinos at the fair that extends beyond the temporal and spatial confines of the fairgrounds. These artistic and scholarly projects reimagine Filipino peoples at the World's Fair as more than injured, abject, mute bodies-in-display by infusing notions of exposition with the experience of travel and showmanship. Their focus on individual and community experiences, and life before, during, and years after the seven months in 1904 demystifies the World's Fair into a time and place remembered from Filipino perspectives, and shared with family, community members, and later generations.

Marlon Fuentes's *Bontoc Eulogy* is an interesting and complex commentary on the intersection of identity formation and Philippine colonial history. *Bontoc Eulogy* is a fictive/experimental documentary that explores the search for identity, the blurred line among fiction, history, and authenticity (represented in the film as "ethnographic materials"—film, photos, memories), and exposes the tension between narrative and facts.[24] There is a dual task to imagining the World's Fair from the eyes of the Filipino peoples in this and other artistic and scholarly efforts. One aspect is the effort to piece together various archives—government-sanctioned documents, oral histories, photographs, and others—to highlight the experiences of Filipinos who participated on this world stage. The other aspect concerns the framing of such reimaginings of the World's Fair. Even as "family," "individual," and "travel" become analytics that counter the logic of muted Filipinos-as-objects on display, one must equally navigate between positing the World's Fair as a personal experience and erasing the historical condition of colonialism that made "*nikimaliká*" possible.

IV. My Manila Belle: Black Brownface in Early-
Twentieth-Century American Musical Theater

The Louisiana Purchase World Exposition is only one among multiple stops for the Filipino/a performing body. It also appears in American musical comedies, this time in a different embodiment of brownface that emerged at the

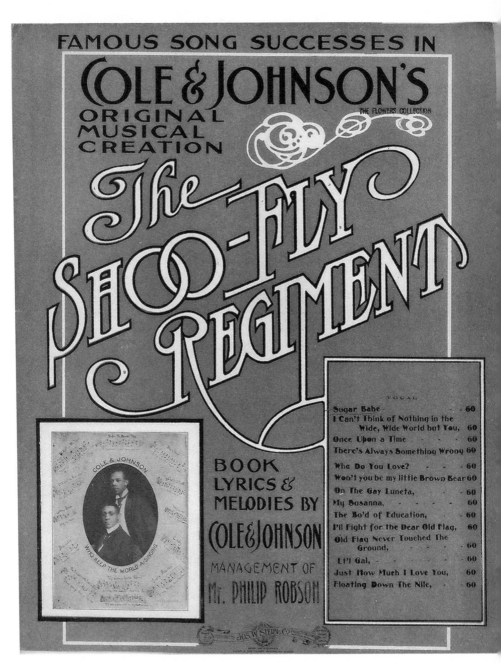

Historic American Sheet Music, "Sugar babe: The shoo-fly regiment," Music B-355, Duke University Rare Book, Manuscript, and Special Collections Library.

intersection of musical theater, nation, and empire building. Musical comedy productions staged an imagined moment of contact between Americans and Filipinos that dramatized a racialized narrative of imperial self-actualization. During the last decade of the nineteenth century and the first decade of the twentieth century, the Philippines and the Filipino/a body appeared in numerous musical productions at a rate that has yet to be matched. Such plays included George Ade's *Sultan of Sulu* (1902), Charles Blaney's *Across the Pacific* (1900), Earl Carroll's *The Wireless Bell* (1910), J. A. Fraser's *Dewey, the Hero of Manila* (1897), Guy Bolton/Jerome Kern's *90 in the Shade* (1915), Clyde Fitch's *Her Own Way* (1903), *Manila Bound* (adopted from *Un Voyage en Chine*, 1900, author unknown), and *The Manila Beauty: An Opera* (1901, author unknown). Alongside the St. Louis World's Fair, chautauquas, and other state- and privately sponsored entertainment circuits, these plays made visible (and desirable) the culture of U.S. empire. Culture, as I invoke it here, refuses the segregation of artistic expressions and the practices of everyday life, a distinction that is clearly impossible within contexts such as the 1904 World's Fair. So too, the musical production of *The Shoo-Fly Regiment* that I analyze below both delineates and blurs the meanings and usage of culture as an art object and as an everyday practice.

If contact zones make us attentive to reaction and interaction among different bodies in contact, the plays that represented Filipinos in this period imagine "what could have happened" during these initial meetings of different cultures (Ade n.p.). Within these plays, the U.S. acquisition of the Philippines is (re)enacted through the conventions of different theatrical genres—comedy, melodrama, musical. The plays, along with legislative decisions, electoral processes, and other forms of cultural labor, actualized and normalized the narrative of the United States' destiny as an imperial power. Theatrical productions during this time of war and nation/empire building were an outlet for patriotic fervor and set the stage for nationalist themes and fantasies that could be fleshed out inside and outside of the confines of the viewing halls.[25] Theater and other forms of embodied performances materialized imaginary exotic locales and peoples; the stage emerged as a pivotal public, cultural space on which thorny contemporary issues could be wrestled with and interpreted in the cultural domain.

Before I proceed, it is important to note the incommensurability between the different performance stages of the early twentieth century. The World's Fair of 1904 was a state-sponsored and -funded spectacle that was held for seven months, and has been extended in the U.S. imaginary through its archival commemoration. Its centrality as a cultural icon is particularly concretized through films such as *Meet Me in St. Louis* (heralded by leading literary scholar Stanley Fish as one of the ten best films in the history of American filmmaking) together with beloved American musical songs like "Meet Me in St. Louis, Louis." The St. Louis World's Fair was also revived in many recent centennial celebrations by different constituencies ranging from the Missouri Historical Society and the 1904 World's Fair Society to the Filipino American Historical Society (FANHS), which commemorated the St. Louis World's Fair in its 2004 conference theme.[26]

The plays noted above have not enjoyed the same longevity, financial support, or governmental attention that the St. Louis World's Fair continues to receive to this day. Many of these plays barely had more than one production; their theatrical run lasted from one night to perhaps two weekends. Some survived in script form, becoming anthologized and published in books (*Sultan of Sulu* and *Dewey, the Hero of Manila*). Others exist in piecemeal form, a hodge-podge of sources put together from artist biographies, one-paragraph reviews, incomplete musical sheets, and, occasionally, images from the production. There is no neat, orderly archive to turn to for these early theatrical productions.

In 1907, Bob Cole and brothers J. Rosamond and James Weldon Johnson, one of the most successful African American music teams of the time, created a musical titled *The Shoo-Fly Regiment*. It is a tale about a young couple, Edward Jackson and Rose Maxwell, whose engagement is interrupted by the Spanish-American War. Edward is a recent graduate of the Tuskegee Institute of Alabama who has been offered a teaching position at the Lincolnville Institute. He postpones his teaching position to volunteer as a soldier in the nation's ongoing war in the Philippines. This decision results in a broken engagement with Rose, who also happens to be the daughter of the principal of the Lincolnville Institute. In the Philippines, Edward leads a successful battle that earns him, and his pal Hunter Wilson from the Lincoln Institute, substantial recognition. He returns a hero, and of course wins back the hand of his beloved. J. Rosamond Johnson plays the role of Edward Jackson and Bob Cole stars as Hunter Wilson. To this day, *The Shoo-Fly Regiment* stands out as one of the earliest all-black productions to shift away from stereotypical characters depicted in minstrel shows.[27] The show toured in the latter part of 1906 to numerous cities in several states, including Texas, Ohio, and Pennsylvania. When it reopened in New York City, at the Grand Opera House and later at the Bijou Theater, *The Shoo-Fly Regiment* had a total of twenty-three performances in the city. At the end of summer 1907, the show went on the road once again, this time extending its tour to Canadian cities.[28]

For scholars such as Paula Marie Seniors, *The Shoo-Fly Regiment* clearly transgressed the norm of musicals during its time through a "change in

Historic American Sheet Music, "I think an awful lot of you; Shoo-fly regiment," Music B-600, Duke University Rare Book, Manuscript, and Special Collections Library.

the representation of African American characters. They discarded . . . Zip Coon, Jim Crow, and Mammy and replaced them with black men as heroic, patriotic, educated, and loving, and black women as literate, virtuous, and romantic" (42). The musical is in three acts, with act 1 being set in Alabama and featuring associated sounds of black musical theater with songs such as "De Bo'd of Education," "I'll Always Love Old Dixie," and "Run, Brudder Possum, Run." The second act, partly set in the Philippines, includes a song titled "On the Gay Luneta," the lyrics written by Cole and the music written by another leading African American musician, James Reese Europe. Music historian Thomas Riis describes this tune as having a "*habañera* rhythm in the bass line of the verse" (131). In the last act, the action returns to the South. Interestingly, though the musical is a romance, the final song—"The Old Flag Never Touched the Ground"—is sung by the whole company but appears to focus only on Cole and J. Rosamond Johnson. Rather than a duet between the primary romantic pair, *The Shoo-Fly Regiment*'s finale features Cole and Johnson's beloved partnership. Along with Bert Williams and George Walker, W. E. B. Du Bois praised these artists for having "lifted minstrelsy by sheer force of genius into the beginning of a new drama" (qtd. in Seniors 93). This final patriotic defense of the U.S. flag not only foregrounds the brilliance of the Cole-Johnson vaudeville act but also firmly situates African American ownership of and belonging in the script of U.S. empire.

I am intrigued by the musical's second act and its placement of the leading man and his fellow African American soldiers in the Philippines. This first "negro-operetta" is one of the few musicals, or perhaps the *only* musical, by an African American creative team that explicitly deals with the American occupation of the Philippines. How did they stage the Philippines? What sounds did they associate with the Philippines? Who performed the "Filipino" characters? What did the Filipino look like in this African American production, noted to be a turning point away from minstrelsy in U.S. black musical theater? These are a few of the pressing questions that came to mind when I first heard of this musical. With the limited available primary resources associated with the musical, these questions are nearly impossible to answer. Very few specifics about the Philippines part of this production can be found in existing reviews and in writings by and about the creative team. Actor Herbert Amos played the role of a Filipino spy and Siren Navarro (sometimes spelled Nevarro) was cast as a "Filipina dancer" named Grizelle. Among a handful of reviews of the Broadway production that ran in the summer of 1907, one noted that the "colored girls appear in Spanish costume" ("Midsummer Listings"). This review signals the production's reliance on costuming to conjure up the Philippines in the second act of the musical.

Two song titles directly reference the Philippines: one, as mentioned earlier, in act 2, titled "On the Gay Luneta" and sung by Lieutenant Dixon and the chorus, and the other, in the third act, "Down in the Philippines," a duet sung by characters Hunter Wilson and Grizelle. In both instances, *The Shoo-Fly Regiment* embodies the Filipino/a and the Philippines in their colonial garb and sounds—"Spanish costume" and "habañera rhythms"—or at least they have been interpreted as such by the critics who recorded what they saw and heard in the show.

In *puro arte* fashion, these historical traces of the Philippines—and the absence of more substantial resources—allow us to shift attention to a minor plot, minor characters, and minor relations in *The Shoo-Fly Regiment*. As mentioned earlier in this chapter, "minor" in this context constitutes what Shih and Lionet propose as an analytical framework that shifts the attention toward a horizontal discourse among racially minoritized subjects. The principal question here is, What narrative labor do the Philippines and the Filipino perform in this unique musical project? In other words, What does brownface and the staging of an exotic locale enable African American artists to express?[29] In staging the proximity between the tropics and the South, does *The Shoo-Fly Regiment* simply recapitulate colonialist visions, or can it also provide a differentiated history of the Filipino/a performing body?

Bill Mullen's concept of "Afro-Orientalism" offers one possible approach to *Shoo-Fly*. Mullen defines "Afro-Orientalism" as a political practice and a counterdiscourse of "U.S. writing on race, nation and empire [that insists] on resistance to the West's most geographically determined form of racism" (xv). Mullen's "Afro-Orientalism" is "grounded in specific terrains," among which are "the experience of black Americans and Asian Americans as indentured servants and slaves in the U.S.; the parallel routes of Western imperialism through Asia and Africa; . . . [and] the attempt by black Americans, from the origins of the Republic, to link with larger radical and revolutionary projects originating outside the shores of the American empire" (xvi). I am drawn here to the political solidarity that is at the heart of Mullen's "Afro-Orientalism" and the possibilities it holds for a more capacious understanding of Filipino/a performance.[30]

For this study on the Filipino/a performing body, *The Shoo-Fly Regiment* is significant as it is a theatrical instantiation of the Philippines as a site of racial uplift for African Americans *through* the practice and imagination of Orientalism. David Krasner cites the musical as one that exemplifies black theater's resistance to racism expressed through "social integration and cooperation" (5). Seniors argues that *The Shoo-Fly Regiment* participates in a project of racial uplift that highlights the struggles of African Americans, and their efforts to claim citizenship in a nation that remained haunted by histories of slavery.[31] While sympathetic to these readings, I would also suggest that *The Shoo-Fly Regiment* expresses the active participation of African Americans in the production of a U.S. imperial imaginary. The Philippines as a *mise en scéne*, and the performance of racial drag—brownface—provides the occasion for a black national identification made possible through the Spanish-American War and the racial "othering" or "Orientalizing" of the Filipino.

Most significantly, *The Shoo-Fly Regiment* advances the metaphorical value of the Philippines and the Filipino/a body: the "Philippines" and the "Filipino" gesture to a world of possibilities in the American imaginary. In the Afro-Orientalist imaginary, performing the Philippines provides the black body with a stage from which to announce its racial distinction from other nonwhite races. The brownface performance of an exotic locale and exotic body constitutes a radical expression of American national identity as heroically black. In the larger repertoire of American theater productions during this period, *The Shoo-Fly Regiment* is among a small yet significant subset of early-twentieth-century American plays that stage U.S.-Philippine imperial relations, through the Spanish-American War, as a backdrop to musical comedies and melodramas. Worth noting here is the Johnson brothers' 1898 operatta *Toloso*, described "as a satire of Spanish-American War," which introduced the work of the Johnson brothers to the movers and shakers of American theater at that time (including "producers and stars of comic operas and musical plays in New York," such as Harry B. Smith, Reginald De Koven, Oscar Hammerstein, George Walker, and Bert Williams) (Riis 35). It was also the production that initiated the partnership with Bob Cole. Though it was never fully produced, songs from *Toloso* were used in later musicals by this creative team (Riis 35-36). Clearly the Johnson brothers had already broached the topic of U.S. imperial pursuits in this earlier work.

Within the repertoire of the Johnson brothers and Bob Cole, *The Shoo-Fly Regiment* actively engages the politics of "Afro-Orientalism." This creative team clearly had an interest in staging African Americans in an "elsewhere" setting and with "an other."[32] *A Trip to Coontown* (1897-1901), noted by the creators as "the first Black musical comedy, with a continuous plot," is one such production (Mates 175). It includes musical numbers such as "The Wedding of the Chinee and the Coon," "All Chink Look Alike to Me," and "The Italian Man" (Peterson 359-60).[33] Though the musical was hailed as "one of the first to break from the minstrel tradition," the slapstick fascination and depiction of racial types—Chinee, Coon, Italian Man—carries over to this groundbreaking musical theater production, known to be the first New York musical written, produced, and performed by black entertainers. Another Johnson brothers and Cole collaboration is *Red Moon,* a production that soon followed *The Shoo-Fly Regiment. Red Moon* explores African American and Native American relations. In both these early productions by this noted creative team, numerous sources have commented on their nonstereotypical depictions of African Americans, casting them in narratives about heroism and romance. Separately, J. Rosamond Johnson, Bob Cole, and James Weldon Johnson also participated in productions that employed the "Orient"— a wide and loose geography that gestured toward and referenced real and imagined embodied expressions of North Africa (Egypt), East Asia (Japan, China), South Asia (India), and Southeast Asia (Philippines). *The Shoo-Fly Regiment's* Afro-Orientalism thus services a patriotic narrative, which in turn services African American citizenship during a time of war. Yet, one cannot but ask what kind of citizenship is being rehearsed in this musical?

The Shoo-Fly Regiment foregrounds African American heroism with the story of an educated young black man whose risks—postponing his teaching career, suspending his romantic relationship to go to war, laying his life on the line of fire—pay off when he returns a war hero. At this historical juncture, it was rare to encounter a theatrical production whose central character depicted a learned black man, a patriotic soldier who claimed a stake in the national project, even though this was a historically accurate story. African American soldiers fought in the Spanish-American and Philippine-American wars, and their participation in them has been well documented and analyzed. The U.S.-Philippine War was the first in which black troops were ordered to fight a "colonial" war in Southeast Asia.[34] African American opposition to the U.S. war in the Philippines is also well documented, in newspapers articles and letters of African American soldiers that appeared in African American journals. Scholar Nerissa Balce has characterized this opposition as simultaneously political and racial—political in the mutual struggle for emancipation it invoked, and racial given the affinity between people of color that it demonstrated ("Filipino Bodies," 53). Most enlightening in the letters and journal entries is the marked ambivalence of the soldiers about their mission, their affinity with Filipino civilians, and their unease with white troops' racist treatment of the local populace, which they equated with the racism they experience as blacks in the military.

The name or phrase "shoo fly" is popularly known through the American folk song titled "Shoo Fly, Don't Bother Me." It has multiple origin stories—in the Civil War, it was equally known as a Pennsylvania Dutch military march song, as a plantation song, as a Negro folk song from Mississippi, and even as a song from the Panamanian work fields.[35] Almost all of these circulating origins stories are grounded in histories of the slave economy. In 1870, *Harper's Weekly* magazine published a political cartoon about the Fifteenth Amendment to the U.S. Constitution with the caption "Shoo Fly, Don't Bodder Me!" It shows an African American man in the act of casting his vote with his right hand while his left hand is swatting flies swarming around him. The flies have human faces and have initials of the states (such as California and Montana) that opposed granting voting rights to African Americans ("XVth Amendment"). During the Spanish-American War, the period of this musical, the significance of "Shoo Fly, Don't Bother Me" was extended to the "flies and yellow fever mosquitoes that plagued American soldiers" ("Shoo Fly, Don't Bother Me").

African American participation in the U.S. nation/empire building is complex, expressed in multiple forms and across a range of ideological positionings. Even though the appearances of the Philippines and the performance of the Filipino/a in *The Shoo-Fly Regiment* are brief, they clearly enable an articulation of African American investment in the U.S. nation/ empire formation. In the musical, Lieutenant Dixon (performed by Theodore Pankey), an officer of Company G, 54th U.S.V., falls in love with Grizelle, the Filipina. Lieutenant Dixon sings "On the Gay Luneta" to convey happy times in Luneta, a famous park in the capital city of the Philippines. It is in "gay Luneta," on "one moonlit night" that the officer meets "this gay Grizelle." He describes this "sweet Manila Belle" as having "soft, dreamy eyes, like the stars in the skies" and "midnight eyes" that are "beaming" (Riis 287-88). This "fair maiden" is the subject of his dreams. Contrary to a gruesome war zone, the Philippines is "a beautiful scene, 'Mid the tropical green," that remains "so calm and serene" (Riis 286-87). In this song, the national body of the Philippines is conflated with the body of the Filipina woman, both feminized into softness and serenity under the desiring gaze of the American military officer.

Grizelle performs a dance at what seems to be the key moment in the musical when the officer becomes infatuated with the Filipina native. Siren Navarro, who plays Grizelle, is billed as the choreographer and also the costume designer for the production. She is best known as a partner to Tom Brown for their Chinese impersonation acts in vaudeville shows from 1900 to 1914. Indeed, Navarro built a career enacting Afro-Orientalism; this was her niche as a performer. As Krystyn Moon writes in her book about early Chinese performances in nineteenth- and twentieth-century American theater and music, "Nevarro continued to do Chinese dances as a solo act for about a year but disappeared from theater columns by 1916" (135). By staging a love connection between an African American and a Filipina native, albeit in her Spanish colonial likeness, *The Shoo-Fly Regiment* suggests an affinity between African Americans and Filipinos. In this world, there exists a complex racial identification that allows for an interracial romantic union that is stridently not a parody or satire. As Seniors points out, "Cole and Johnson centered the number on the interracial romance between the two characters in the Philippines and simultaneously broke the love scene taboo and the taboo against interracial romance" (67). Within the realm of romance, a harmonious nonwhite, interracial, and perhaps even international union is made possible. One could well argue that such moments are precisely where we see the limits of the Afro-Orientalism paradigm. This interracial union transpires between minor characters and is sanctioned because the lead romantic pair, an upstanding middle-class black man and woman, happily reunite. It is also sanctioned because the main black male protagonist leads a successful battle in the name of the U.S. nation/empire. Could such an interracial union have been staged if the hero had been one of the few dissenters, if he had denounced U.S. occupation of the Philippines and joined the opposition instead? The interracial union between Lt. Dixon and Grizelle displaces the possibility of an ideological affinity with the Filipino people's struggle against U.S. imperialism and their pursuit of an independent nation.

In purely historical terms, the Philippines serves as an appropriate setting for a military musical that casts Africans Americans at the center of the story because black soldiers were indisputably active in the Spanish-American War and, later, the Philippine-American War. Biographer Reid Badger, in writing about *The Shoo-Fly Regiment*'s musical director, Thomas Reese Europe, comments on the popularity of military plots in theater: they "encouraged plenty of crowd-pleasing action on stage and provided an opportunity to exploit a resurgent national pride through patriotic songs" (33). For this musical, the Philippines provided a new backdrop to spice up romance, a faraway location filled with exotic spaces and bodies. Such a turn to the Philippines was commensurate with larger forms of spatial experimentation that enlivened the American artistic imaginary in the early twentieth century. Extranational plots allowed for an exploration, for a different look, with aesthetic elements on stage. Within African American theatrical and creative efforts, these enactments of other exotics were opportunities to demonstrate the malleability of the black body. As artists such as Cole, the Johnson brothers, and the performing team of Bert Williams and George Walker struggled to establish new forms of black expression, productions such as *The Shoo-Fly Regiment* and *The Red Moon* demonstrate possibilities for the black performing body beyond stereotypical images embedded in the tradition of black minstrelsy.[36] Performance Studies scholar Daphne Brooks argues that "minstrelsy sought to naturalize the spectacularly abject and hyper excessive black body in the 19th Century" (28). She contends that African Americans, as new bodies of modernity following emancipation, "work out corporeality in a new period of autonomy, . . . [and the] culture of performance responded to the uncertainty of corporeal autonomy by producing a range of liminal and embattled types and icons" (23). Nearly a century later, in the era of Jim Crow, African American performers continued to wrestle with the dominant mode of minstrelsy as their primary currency of evaluation. As I have argued, such struggles may have advanced African American emancipation, but these efforts, in the case of *The Shoo-Fly Regiment*, were still waged at the expense of the Filipino/a body.

V: A Centennial Later: Fair Legacies and Beyond

Both the 1904 World's Fair and the musical production *The Shoo-Fly Regiment* present brownface performances that were clearly instrumental in U.S. nation/empire building. The stages of the St. Louis World's Fair displayed Filipino/a bodies from the "Visayan maidens" to the dog-eating "Igorots," from the "the little naked Moro boys" to the more respectable members of the Philippine Constabulary Band. In doing so, they produced the everyday life of Filipinos as a spectacle of extreme racial difference and barbarism, thereby sanctioning the civilizing mission of U.S. imperialism. Within the context of this state-sponsored, made-for-the-purposes-of-imperialism performing stage, the Filipino/a body became a brownface performance through the literal strength of its material presence within the fairgrounds. As for the all-black musical theater production, *The Shoo-Fly Regiment*, black bodies acting Filipino and staging the Philippines aided black citizenship as it struggled with anxieties over national belonging. More specific to the black performing body, brownface performances were attempts at exploring its capacity to represent, its potential to transform, by translating to a racial script distinct from its own. In both versions of "brownface," performing Filipinos as racially different provided white and black Americans a form of mobility that consolidated self-transformation through the language of empire. How are these brownface performances of one hundred years ago visited upon the contemporary Filipino/a performing body today? When and under what circumstances are these early representations confronted in contemporary Filipino/a American performance works?

In 1998, a number of Filipino/a American artists collaborated to combine various international events commemorating one hundred years of U.S-Philippine relations. Artists Wilma Consul, Allan Manalo, Joyce Manalo, Alleluia

Panis, Sony Ley, and Pearl Ubungen, mostly based in the San Francisco/Bay Area at the time, produced the Post Modern American Pilipino Performance Project (POMO), "created to focus, highlight, promote, and elevate American Pilipino post-modern aesthetics" ("Post Modern American Pilipino Performance Project [POMO]").[37] POMO is now held yearly in San Francisco, and has successfully presented the works of many Filipino/a American artists, including Tongue in a Mood, TnT (Teatro ng Tanan), Sean San Jose, Gigi Otalvaro-Hormillosa, 8th Wonder, Simeon Den, Rex Navarrete, Alyson de la Cruz, Kennedy Kabasares, Dewayne Calizo, Jen Soriano, Anthem Salgado, and the Alleluia Panis Dance Theatre. The POMO Festival embodies a strategy taken up specifically by contemporary Filipino/a American artists to contend with what Alicía Arrízon has analyzed as "the unresolved upheaval and cataclysm" of imperial representations (94). In analyzing the POMO Festival in these terms, my aim is to elaborate a relationship to performance that thinks through the weight of historical representation rather than simply against it.

POMO's critical programming strategy of showing the colonial stagings of the Filipino/a alongside the dominant logic of multiculturalism confronts the continued display of Filipinos and other racialized bodies as exotic, in isolation, and decontextualized from the century-long U.S.-Philippine imperial relations. Such a confrontation of the centennial and multiculturalism is of course possible because of a long history of Filipino American cultural production in the Bay Area.[38] Muriel Miguel (of the Kuna and Rappahannock nations), an actor, playwright, director, choreographer, teacher, and member of the feminist Native American performance ensemble Spiderwoman Theater, once said, "When I hear 'multiculturalism,' I hang on tight to my clothes, even my underwear." Miguel's sardonic comment richly sums up many artists of color's critique of the liberal pluralist logic of multiculturalism that became dominant in the 1990s. Multiculturalism provided a platform, an opportunity, and visibility for Filipino American and other racialized artistic projects. U.S. multiculturalism, as practiced by the nation-state and as understood in popular discourse, is a response to U.S. monoculturalism. Its liberal pluralist approach sought to treat all the cultures that make up the United States as equal. While the notion of U.S. multiculturalism advocates plurality, it diverts attention from continuing inequities among different racialized communities. It does so by privileging the discourse of difference through a celebratory, apolitical mode. More so, as captured in Miguel's reaction to the very utterance of the word "multiculturalism," racialized performing bodies are spectacularly made to service the regime of multiculturalism, touted as the realization of a truly pluralistic, democratic society. Yet, many artists, even those who benefited from programming

Postmodern American Pilipino Performance Project. 2002. Produced and Presented by KulArts, Inc., in association with the Yerba Buena Center for the Arts. Photos: *Clockwise from top left*: Kennedy Kabasares; Traci Kato-Kiriyama and Edren Sumagaysay; Michelle Ferrer and Mariel Flores Viñalon; Gigi Otálvaro-Hormillosa. Graphic designers: Tina Besa and Julie Munsayac. Permission granted by Alleluia Panis of Kul Arts, Inc.

that supported their work, understood multiculturalism as a disciplinary measure that limited their range of artistic expressions. Their conditions of labor and creativity were still being measured within and against a dominant aesthetic value that treated artists of colors as tokens and evaluated their work in terms of quotas to be met in order to subscribe to the multicultural order. Though not as literal as the World's Fair fairgrounds, the racialized performing body was still made to serve an agenda that sought to mask and mobilize U.S. imperial ambitions.

Centennial celebrations between 1996 and 2006 approached the state-sanctioned remembrance of one hundred years of U.S.-Philippine contact on multiple fronts. Many local and state-sponsored celebrations focused on the contributions of Filipinos in U.S. labor and cultural economy, thereby putting the burden of memory on Filipino Americans.[39] Yet, projects such as POMO and others by individual Filipino American artists took up the centennial as an opportunity to lay bare the historical, economic, social, and cultural conditions through which Filipino/a radicalization had been made possible. Many also used the commemoration as a way to examine the relations of power that facilitate Filipino/a global mobility. The inauguration of the POMO Festival constitutes a unique and challenging approach to the U.S.-Philippine centennial. Rather than reiterate the two states' benevolent intent to memorialize their friendly relations, the POMO Festival subverted the occasion, making it a platform to comment on the imperial contact zone's continuing impact on Filipino/a racialization. The performance festival was turned into a reverse spectacle that set the celebratory visibility of the Filipinos at the centennial against their prurient visibility in the imperial past. For example, in 2002, Gigi Otalvaro-Hormillosa was a featured performer in POMO. Otalvaro-Hormillosa's works, *The Inverted Minstrel, Cosmic Blood,* and a short film titled *Dimension of IS,* take up the legacy of the World's Fair as sites for display of queer and colored bodies.[40] These performance pieces explore the connection among freak shows, queer and colored bodies as spectacles, and performance through the genre of speculative fiction. Equally important about Otalvaro-Hormillosa's work is that it situates the spectacle of the Filipino/a hybrid body in the longer history of the conquest of the Americas. Also presented in the same program were performance excerpts from the play-in-verse *Coconut Masquerade,* written by Melinda Corazon Foley and the poetry/performance ensemble *zero 3,* which consists of Los Angeles–based artists Kennedy Kabasares, Tracey Kato-Kiriyama, and Edren Sumagaysay.

In its response to the centennial celebrations, the POMO Festival directly engaged the historical and political terms through which the Filipino/a

American performing body "puts on a show." In doing so, POMO defies the "basic food group" approach of multiculturalism, where only one artist of color can be represented in a long laundry list of differences. Simply put, under the multicultural agenda, the artistic value of Filipino Americans gathers currency only through its performance of so-called traditional Filipino art forms. Creative capacity is recognized through a fantasy of cultural preservation, not innovation or experimentation. POMO places emphasis on "American Pilipino post-modern aesthetics" as a strident response to the constrictions of "traditions" that otherwise sanctioned the racialized performing body's creative value. This is not a facile critique of "traditional" art forms; after all, Panis and KulArts, Inc., have a vibrant arts program that works with contemporary master artists of tribal arts in the Philippines. The consortium understood the practice of traditional performing arts as equally innovative, modern, and not at all static. Rather, the focus of the criticism is more on how multiculturalism reifies ethnic and racial identities and forms of cultural expressions. In contradistinction to the flattening logic of multiculturalism, the POMO Festival stages Filipino/a American performance in its myriad forms, embracing the legacies of its colonial past as the critical impetus for its creative future.

In this chapter, I have been grappling with the metaphorical value of the Filipino/a and the Philippines as realized in two forms of brownface performances—in the 1904 World's Fair and the musical theater *The Shoo-Fly Regiment*. During the early years of U.S.-Philippine imperial contact, the newly acquired imperial possession and its subjects seemed to offer the possibility of mobility for African American men and white American women. As we see from the emergence of the POMO Festival, contemporary performances continue to wrestle with the impact of the colonial legacies on Filipino/a racialization in the United States. These Filipino American artistic projects foreground the link between early representations of the Filipino/a performing body and the Philippines and the logic of late-twentieth-century multiculturalism. In the next chapter, I continue to consider the metaphorical value of the Filipino/a performing body as it comes into close contact with other American bodies. I follow the Filipino/a performing body to the U.S. taxi dance halls of the 1920s and 1930s. As the imperial metropole comes face to face with the splendid Filipino dancing body, a new "Filipino problem" emerges: the migrant subject.

2

"Splendid Dancing"

Of Filipinos and Taxi Dance Halls

"The Filipino Is The State's Next Problem"
—editorial title, *Watsonville Evening Parajonian,* 1930

Filipinos as a rule are *splendid dancers.*
—Jeanne De la Moreau, taxi dancer, *Los Angeles Times,* 1931

A 1904 photograph shows Mrs. Wilkins, a white patron at the St. Louis World's Exposition, gleefully holding hands with a muscular, scantily dressed brown man identified as an "exhibit" from the popular Philippine Village. The caption to the photograph reads, "Mrs. Wilkins teaching an Igorot the cakewalk" (de la Cruz, Baluyut, and Reyes 44). A little less than three decades later, the instruction continues, albeit with some subtle differences. A second photograph, this time of a well-dressed Filipino man, his arm around a white taxi dance hall dancer, carries the caption, "An American Taxi Dancer and Her Filipino Escort Outside a Dance Hall" (de la Cruz, Baluyut, and Reyes 45). Several factors are inverted *and* reproduced in these two startling images. In the 1904 World's Fair photograph, the white woman plays the role of the patron, with the savage "Igorot" as pliant student. In the second image, the dapper Filipino man performs the role of the patron, with the white female dancer as his willing partner. For many Filipino patrons, going to taxi dance halls was often referred to as "going to class." The taxi dance hall was a valuable social institution that "provided social contacts

with American young women, . . . it was a school by which he [the Fili-
pino] gained self confidence and a certain degree of social ease when among
Americans," and that "acquainted the Filipino with American life" (Cressey
174). The Filipino man's access to whiteness and American social practices
is mediated by and through his desire to learn, mimic, and ultimately perform. The organizing structure that brings together the two photographs is
tutelage.

The two images referenced above were first juxtaposed in a landmark
collection, *Confrontations, Crossings, and Convergence: Photographs of the
Philippines and the United States, 1898-1998*. Described by its editors as "a
centennial reflection on the complex relationship between the U.S. and the
Philippines through the medium of photography . . . [containing] prints
from governmental archives, libraries, museums and personal collections in
Asia, Europe, and North America," this collection is indeed a rare compen-
dium of the Filipino past (de la Cruz, Baluyut, and Reyes 15). Multiple readings are implied by the juxtaposition of these two images entitled "Dancing
as Transcendence" (44). Placing these images left to right suggests an evolutionary narrative, a before and after storyline made possible by the graces of
colonial tutelage. Through benevolent assimilation, and careful education in
the ways of American life, the Filipino savage grows up, matures into a fine
club patron, where he continues to learn about the subtleties of "American
life." The two images center the pivotal role white women and performance
played in the American civilizing mission. In both images, access to American social practices is guaranteed through and by contact with white women.
The text that accompanies the two images explains their visual coupling:
"Illegitimate Desires: Widespread fear of 'racial contamination' led to pro-
hibitions against Filipinos. Nonetheless, Filipino men and American women
discovered creative ways to transcend the barriers" (de la Cruz, Baluyut, and
Reyes 18). Placing these images side by side, the editors propose, highlights
the ways in which Filipino men, and the white women who danced with
them, transcended social and racial barriers through dance. Their forbidden
dance becomes a site of potential defiance.

This chapter follows the Filipino patron in American taxi dance halls of
the 1920s and 1930s to situate and interrogate the visibility of the migrant Filipino performing body. Three key concerns animate my interest in the relationship between Filipino male migrants and taxi dance halls. First, through
their *puro arte*, through their "exceptional" mastery of popular American
dance steps, I consider how Filipino bodies become at once desirable and
racialized. Second, what happens when the migrant/colonial body of the
Filipino reroutes the script of racial oppression through his own "splendid"

dancing? Third, how does the success of the Filipino as dancer and patron complicate extant discourse on the taxi dance halls, one of America's unique social institutions?

In order to attend to these concerns, it is important to first clarify the specific historical connection between the Filipino and the taxi dance hall. In the 1920s and early 1930s, Filipino men patronized the popular American social institution of the taxi dance hall, comprising "at least a fifth of the total patronage" in major cities such as Detroit and Los Angeles (Cressey 145).[1] Taxi dance halls were at the height of their popularity during this period, often serving as a key site of sociality among and between immigrants. Women were employed as dancers for hire, and men, predominantly immigrants, were their principal patrons. Filipinos, workers and students alike, came dressed in McIntosh suits, eager to spend their hard-earned wages on taxi dancers.[2] Here, Filipino men made rare social contact with women—taxi dancers who were largely white, occasionally Mexican, and very rarely Filipina. Filipinos would purchase their dance tickets, choose their favorite girl within a group of taxi dancers, and move to the music of a live band. For ten cents per dance number, slow or fast, Filipino men could choose to stay with a partner until their tickets ran out or opt for the pleasures of another. Like a taxi ride, each dance came with a ticketed price and the expectation of a tip, in the form of either a drink, a sandwich, or perhaps even a marriage proposal.

Filipino patrons' dancing skills drew passionate comments from dancers as well as early scholars of American taxi dance halls. For example, in "Confessions of a Taxi Dancer," Jeanne De la Moreau excitedly declares that "Filipinos as a rule are *splendid dancers*," noting that one Filipino patron was even nicknamed "God's Gift to the Taxi-Dancers!" (E5). De la Moreau is not alone in her rhapsodic characterizations of the Filipino dancer in the taxi dance halls as physically "splendid." For many observers, the Filipino male was arguably the best dancer among the patrons of taxi dance halls at the peak of this social institution's popularity. In particular, his exceptional kinesthetic abilities (variously described as "splendid," "spectacular," "fancy") were a source of repeated commentary. He was dazzling in his knowledge of the latest American dance steps of the period (such as the lindy hop, the swing, and the shimmy). The Associated Filipino Press reports of Filipinos at the Hippodrome Dance Palace in Los Angeles further aggrandize the status of the Filipino male dancers, describing them as "fancy dancers in excellent pairs . . . gliding jovially on the floor until the wee hours of the morning" (qtd. in Maram 15).[3] "Filipino conduct" *in* the taxi dance hall is also equally exemplary, as "one which he can point to with pride. He is seldom guilty of sensual dancing, and is much more the pursued than the pursuer in his contacts with taxi dancers" (Cressey 155).[4] So iconic is the Filipino male dancer that American sociologist Paul Cressey goes so far as to say that the Filipino's exceptional dancing skills demonstrate his knowledge of American ways and his "all too rapid" assimilation into American society.[5]

The discourse of exceptionality framing the perception of the Filipino dancing body draws directly from the production of American empire and its implementation. This representational coupling of exceptionality with the Filipino dancing body coincides with the established metaphorics of United States imperialism. Filipino Studies scholars, most notably Oscar Campomanes, have linked "American exceptionalism" to the denial of U.S. imperialism and to the historical "amnesia" surrounding the U.S. invasion of the Philippines. Epifanio San Juan Jr., a leading scholar of the U.S. invasion in the Philippines, offers this critique: "The United States as a political formation is 'exceptional,' according to the Establishment historians, because it did not follow the European path to colonial expansion. The discourse and practice of 'American exceptionalism' as part of Cold War strategy has been criticized acutely 'as an outgrowth of technocratic modernization and developmentalist thought'" (16). Within the context of U.S. empire in the Philippines, "exceptionalism" emerges as a hegemonic construct that "forgets" the calculated pursuit of the Philippines by the United States. Furthermore, it erases the violent implementation of American imperial rule in the Philippines.

Of significance here is that the trope of "exceptionalism" problematically sanctions, even mandates, the violations of U.S. empire.[6] A related project of sanctioned imperial amnesia, I want to suggest, emerges within the myriad depictions of the Filipino body as "exceptional." Routed through the "splendid" discourse of Filipino dancing, the language of exceptionality instead sediments and extends U.S. colonial modes of commodification and racism. Taxi dance halls, for instance, facilitated one of the few spaces of social interaction between Americans and Filipinos. Within spaces such as the taxi dance halls, the spectacle of the Filipino dancing body emerges as a vibrant and potentially violating instantiation of the effects of U.S. imperialism. This "brown menace's" "splendid dancing" is a corporeal testament to one of the key anxieties of American men.[7] Filipinos competed for jobs in a rapidly shrinking American labor market, even as American men warily regarded Filipinos and their appeal to white women as *the problem* of the decade ("The Filipino Is This State's Next Problem"). Unlike "other Orientals," whose masculinity was defined as asexual, the Filipino's supposed hypersexuality fueled the very fire that ignited his eventual exclusion. Part of my contention here is that the persistent reading of Filipino corporeality (as "splendid dancers

Mrs. Wilkins teaching an Igorotte boy the cakewalk at the 1904 World's Fair. Missouri History Museum, St. Louis.

and passionate lovers of white women") through the lens of "exceptionality" equally circulates and corrupts the very languages of U.S. imperialism.

In what follows, I explore the following questions: What do we make of the characterization of the Filipino dancing body as "exceptional" within the context of a heightened anti-Filipino U.S. politics? How do we understand the complimentary descriptions of the Filipino on the dance floor, when *outside* the dance halls these "beloved" patrons were being hunted by white mobs? Was the dance hall a haven from the violence of anti-Filipino sentiments, and did dancing in fact transcend the battles between anti-immigrant nativists and their "problem"? I am also interested in how this phenomenon of the Filipinos in taxi dance halls has been mobilized in contemporary narratives of Filipino America. In this chapter, I propose an understanding of the exceptional Filipino dancing body through a set of overlapping readings that can be differentiated in political, historical, and performative terms. The first section introduces the Filipino dancing body as an archival embodiment of the anti-Filipino sentiments of the 1920s and 1930s. Here, I engage with the existing scholarship on Filipino dancing in taxi dance halls, specifically the perception of "dancing" within and against various social forces. The next section examines what I term the "geopolitics of the taxi dance halls" and details the racial workings of the taxi dance halls that fueled anti-Filipino sentiments. The analytic of "geopolitics" shifts the understanding of taxi dance halls as solely an urban sociocultural formation, as they were characterized by early taxi dance hall scholars, to an understanding of the taxi dance hall as a complex social institution shaped by foreign policy, immigrant communities, and race politics. The last section returns to the Filipino dancing body in the taxi dance halls as a figure of "corporeal colonization" (Choy, "Salvaging the Empire," 40). Framed within the concept of *puro arte*, the Filipino's "dazzling steps" and "splendid dancing" are thus situated alongside the American empire's spectacularization of the Filipino body as inferior, infectious, and ultimately savage. I conclude this chapter with an analysis of contemporary Filipino/a American narratives that articulate the social phenomenon of the taxi dance halls as a differentiated space of consolation and condemnation.

I: Taxi Dance Halls, Immigrants, and Social Relations

The Filipino dancing body in the taxi dance halls presents "an archival embodiment" of a crucial moment in Filipino American history (Román, "Dance Liberation," xxiii).[8] Archival embodiment, in this chapter, gestures to the corpus of Filipino American history and records, choreographed by

Untitled. Courtesy of Visual Communications Photographic Collections.

and onto the Filipino body. As has been previously noted, the taxi dance halls and their Filipino patrons played critical roles in the landmark Tydings-McDuffie Act. The Tydings-McDuffie Act, paradoxically also called the Philippine Independence Act *and* the Filipino Exclusion Act, was passed in 1934. It declared the Philippines independent, thereby changing the legal designation of Filipinos from nationals to aliens and, consequently, limiting Filipino immigration to the United States to fifty persons per year.[9] Nativist sentiments in the form of violence against Filipinos marked a distinct shift in the racial and social status of Filipinos both within and outside the United States. The Filipino's exceptional dancing thus gathers its representational significance within the fraught historical context of U.S.-Philippine relations. What is key here is that many anti-Filipino attacks occurred in social settings such as taxi dance halls rather than in work places. My particular focus is on the Filipino dancing body as "an archival embodiment" of the link among immigration, foreign policy, social institutions, and Filipino corporeal colonization.

Early sociological scholarship on the taxi dance halls, specifically by scholars from the emerging American School of Sociology in Chicago at that time and eventually in other American universities, situated its emergence within a period of transition. The development of an urban culture and commercialized mass entertainment ushered in new forms of sociality. Growth of urban spaces also meant increased crime, delinquency among youth, and tension between new bodies of people interacting. The American School of Sociology in Chicago produced scholarly assessments of the role of taxi dance halls in the changing social landscape of burgeoning urban spaces. In a republished version of Cressey's *Taxi-Dance Hall* in 1969, Ronald Vanderkooi refers to the taxi dance hall as a "transitory social institution, developed to meet certain needs in an American era of rapid urbanization and dramatic cultural exchange" (xi). Taxi dance halls thrived in cities because urban life, as sociologists such as Cressey and Ernest Burgess concluded, prioritized the individual and did not facilitate social integration.[10] Taxi dance halls were commercialized recreation and fostered "casual association" versus wholesome expression (Cressey xvi). The taxi dance hall was constructed as an institutional testament to the disappearance of a collective way of life.

Early scholars of taxi dance halls characterized their methodological approach to social processes as systemic, objective, and empirical. However, their analyses were clearly marked by anti-immigrant bias, framed as reform or a period of social transition. Cressey's study (with a preface written by

Burgess) repeatedly laments the new social relations fostered by the taxi dance halls, pointing to "the loss of community-oriented recreations to large scale commercial forms" (Vanderkooi xiii). This bemoaning of a "collective way of life" reads as a cautionary tale for the immigrant communities' invasion of the public sphere.[11] It is significant that these studies circulated beyond conventional academic readership. For example, Cressey served as a caseworker and special investigator for the Juvenile Protective Association while he was conducting his research on taxi dance halls.

Despite such early moral leanings, scholarship on Filipinos in the taxi dance halls has been, by and large, productive and generative in analyzing the ways in which a racialized immigrant community negotiated its presence in a dynamic public social space. For example, in his 1934 M.A. thesis at the University of Southern California, Benicio Catapusan Jr., under the aegis of the eminent sociologist-scholar Emory Bogardus, researched the social activities of Filipinos in Los Angeles. Catapusan specifically examined taxi dance halls and pool halls to describe Filipino immigrants' social adjustment. Later scholars have turned to feminist theory and theories of racial and gender formation to extend and thicken our understanding of Filipino patrons' participation in the taxi dance hall economy. In her essay "'White Trash' Meets the 'Brown Monkeys,'" Rhacel Parreñas proposes a relational understanding of the Filipino patrons' and the white taxi dancers' social formation in the taxi dance halls, concluding that an alliance emerged between these two based on their immigrant worker status as well as their deviant sexuality. Linda Maram, in *Creating Masculinity in Los Angeles' Little Manila*, discusses Filipinos in taxi dance halls within the context of policing youth immigrants of color. Both Parreñas and Maram comment on the meaning of dance for Filipino patrons within histories of gender, race, immigration, and the taxi dance hall. For Parreñas, dancing counters the subjectification and disciplining of Filipino men "through the maximization of their bodies as machines" (120).[12] For Maram, Filipino dressing and dancing in the taxi dance halls are alternative ways of being, beyond being workers subjected to harsh labor conditions. Such an approach regards the Filipino dancing body as contrary to the much-maligned Filipino masculinity. Other scholars contend that the Filipino dancing body in taxi dance halls is crucial evidence of the presence and contributions of Filipinos in the American cultural fabric.

In this chapter, I consider a different problematic, one that explores the exceptionality of the Filipino body without recourse *only* to its resistant potentiality. I want to be clear here that my aim is not to facilely elide early readings; rather, I am committed to expanding the scholarship to include questions of aesthetics, performance, and culture—to suggest, in other words, that the trope of "exceptionalism" in the form of aesthetic accolade can also work to contain and domesticate the unwieldy colonized Filipino body. Dancing in taxi dance halls clearly worked as a profound spectacle of colonial mimicry. On the one hand, mimicry here is the strictest form of ideological disciplining; after all, dancing bodies are *not* overtly being prompted to dance splendidly for the master. On the other hand, it is also the ultimate corporeal evidence of the "success," if we recall Mary Talusan's argument about Philippine brass bands in the St. Louis World's Fair, of the American imperial project: in just two decades, Filipinos had progressed from savage to civilized, shimmying their way into American society. Yet, the Filipino's mastery of "Occidental ways" equally enacted the worst nightmare of those who had foreseen the effects of the conquest of the Philippines.

Filipino patrons' "splendid dancing" and "dazzling performance" clearly require complex historical analysis that is mindful of the dangers of hypostatizing their kinesthetic abilities. In other words, what is the material history of the Filipino dancing body? How did the Filipino gain this infamous kinesthetic knowledge that garnered such attention and caused so much tension in the taxi dance hall? Dancing as a kinesthetic practice performs sociality and facilitates corporeal relation, often rendered as liberatory because of the fantasy of a shared space (Román, "Dance Liberation," x). In the dance hall, dancing is viewed as an unregulated, unmediated, and uninhibited movement. Yet, dance cannot be totally uninhibited or unregulated. Sociality in the dance hall, through dancing, is also about the negotiation of power. Dance moves are measured and calculated, structuring a relation or exchange, as much as they are about associating pleasure with moving freely. The "splendid dancing" of Filipinos in the taxi dance hall gained attention, yet it did not necessarily garner the Filipinos a sense of belonging outside the dance hall. In fact, this very performance of bodily knowledge and ability further enhanced Filipino difference and contributed to the hostility toward Filipinos.

II: The Geopolitics of Taxi Dance Halls

I view the taxi dance hall as a differentiated space of consolation and condemnation for Filipinos, as a space that best embodies the workings of *puro arte*. As noted, the taxi dance hall was a prominent space of anti-Filipino sentiments that led up to the Philippine Independence Act. Immigration, foreign policy, and race relations substantially impacted the functioning of this social public space. Filipino immigrant social interaction within these public spaces was thus highly regulated, and they were not simply a safe haven for dancing and leisure.[13] Forms of control included surveillance by the police as well as white patrons who hung out in these social establishments waiting for "something" to happen.[14] Euphemistically involved in "waiting" processes, white men regularly harassed and intimidated Filipinos.

An analysis of the location of the dance halls provides a clearer insight into the geopolitics of these spaces in the 1920s and 1930s. Cressey coins the term "interstitial areas" to describe the location of the taxi dance halls. He notes that they were "in the central business district and the rooming house area, near the residence of a majority of its regular patrons," or at least easily accessible to potential patrons through public transportation (224, 226). Aptly termed "interstitial," these areas fell outside the moral radar of the "community conscious" and were thus not vulnerable to protest or policing. Many taxi dance halls were concentrated in Los Angeles' downtown area. Shifting boundaries and increasing ethnic and racial communities characterized the city's growth as the "downtown and central district . . . housed more than half the population" in 1919. But by 1929, "less than a third of the population lived in the downtown, East Los Angeles, Hollywood, and Wilshire districts" (Tygiel 2).[15] One of the taxi dance halls frequented by Filipino patrons was the Hippodrome Dance Palace in South Main Street. Once known as the Adolphous, the Hippodrome was a site of various forms of nightlife activities. It opened as the largest vaudeville house in 1911, with a capacity of twenty-one hundred people (Crowley and Melnick). The Hippodrome routinely competed as one of the most popular vaudeville and movie houses in Los Angeles until the decline of vaudeville as popular entertainment in the early 1930s. It appears that the Hippodrome was simultaneously a vaudeville theater (which also showed moving pictures) with a taxi dance hall on the second floor.[16] In this instance, this social space was already identifiable as an establishment of commercial entertainment, frequented by a variety of patrons. Filipinos also patronized other Main Street dance halls, such as the One Eleven Dance Hall and Danceland, and the Rizal Cabaret on Spring Street (Catapusan, "Filipino Occupational and Recreational Activities," 45).

During this period of transition, new residents of Los Angeles were developing a proprioceptive awareness of the city and one another. Jules Tygiel's introductory summary in *Metropolis in the Making* describes the interaction between the "overwhelmingly Caucasian and Protestant" Angelenos and the migrants displaced in Los Angeles:

> The Ku Klux Klan found a ready following in the 1920s Southern California. Employers in many industries, especially the expanding white-collar sector, as Clark Davis illustrates, sought to hire only "red-blooded Americans."

According to Hise, the "imaginative geographies" envisioned by local leaders and planners stressed whites-only policies, and zoning in towns like Torrance specifically barred non-Caucasians. Restrictive housing covenants in most sections of the region prevented nonwhites from moving in. The Legal Committee of the NAACP, writes Flamming, found ample work warding off police brutality against minorities and segregation in housing and public swimming pools. Exclusion persisted even in death. At Forest Lawn, notes Sloane, "only people of Caucasian descent were welcome to purchase lots." (8)[17]

Filipino Americans were also subjected to the racism already plaguing Los Angeles. In his memoir, Manuel Buaken records the racism practiced against Filipinos in Los Angeles by way of segregation in the 1920s. He writes of his repeated rejection in his search for a place to live. An excerpt from *I Have Lived with the American People* reads,

> These flats around Pico Boulevard were also built to cater to the discriminating public, yet the rents ranged from $25 to $50 monthly. . . . Since my friends and I were also financially able to rent a similarly priced flat, I tried one of these. But the lady said, "I am sorry, Orientals are not allowed here." I went to the next house. Striding to the door again and beginning in the usual manner, I greeted another dignified lady. "What do you want here?" was her question, fired at me before I had a chance to speak. I replied, "I wanted to rent a place to live." She snapped at me, "Only whites, in this neighborhood." I tried the other six vacant flats on this street, and I got the bitter and more tumultuous reply "no," in all of them. (68)

Segregation and exclusionary practices based on racism operated in taxi dance halls as well. Few Filipinos were to be found in taxi dance halls such as the Liberty (later reopened under the name Tiffany Dance Hall), Olympic, and Royal Palais. Some dance halls unapologetically refused entrance to Filipinos and Chinese.[18] This exclusionary practice was rendered as a way to manage the possible violence that might (and did) ensue between the Filipino and white patrons. This preventive logic sought to protect the interests of the business owners, their clients, and their workers. An alternative cause of segregation was the alleged "preyed upon by every leech" Filipino men, who would "give anything to get the attention and date from the 'white' taxi dancer." In an ironic twist, "popular dance halls were closed to protect naïve *Filipino men* from predatory *white women*" (Park 115). On this occasion, however, the taxi dancers, mostly Eastern European immigrants and Mexican Americans, were rendered the aggressors, and the Filipino patrons were infantilized as naïve, subject to trickery and fleecing by gold-digging taxi dancers. Here, barring Filipinos and other racialized patrons was justified through a discourse of protection and security. The figure of the antagonist and the injured party may have been reversed, but the racism motivating this system of segregation clearly continued.

Relatedly, taxi dance hall development in the 1920s and 1930s accommodated growth and expansion largely due to migrant and immigrant communities. Immigrant destinations were not simply concentrated in cities. They were in rural towns such as Palm Beach (Salinas Valley), Watsonville (Salinas Valley), Stockton (Delta Region), and El Centro (Imperial Valley). Such activity is writ large in excerpts from California newspapers of the day. A *Los Angeles Times* news report titled "Filipino Race Clashes Laid to Red Agitators" contained the following in its first paragraph: "[R]ecent Filipino Riots at *Watsonville* and *Exeter* began with fisticuffs over 'taxi-dance-hall' Girls." An Imperial Valley newspaper, *El Centro*, carried the following headline: "Dancers Held in Shooting; Shot through the Back and Stabbed through the Stomach." The following *Los Angeles Times* article details the historic anti-Filipino riots in Watsonville:

> The Pajaro Valley, scene of numerous clashes between white residents and Filipino laborers, was quiet last night and today, but official watchfulness continued, fearful of a resumption of rioting.
>
> Three of the seven white men jailed yesterday on rioting complaints are additionally charged today with assault with deadly weapons with intent to commit robbery. ("The Pajaro Valley Riots Quelled," 4).

As is evident from these excerpts, the characterization of Filipino patrons as disruptive does not change, even as one shifts from city centers to rural outposts of the U.S. landscape.

The emergence of taxi dance halls in the rural towns can be attributed to the migrants working in these arterial agricultural towns. As Brett Melendy, a noted scholar of early-twentieth-century immigrant labor in the United States, writes,

> The state's farming regions—the Imperial Valley, San Joaquin Valley, Delta Region, and Salinas Valley—relied upon cheap migratory labor to produce a variety of crops. During the 1920s most Filipinos in the Delta area, near Stockton, worked in the asparagus fields. The Salinas Valley, another major Filipino center, has over the years provided seasonal work in the lettuce fields and packing sheds. (Melendy, "Filipinos," 527)

In the 1920s, El Centro was also becoming the central town of Imperial Valley, rapidly increasing in size. At this time, Watsonville underwent severe changes as it shifted from a largely apple-producing town to a lettuce-producing area. By 1930 lettuce interests had transformed the economy as corporations took over the agricultural industry, reducing wages and creating deplorable labor conditions (Dewitt 42). Of interest to my argument, taxi dance halls in nonurban towns such as El Centro, Stockton, Exeter, Watsonville, and Palm Beach were the seat of anti-Filipino sentiments and movements that would come to a head in the 1930s. Howard Dewitt's writings on anti-Filipino movements astutely recognize the *centrality* of taxi dance halls: "Taxi dance halls brought the first organized resistance to Filipinos in the labor market" (18). He concludes that the "rise of an anti-Filipino movement was a complex phenomena [sic], and it was related to social, economic, and political tension" (38).

The volatility of taxi dance halls is apparent in most histories of the region. In January 1930 a mob of white men attacked Filipinos in Watsonville. This riot lasted for days and culminated in a newly opened taxi dance hall in nearby Palm Beach. Anti-Filipino sentiments had been building, but the Watsonville riot became a focal point in the deliberations for the legislation that would become the Tydings-McDuffie Act.[19] The Watsonville riot was an often-cited incident in arguments for Filipino exclusion by way of Philippine independence. Influential local, state, and national aldermen who proposed anti-Filipino/exclusion resolutions, such as Judge Rohrbach, Representative Richard Welch, V. S. McClatchy, and Senator Samuel Shortridge, used the catalytic incident in the Palm Beach taxi dance hall to support their cause.

It is worth noting here that the actions leading up to the declaration of Philippine independence were centrally motivated by racism against Filipinos. If Philippine independence were declared, the legal status of Filipinos would shift from national to alien. Whereas their standing as nationals afforded Filipinos mobility, they would no longer have such privileges once they became "aliens."[20] As nationals, they were able to migrate up and the down the Pacific coast and to and from Hawaii, following the trails of seasonal labor. Large corporations benefited from the status of Filipinos as nationals as they had control of agribusiness and other businesses booming at this time. Once declared aliens, Filipinos forfeited their mobility, even as they had ironically been granted "independence" from U.S. control. Just as the Filipino migrant workers were afforded mobility in urban and rural California, across the continental United States, and in Hawaii and Alaska, Filipino patrons also performed an adept mobility in the taxi dance halls. Both instances of Filipino corporeal mobility, however, are examples of sanctioned and detrimental itinerancy. Movement is granted, and celebrated, only at the expense of the laboring Filipino body.

III: Corporeal Colonization: The Discipline of Movement

The "splendid" Filipino, I have been suggesting thus far, is an archival embodiment of corporeal colonization through dance. That is not to say that such colonization works seamlessly; rather, the corporeality of the Filipino body testifies to the uneven successes and limits of U.S. empire. The disciplining of the Filipino immigrant body preceded his arrival in the United States. His "knowledge of American ways" coincided with the onslaught of colonial rule in the late nineteenth century. Two decades into U.S. rule in the Philippines, Filipinos were already dancing, singing, and performing American popular culture masterfully. In addition to establishing a colonial government, or a repressive state apparatus, through which the United States could enact its formal and material rule over Filipinos, the United States also set in motion ideological state apparatuses through education, culture, and health care.[21]

By the end of the decade, the touted Filipino "invasion" had moved into the taxi dance halls. There, patrons engaged with the visible and live effects of "forgotten" American imperialism in the form of the kinesthetically "gifted" Filipino on the dance floor. Joseph Roach's meditations on the linkages among mimicry, performance, and identity speak directly to the colonial panic surrounding the arrival of the "gifted" Filipinos. Roach contends that "performances propose possible candidates for succession" whereby "the anxiety generated by the process of substitution justifies the complicity of memory and forgetting" (6). In true Calibanesque fashion, even as the Filipino dancing body excels in the "gift" of the master language, its arrival and success exposes the stress and fears of such exchanges.

Catherine Ceniza Choy's concept of "corporeal colonization" speaks directly to the U.S. empire's disciplining of Filipino subjects, more specifically of the Filipino body.[22] Prior to the 1920s, the spectacle of Filipino corporeal colonization was disparately present within the U.S. cultural imaginary. For example, Choy cites the 1904 St. Louis World's Fair as a classic locus of "corporeal colonization" where over one thousand Filipinos from various regions were displayed; of note were the "[d]og-eating and head-hunting tribal savages" (40). In the context of the taxi dance halls, Choy's concept of "corporeal colonization" must necessarily be expanded to include the workings of American popular dance and music, fashion, and social mores as ideological state apparatuses that extend U.S. cultural hegemony. Unlike violent reinforcement through repressive state apparatuses such as the police or military, the cultural forces of American popular dance and music operated more insidiously through registers of desire and pleasure.[23] American imperial ideology became (and continues to be) naturalized through seemingly benign technologies of cultural expressions, creating a hierarchical system that displaced already existing Filipino cultural practices. As historian Barbara Gaerlan has noted, by the 1920s, "The old dances were dying out and American dances were extremely popular, especially in the urban centers and areas reached by American cultural and educational influence" (264). Just as the Filipino becomes "exceptional" through his exuberant translation of American modes of dance and performance, no mention is ever made of how and whether Filipino performance traditions permeate such renditions of colonial mimicry. The taxi dance hall, I want to suggest, is equally a "scene of subjection," to use Saidiya Hartman's term, where the Filipino dancing body personifies the spectacle-embracing aspect of *puro arte*.

By focusing on U.S. colonial implementation through culture, specifically dance and performance, I am not suggesting that American colonialism was primarily responsible for the transmission of Western dance and cultural practices. After all, Spain had colonized the Philippines for more than three hundred years before the arrival of the Americans. Spanish cultural practices have been so thoroughly incorporated within the daily life of Filipinos that they are often read as indigenously Filipino. The history of Filipino corporeal colonization thus clearly extends beyond the American imperial invasion. Such longer histories of colonialism are even evident in the American characterizations of the Filipino dancers. For example, taxi dancer Jeanne De la Moureau and sociologist Paul Cressey both take note of the "Filipino's Passion" and his gentlemanly ways, which they both attribute to the Filipino's "latin mores" (Cressey 148). Within such formulations, the Filipino's "splendid dancing" must necessarily be read as both an effect of, and a response to, multiple and variegated genealogies of colonialism and performance.

The language of corporeal colonization also allows us to complicate existing interpretations of Filipino "splendid dancing." As argued earlier, previous scholarship on the taxi dance halls casts dance as liberatory within the restrictive and exclusionary circuits of empire. Scholars contrast the vibrant Filipino dancing body to the mute Filipino worker's body that is contained, exhausted, and made to perform monotonous physical labor. Thus, dance and the dancing body become the enduring corporeal evidence of Filipino resilience, agency, and perseverance despite all odds. The Filipino dancing body (in all its privileged "exceptionality") becomes a rousing avatar of "kinesthesia's pull against other representational frames" (Desmond 18). My turn to the concept of corporeal colonization emphasizes the conditions of possibility that *equally* create "splendid dancing" and monotonous physical labor. Corporeal colonization connects two seemingly competing sites through the leveling practices and ideology of U.S. empire. In both cases, the labor of the Filipino body becomes the representational playing field for the enactment of violent forms of social and political control.

Such forms of control are enacted visibly within taxi dance halls. Each taxi dance hall had its own codes of "citizenship" or belonging, with the Filipino patron's "reputation" about his kinesthetic ability securing him access to some of the taxi dancers. Indeed, the rules of conduct on the taxi hall dance floor, although not disconnected from the outside world, had different criteria. Filipino patrons gained recognition because of their "splendid dancing," "their dazzling suits," and their gentlemanly behavior in the hall. Their visibility and acceptability on the taxi dance floor was based on their ability to perform and to dazzle with their skills of mimicry as good colonial (albeit unacknowledged) subjects. Yet, these markers of recognition highlight the Filipino performing body as "excess." That is, the very markers that make Filipinos visible are also the very signs that make impossible their acceptability in and belonging to American political, social, and cultural fabric. Kinesthetic ability, although a marker of skill and popularity, does not guarantee national belonging or national citizenship. The Filipino patron's knowledge of and ease with American ways—including the latest dance steps—simultaneously strays from and stays within the script set for racialized, immigrant, worker bodies.

A closer look at the exceptional Filipino dancing body reveals its embeddedness in the languages of empire. The Filipino body's smooth gliding across the dance floor was inseparable from the growing threats of miscegenation and contagion. Nativists' paranoia about these threats (which took the form of moral and physical concerns) converged repeatedly on the errant Filipino dancing body. Filipinos in taxi dance halls were routinely narrated as the corporeal icon for miscegenation between Filipinos and white women, even as those narrations continued to be challenged and negated. Fears of the Filipino's "hypersexuality" gathered force through "conclusive" observations by "area" experts such as David Barrows. Barrows, a professor at and president of the University of California at Berkeley, and secretary of education for the Philippine government, testified at the United States House of Representatives Committee on Immigration and Naturalization on the "cause" of Filipino "problems": "an aroused sexual passion and natural tendency for vice and crime" (qtd. in Dewitt 46). Barrows, of course, was not the only one to make such incendiary claims. "Contagion," the other staple of moral concern, is an established motif in colonial rule. The works of Choy, Nayan Shah's *Contagious Divide*, and Warwick Anderson's *Colonial Pathologies* specifically explore contagion by linking U.S. empire, Asians/Filipinos, health, and bodily reform. Barbara Browning's *Infectious Rhythm* is particularly useful because it decisively conjoins "metaphors of contagion," race, pathogen, and culture. "Metaphors of contagion," she notes, "often take seemingly benign forms ('infectious rhythm' as a dispersal of joy), but can also often lead to hostile, even violent, reactions to cultural expressions" (7). Such "contagion" is most evident in the conflation of physical and moral discourse regarding Filipinos in the taxi dance halls. Popular and scholarly discourse on Filipinos and the taxi dance halls rarely made a distinction between the new immigrants' *conditions* of living and their *ways* of living. The infamous resolution passed by the Northern Monterey Chamber of Commerce specifically charged Filipinos with "living unhealthily . . . sometimes fifteen or more sleep in one or two rooms" (Dewitt 92). The taxi dance halls, with all their promise of intimacy and mobility, were a perfect target for the fear of infection as Filipino dancing bodies collapsed sanctified distances of race and gender.

Headlines such as "Taxi Dancers Start Filipinos on the Wrong Foot" (1920) illustrate the possible infections exchanged in such an establishment. Here, the colonial order is ostensibly reversed as the lascivious and predatory ways of the white taxi dancers are seen as capable of corrupting and infecting gullible and defenseless Filipino immigrants. Once again, the trope of the infantilized colonial subject is invoked. Combating such an infantilization of Filipinos are equally problematic declarations of Filipino moral superiority. In 1931, Amado Dino, the editor of a U.S. publication entitled *Filipino Youth,* wrote a statement against the taxi dance halls and Filipinos in the *Seattle Review*: "these young men are dragged down by such degenerate and low association, the result of which is an utter detriment to the manhood of Filipino youths." He goes on to say, "Therefore, we Filipinos are to blame. . . . One remedy for this is our government to RESTRICT the coming of Filipinos to America and Hawaii, but most emphatically to America." Dino critiques the U.S. racist perception that Filipinos fawn over white women just because they are white. For Dino, Filipinos are emphatically morally superior, and their association with the taxi dancers is a mere social necessity, open to condemnation and refusal.

The physical benefits of dancing were equally a subject of these moral debates. In a telling example, a taxi dancer responds strongly to the denouncements of dancing in taxi dance halls as a reproachable activity for

Filipinos. Writing in the *Philippine Advocate,* Emily Angelo (1930) proposes dancing as a healthy and enjoyable form of physical release:

> Since the boys have come back from Alaska, it's all for one and one for all. Who is to gain and who is to lose? Gambling houses or taxi dancers? Arroyo, in his last article of this paper encouraged gambling and discouraged taxi dancing. I, a taxi dancer, encourage neither, but can honestly state that a man in gambling can certainly lose more in fifteen minutes of gambling than in six hours of dancing provided he doesn't meet some of these vicious gold-diggers, so to speak. All of us know that gambling is a detriment to proper sanitation whereas in the proper form of dancing we can derive relaxation of mind and a source of exercise and poise.

Angelo favors the activity of dancing as a healthy physical and mental outlet. Her comment carefully disentangles dancing from the vice of gambling and from related terrains of criminality. As an activity in itself, dancing, we are told, is not morally reprehensible, unlike gambling, which involves a loss and danger to one's life and property. What is key here are Angelo's careful efforts to evacuate any and all discussions of "morality" from dancing. She minimizes the connotation of dance as an inherently sensual activity and focuses instead on a safer mythos of relaxation and exercise. Taxi dancers are certainly not "vicious gold-diggers." Despite such careful semantic moves, it remains indisputable that social dance involved social exchange (a different mode of gambling), and, as I have argued, power relations clearly choreographed the "relaxing" effects of dancing in taxi dance halls in the 1920s and 1930s. There were other, less flattering accounts of taxi dance hall dancing that dismissed Angelo's call for such healthy habits. An early study of Filipino immigrant life in Los Angeles in the 1930s contends that taxi dance halls were in fact detrimental to one's health and "fostered a lifestyle that required late nights" (Catapusan, "Filipino Occupational and Recreational Activities," 50). Such a practice, Catapusan argues, diminishes worker productivity and morale as workers endure sleepless nights in search of pleasure at the taxi dance halls. Catapusan ends his study by unequivocally declaring dancing in taxi dance halls as noxious to Filipino prosperity and progress.

IV: Sanctioned Dancing: Contemporary Narratives

Contemporary cultural productions have equally turned to the Filipino performing body in taxi dance halls as a site of "intersection among the variegated differences that discourses of sexuality, empire, race, and nation bring into critical visibility" (Chuh 34). While Kandice Chuh interprets "Filipino America" as the site of such an intersection, the particularity of the Filipino performing body in taxi dance halls unfolds as a material figuration for the recuperation of a "wounded Filipino masculinity" and history. Works on Filipino American history, immigrant labor, and racial violence have noted the prominence of taxi dance halls in the increased and marked violence against Filipinos.[24] Geoffrey Dunn and Mark Schwartz's *A Dollar a Day, Ten Cents a Dance: A Historic Portrait of Filipino Farmworkers in America* (1984) is a documentary film about Filipino immigration in the United States. In this film, as is evident in its title, Filipinos in taxi dance halls epitomize early Filipino American history. In other words, Filipinos in taxi dance halls become the very embodiment of Filipino experience in the United States.

Filipinos in taxi dance halls have also been the focus of several theatrical works. Some of these plays/performances are Theo Gonzalves's *Taxi Dancing*, Chay Yew's *A Beautiful Country*, Alleluia Panis's *Heroes*, and Marina Feleo Gonzales's *Song for Manong*. Other creative works that take inspiration from Filipinos in taxi dance halls include a poem by Al Robles titled "Taxi Dance" (1993) and Catalina Cariaga's "A Dime" (1993).[25] Here, I am particularly interested in creative works that turn to performance and performative sites, such as the taxi dance hall spaces, to transcend pathologizing histories of race and gender. In these narratives, Filipino bodies take on a salvific centrality, with the taxi dance halls becoming spaces of mobility and empowerment. These creative texts counter racist and sexist stereotypes of a predatory Filipino masculinity with images of more complexly gendered bodies. For example, popular and scholarly references to the colonial era consistently refer to Filipino men as hypersexual and prone to lascivious contact with white women. Sociological and anthropological journals are littered with articles such as Panunzio's "Intermarriage in Los Angeles, 1924–1933," Hunt and Coller's "Intermarriage and Cultural Change: A Study of Philippine-American Marriages," W.I.C's "Marriage: Miscegenation," and Hayner's "Social Factors in Oriental Crime."

As a narrative, the theme of Filipinos in taxi dance halls lends itself to a promising theatrical form. Its staging has been imagined to include dance choreography of popular dances, a variety of musical genres, a live band, and period costumes. For example, Chay Yew's Asian American epic play *A Beautiful Country* enlists the story of Filipinos in the taxi dance hall as the representative narrative to dramatize the plight of early Filipino migrants. The narrative of Filipinos in the taxi dance halls is set alongside the history of one hundred years of Asian diaspora to the United States, woven together

by the performance of an immigrant Malaysian drag queen. Scholar David
Román applauds Yew's *A Beautiful Country*:

> [The play] stages the various contradictions of Asian American experi-
> ence, the ways in which racial and national identities are forged histori-
> cally through—in Lisa Lowe's telling phrase—"immigrant acts," a term
> that at once summons forth the exclusionary practices of U.S. immigration
> laws and policies and the performances generated by Asian immigrants
> and Asian Americans who have found themselves often enmeshed within
> these shifting historical conditions and constraints. (88)

The play opens with Ms. Visa Denied's entry interview, setting the stage
for a performative and theatrical interpretation of key historical moments in
Asian American history. For example, Yew depicts early anti-Chinese sentiment by restaging Henry Grimm's 1879 play *The Chinese Must Go!*—a popular
play that uncritically dramatized anti-Chinese sentiment in the United States
in the late nineteenth century. A second reminder of the weight of history is
the depiction of anti-Japanese campaigns in the United States during World
War II as a campy fashion runway show titled "How to Tell Your Friends from
the Japs." In this landscape of xenophobic popular theater and fashion run-
ways, Filipino Americans are introduced as historical presences through the
space of the taxi dance halls of the 1920s. One scene, entitled "The Dance of
Filipino Migrants," begins with movements derived from cannery work:

> WORKER:
>> Slice head
>> Cut tail
>> Hack fins
>> Gut guts
>> Half a minute
>> Alaskan salmon in a can

As this goes on, the choreography reveals the physical dangers and risks at
work:

>> In poor light
>> Luis he cuts the—
>> Luis!
>> Watch the—!

Watch out—!
Cutting machine!
Right arm—!
Right—!
Arm—!
You—!
Slash!
It—!
Off! (202)

Such a relentless and machinelike monotony of movement marks the bodies
of Filipino men. The mesmerizing movements of the cannery workers merge
with the splendid dancing of the Filipino taxi dance hall patron, creating, as
it were, a numbing choreography of colonialism's violence.

Later in the scene, at the Manila Dancehall, the same workers transform
to "princes of the city," albeit for a brief moment:

Suits snappy
Fingers snapping
Hair back
Hands cologned
Hands with tickets
Ten cents a ticket
Ten cents a dance
With Girl American. (208)

In this transition from work movement to dance hall dancing, a moment
opens up, and we are presented with three minutes of "dancing with dream
American" (209). Yet, Yew does not valorize these three minutes as *the* site of
possibility. In fact, we are reminded of the cost of these three minutes—"worth
a life of bedding Alaskan salmon." These brief minutes are costly and have
long-term consequences. "The Dance of Filipino Migrant Workers" ends with
"wages / earnings / evaporate / dwindle to zero," worker's tickets all spent, torn
up: "in an ocean of tickets torn / I wait / wait / wait / and wait" (209).

Plays such as Chris Millado's *PeregriNasyon*, Marina Feleo Gonzalez's
Song for Manong, and Alleluia Panis's dance-theater piece *Heroes* stage Filipino lives in the United States in the early twentieth century, all incorpo-
rating a scene with taxi dance halls. One clear objective of such projects is
to narrate Filipino experiences in the United States from the perspective of

Filipinos. In all three pieces, the taxi dance hall scenes generate both levity and gravitas as they grapple with the everyday lives of migrant Filipinos: Filipino workers emerge not just as laboring migrants but as emboldened subjects who participate in social exchanges, such as dancing. During such dance scenes, the stage is fully occupied as lively and skillful partner dances are showcased. Yet these scenes are often interrupted or transition into others that register rejection or racism toward the Filipinos who dominated the floor with their fancy moves, McIntosh suits, and dancing with the white taxi dancers. These contrasting scenes of pleasure and pathos transform Filipinos in the taxi dance halls into scenes of national abjection who "occupy the seemingly contradictory, yet functionally essential, position of constituent element and radical other" (Shimakawa 3).

Filipinos in taxi dance halls further provide creative impetus for the reparation of Filipino masculinity. The photograph of the white taxi dancer with the Filipino patron that inaugurates this chapter is often recuperated as testimony to the resilience of Filipino men. For example, in Peter Bacho's *Dark Blue Suit and Other Stories*, as well as in Linda Maram's chapter on the taxi dance halls in *Filipino Masculinity*, the bachelor community of Filipino men consists of sharp dressers, sweet talkers, and overall the best dancers in the halls. These works rally against the criminalization of Filipino men who have been (falsely) cast as predators of white women. While I find such recuperations of Filipino masculinity laudable, I want to end this chapter with a different rendition of the gendered body of the Filipino dance. A short story by Veronica Montes entitled "Bernie Aragon Jr. Looks for Love" mobilizes the narrative of Filipinos in the taxi dance hall beyond its resistive recourse, to reevaluate what has become a central allegory for Filipinos in the United States itself. Montes's "Bernie Aragon Jr. Looks for Love" ruptures the assumption that all Filipino men desire white/American women. In Bernie Aragon Jr.'s romantic quest for love, taxi dancers and Filipinas are interchangeable objects, one standing in for another:

> Bernie often imagined—and why should he not?—that the pretty and not-so-pretty girls he held in his arms under the dimmed lights of Paramount Dance Hall were the girls he had grown up with in Bacolod. That their hair carried not the flowery scent of drugstore shampoo, but the perfume of coconut oil. . . . "I'm Kathy," one would whisper into his ear. "That's beautiful," he would answer, silently re-naming her Pansing, Naty, Marites. (par. 6)

In an ironic reversal of racialized hierarchies, this opening passage sets up white taxi dancers as mere flesh substitutes to Bernie's real fantasy—Filipinas.

Bernie, as the title describes, is in search of love. He summons women in his dreams and considers himself a "romantic martyr" (Montes par. 17) When Bernie finally falls in love with a nineteen-year-old transplant from Seattle to Watsonville, Charito "Chito" Bautista, he purifies himself of gambling, smoking, and taxi hall dancing. Montes, however, does not give us a romantic ending. Chito ends up being a woman of serious substance, not quite the girl of Bernie's dreams. Unlike her youthful counterparts, Chito is anxious to get old, to get to a place where no one will care if she is "ugly." In her spare time, Chito enjoys the company of older men and a good smoke. It is only after a protracted fistfight with one of the older men that Bernie realizes that Chito is not the right girl for him. The story ends with Bernie, and his foe-turned-friend Efren, back at the Paramount Dance Hall: "Bernie Aragon, Jr. danced until midnight. He danced until he had held every pretty and not-so-pretty girl in his exhausted arms, until his eyes closed in semi-sleep, until torn dancehall tickets littered the floor" (Montes par. 37). In this evocative narrative of Filipino masculinity, the dance halls are a site of redemption and withdrawal, desire and destitution.

There is perhaps some risk involved in foregrounding the contradictory role Filipino dance hall patrons played within the project of U.S. empire. My attempt here has been to extend the field of historical signification within which such iconic figures are placed. "Splendid dancing," ultimately, must make way for a more enduring analysis, one that must expand representational possibilities and interpretation beyond oppositional recourse. Kandice Chuh sees a potentiality in "Filipino America," particularly its nonequivalence to "Asian America," to compel us "to hold as suspect the promise of justice through the achievement of subjectivity" (32). In many of these narratives, the Filipino performing body in the taxi dance halls proffers a different sightline of visibility. These representations function to acknowledge the Filipino performing body as an equally desiring and desirable subject, alongside its white, American counterpart. Chuh's reading of "Filipino America" as "holding suspect the promise of justice through the achievement of subjectivity" provides a shift from visibility as *the* political project of justice to visibility as one of many avenues of racialized subjectivity.[26] Chuh sees Filipino America's intervention as challenging the liberal limits of such narratives' humanizing impulse, which render Filipinos as gratifyingly virile and honorable. In other words, Montes goes beyond representing Filipinos as a desiring and desirable subject; rather, her depiction presumes such a complexity already. In "Bernie Aragon Jr. Looks for Love," the Filipino dancing body's potentiality is not simply in the recognition of its desirability (to white women) or its resistance against white oppressive forces. We encounter Bernie Aragon Jr. in his romantic, naïve, and desiring self.

The Filipino dancing body in the taxi dance halls performs multiple functions: it is a corporeal metaphor for the ambivalent status of Filipinos as U.S. colonial subjects; it is an archival embodiment of and against anti-Filipino movement through dance; and, finally, it serves as material evidence of the "success" of the American imperial project. While in this chapter I challenge romanticized readings of Filipino dancing as a figuration of resilience and resistance, it is equally clear that the disciplining of colonial subjects through dance (or any other bodily expression) does not foreclose the possibility of enjoyment or subversion. I have instead attempted to link the "exceptionality" of U.S. empire to the "exceptionality" of "splendid dancing" by Filipinos in the taxi dance halls. Terms such as the "geopolitics of the taxi dance halls" have further illustrated the spatial continuity of the racist workings of the U.S. empire in the domestic sphere. Through an elaboration on the concept of corporeal colonization, I have labored to situate this icon of Filipino corporeality within the machinations of U.S. cultural hegemony.

* * *

Thus far, I have focused on the Filipino performing body's *puro arte*, highlighting locations of visibility, stages of performance, and enactments of fraught imperial relations. *Puro arte* has allowed me to elaborate on the Filipino performing body's complex mobility in the early years of U.S. colonial occupation of the Philippines. Mobility, as I invoke here in the case of the Filipino patron in U.S. taxi dance halls, is not an uncritical celebration of Filipino upward movement toward whiteness or even color-blindness in the racial hierarchy in the United States. For instance, I do not uphold Filipino splendid dancing in the taxi dance halls as an example of upward mobility in the U.S. social ranking. Nor have I argued that this remarkable corporeal dexterity is an innate racial trait. I highlight *puro arte*'s attention to the webs of relations in which the Filipino performing body has been entangled or must negotiate. Dance Studies scholar Cynthia García argues that social mobility for Latinas in Los Angeles salsa dance clubs is centrally concerned with "effectively navigating the patriarchal nightclub economy, not necessarily about undoing it" (204). This insight is helpful to my treatment of the Filipino performing body beyond its capacity to embody resistive or complicitous practices. Rather, I privilege what these acts afford and cost the Filipino performing body as it negotiates U.S.-Philippine relations in its specific historical juncture. This attention to specificity does not facilely underscore Filipino difference; it insists more on the "relationship of forces" (Foucault) through which such forms of difference emerge.

3

Coup de Théâtre

The Drama of Martial Law

The skits and stories are in the everyday news, on the pages of society magazines and leftist publications, not from 25 years ago, but
yesterday, 10 minutes ago, now.
—Patricia Evangelista, *Philippine Inquirer*, 2007

This chapter turns to the variegated drama(s) of Philippine Martial Law under
the dictatorship of President Ferdinand Marcos. In it, I consider how the Filipino performing body enacts the drama of Martial Law in two seemingly disparate sites: the protest performances of Sining Bayan, a cultural arm of the radical
Filipino American political group Katipunan ng mga Demokratikong Pilipino
(KDP), and the multiple productions of *Dogeaters: A Play* by Jessica Hagedorn.
Both cultural sites, I suggest, dexterously mobilize the logic of *puro arte* through
their use of spectacle to undercut discourses of exceptionality surrounding the
Martial Law regime and its placement in Philippine national history. In these
performances, *puro arte* provides the conceptual pivot that enables a differentiated understanding of Filipino subjecthood and subjugation in the shadow of
Martial Law. Within these stage(d) acts, we are confronted with a Filipino performing body actively engaged with the embattled conditions of its historical
possibility. Improvisation, humor, and defiance take center stage as we are confronted with a history of performance punctuated by contradictions, eruptions,
and relentless continuities.

Sining Bayan's turn to political theater as a mode and practice of political praxis is *puro arte* in its full artful expression. We see *puro arte* at work in the protest art of Sining Bayan as they transform and revitalize political practice for Filipino diasporic communities in the United States. From 1973 to 1981, Sining Bayan infused a transnational and historical agenda into the Philippine national democratic movement as it staged theatrical productions that included plays about early Filipino migrant workers in the United States, the shared land struggle between Christian Filipinos and Moros in the Philippines, and the campaign to free two Filipina nurses accused of multiple murders in a veterans hospital in Michigan. Even as Martial Law plays a central role in Sining Bayan's production, their performances continually linked the freedom of the Filipinos and the well-being of immigrant communities. Such forms of connectivity and protest are equally evident in the early-twenty-first-century productions of Jessica Hagedorn's *Dogeaters* in the United States and in Manila, Philippines, as these productions grapple with the narrative of Martial Law and its place in national and diasporic histories nearly thirty years later. Both Sining Bayan's spectacle-for-agit-prop and *Dogeaters'* defiant humor(s) confront Martial Law less as an extraordinary moment in Filipino history than as an enduring theater of imperial subjection and affect.

In some narrations, the Martial Law period has been regarded as a stain in the country's modern history, one that has damaged the Philippines' image as, in Stephen Shalom's words, "America's Next Top Model" of democracy.[1] It is marked as an exceptional moment in which the country deviated from its righteous democratic path. Though President Laurel declared Martial Law in the Philippines in 1944, during the Second World War, the 1972 declaration is the one cited as a "harbinger of doom for the future of the Philippine Republic" ("Proclamation 1081"). Yet radical protest narratives offer a differing view. The declaration of Martial Law, for anti-Marcos activists, in fact exposed the failed system that the Philippines had been under. Martial Law sanctioned corrupt and repressive government methods that were already in practice. In other words, anti–Martial Law/anti-Marcos activists built their oppositional politics to expose Martial Law as what political theorist Giorgio Agamben calls a "state of exception." Agamben develops the notion of "state of exception" to describe state-sanctioned violence that occus when the state, during times it considers moments of crisis, legalizes the right of the government to suspend civil liberties and other laws protecting individuals' freedom of action. He concludes that the "declaration of the state of exception has gradually been replaced by an unprecedented generalization of the paradigm of security as the normal technique of government" (14). Hence, security is not only naturalized as a mode of rule; it is also tightly coupled with

Proclamation 1081. The law provided the president executive authority to centralize government power, to suspend civil rights, and to regulate law through military rule. Marcos's justifications were numerous, including oligarchy and the threat of communism. One oft-cited incident behind his decision to declare Martial Law was an alleged assassination attempt against the life of his defense minister, Juan Ponce Enrile. Marcos held responsible those who

> have been and are actually staging, undertaking and waging an armed insurrection and rebellion against the Government of the Republic of the Philippines in order to forcibly seize political and state power in this country, overthrow the duly constituted government, and supplant our existing political, social, economic and legal order with an entirely new one whose form of government, whose system of laws, whose conception of God and religion, whose notion of individual rights and family relations, and whose political, social, economic, legal and moral precepts are based on the Marxist-Leninist-Maoist teachings and beliefs. ("Proclamation 1081")

Marcos also referred to Batas Militar as the "September 21st Movement," proudly claiming his New Society to be a much-needed "revolution from the center." By describing Martial Law as a national "movement," Marcos appropriated revolutionary and radical impulses attached to the term—concern for the poor, social justice, collective action—to rework them as constitutive of the New Society. He insisted that all necessary change must be "led by the government" so as to enact "drastic and substantial reforms in all aspects of national life" (*Revolution from the Center*, 32). The revolution was to be bloodless and nonviolent, envisioned to inaugurate a "movement for great reforms in all spheres of national life, a remaking of society, towards national survival" (36-38). Marcos repeatedly emphasized that the path to the "September 21st Movement" was legal and constitutional (hence "center"), and in distinct contrast to the disruptive ways of the Communists, who were more attached to "unceasing struggle" (*Notes on the New Society*, 44). In other words, Marcos offered the model of Martial Law as a rational, enlightened, modern form aimed at a dramatic restructuring of the Philippine government and society. The Martial Law, in this sense, is a progressive rule of law, a relief from "unceasing struggle."

Together with social reforms such as the agrarian "Green Revolution," the cultivation of a culturally rich nation presented a benevolent image of what Nati Nuguid calls a "compassionate society" (33). This "compassionate society" of dictatorial rule advances values such as "concern for once neglected segments of society" (33). The culture of/for Martial Law justi-fied totalitarian rule through its display of a kind, gentle, civil, and modern state. What does it mean for a dictatorial, militant state to be compassionate? How can a dictatorship be "compassionate"? There is "nothing clear about compassion," feminist Queer Studies scholar Lauren Berlant notes, "except it implies social relations between spectators and sufferers, with emphasis on spectators' experience of feeling compassion and relation to material prac-tice" (1). Berlant's theory of compassion is useful here as it illuminates the stakes of an emotional state, or how and when the ruling power chooses to describe itself through the language of emotion. In particular, by character-izing itself as compassionate, and promoting its policies and philosophies as such, the regime of Martial Law humanizes itself. Marcos's Bagong Lipu-nan distinguished itself as a humane regime with its claim to compassion. It further reinforces the state as a moral institution, providing guidance on how to behave. A moral state is a conflation of contradictions, for oftentimes morality is depicted as transcending the bounds of the law. Furthermore, a compassionate state, Berlant argues, presumes "all social membership as vol-untary," thereby equalizing the roles and responsibilities of the state, local institutions, and citizens "to take up the obligation to ameliorate suffering" (3). In the case of the Marcos regime, the idea of a "compassionate state" was solidified through its attachments to and mobilizations of the idea of culture. Cultural products, such as music festivals, fashion shows, and beauty pag-eants, were deployed to perform the salvific miracles of Marcos's "compas-sionate state."

How did culture play a role in creating, naturalizing, and regulating authoritarian rule? In other words, what was and is the culture of/for Martial Law? There is, for instance, ample evidence that the "September 21st Move-ment's" mobilization of cultural production and artists secured moral and judicial authority for the Marcos regime. Under the New Society, "Philippine culture" became visible as a modern society to the world at large. Imelda, partner to what writer Primitivo Mijares calls "conjugal dictatorship," over-saw the nation's artistic enhancement projects as the head of the ministry of culture. Imelda's numerous cultural initiatives were a stunning deploy-ment of spectacle to blind the world and Filipinos themselves to the pov-erty, corruption, and murder ongoing under this administration. A list of world-renowned artists who visited the Philippines during this time includes the San Francisco Ballet, the Boston Opera, and the London Symphony, and events such as the 1974 Miss Universe Beauty Pageant and the Interna-tional Film Festival were held in the country. While their agenda valorized Euro-American cultural domination, Nicanor Tiongson also argues that the

Marcos government "consciously cultivated an image of itself as the patron of nationalist culture" with events such as Kasaysayan ng Lahi (a massive parade representing the history of the Philippine nation and Filipino people); Bagong Anyo/New Year fashion shows featuring contemporary designs of Filipino national costumes, including the *terno* and the Maria Clara; the Metro Manila Popular Music Festival, which yielded musical talents such as Freddie Aguilar; and the National Artist Awards program. Famously touted as an example of Imelda's "edifice complex," the Cultural Center of the Philippines Complex (CCP) was also erected at this time (Lico). The CCP includes the Philippine International Convention Center, the Folk Arts Center, the Philippine Film Center, the Coconut Plaza, and the Philippine Village Hotel.[6] "State propaganda" cultural productions, as coined by Philippine literature scholar Bien Lumbera, were designed to promote the values of the New Society to engender what Marcos called a genuine "revolution from the top." World-captivating events such as the International Film Festival and the Thrilla in Manila event (a high-stakes boxing match between two American champions, Muhammad Ali and Joe Fraser) were widely advertised in an effort to draw international audiences. Art historian Pearlie Baluyut argues,

> Through these highly centralized institutions, which had the ability to cultivate, strengthen, and disseminate the value systems, traditions, and beliefs of the Filipinos as a people, as well as cross the lines of political constituency, kinship ties, and special interest groups, the Marcos rule engendered a condition of cultural rebirth in a magnitude and scale never to be seen again in the Philippines. (xvii- xviii)

Under the aegis of their "New Society," the Marcoses carefully undertook the refashioning (as it were) of Philippine national history, mobilizing personal and national narratives to construct the (favorable) inevitability of the Marcos regime. The Marcos Bust built on a Benguet hillside on the 355-hectare Marcos Park and the history book President Marcos penned, *Tadhana:The History of the Filipino People*, explicitly insert the Marcoses into Philippine history.[7] Vince Rafael argues that such a staged sampling of personal and national histories made "it appear as if they were always meant to be the First Couple" (127). Not content with populating the contemporary national landscape with busts and writings, the Marcoses even tampered with the iconic creation myths and legends of the Philippine nation. For example, they commissioned paintings of *Malakas* (strong) to feature Ferdinand himself and *Maganda* (beautiful) in the likeness of Imelda. The first couple assigned themselves legendary status as the "first Filipino man and woman who emerged from a large bamboo stalk"

(Rafael 122). The very notion of "revolution from the center" crafts Marcos as a revolutionary, as if his regime was put in place by a movement that reprised the nation's founding struggles against Spain. In these ways, Marcos constantly proclaimed the exceptional character of his presidency: "Thus martial law in the Philippines takes on a unique character from the untenable strategy of protecting or restoring the status quo to a militant, constitutional, and legal strategy for creating and building, from the ashes of the old, a new society" (*Notes on the New Society*, vii). Invoking the phoenix rising from its own ashes, the mythological symbol of life, resurrection, and immortality, Marcos created a cultural mechanism to legitimize his rule as a personal and national *tadhana* (fate or destiny). Marcos's notion of destiny is a "kind of transhistorical and thus natural right to rule, [and] is made to function as the unassailable context determining not only his past but that of other Filipinos as well" (Rafael 128).

If the Marcos dictatorship deployed cultural spectacle, the Marcoses' own version of *puro arte*, to successfully sediment "compassionate" rule, then what were the forms of resistance and opposition against it? After all, for most ordinary Filipinos, the "New Society" represented an escalation of suffering, terror, violence, fear, torture, and threat. A different revolution was needed, parsed through and against the very idioms of culture mobilized by the Marcos regime—a revolutionary culture against Martial Law. Culture would prove to be a site of fierce contestation. Even as it was utilized to enforce and naturalize a highly centralized governance and military force, culture also became a site of oppositional practices.

II. Culture against Martial Law: Toward a Theater of the People

The fractures within the U.S. nation and the Philippines' Martial Law set the stage for Sining Bayan's drama. Sining Bayan's emergence within these historical contexts and political moments illustrates Filipino American participation during an intense period of reimagining social relations in both the Philippines and the United States. The turbulent political upheavals of the post–civil rights era produced a dynamic cultural movement in the United States. The racist and imperialist Vietnam War was a galvanizing cause, an event that opened the eyes of many Americans to the dark underbelly of the American nation. Yet for many racialized communities in the United States, the Vietnam War was only one among a long list of long-held grievances. As Harry Elam writes,

> At the outset of the 1960s the nation watched intently as civil rights protesters in the South valiantly resisted Jim Crow laws and mob violence,

water hoses and attack dogs, racial segregation and discrimination. Out in the Far West migrant workers in the San Joaquín Valley of California, impatient and frustrated with their substandard wages and inadequate housing, followed the lead of the civil rights activists and organized a plan of resistance. (20)

This period witnessed a new phase of racial awareness with political projects such as the Black Power Movement, the American Indian Movement, and *La Huelga* Movement that were not simply identity-based calls for inclusion of the black community, the Native American community, and the migrant worker in the American social fabric. These movements pushed for a radical reimagination of subjectivity that took to task the white, liberal subject as *the* marker of not just who is an American but who is *human*. This reconceptualization of subjectivity is thus inextricable from what state, culture, and the core of social relations might look like from a nonwhite, liberal point of view. As Cynthia Young argues in *Soul Power*, "U.S. Third World Leftists . . . turned to Third World anticolonial struggles for ideas and strategies that might aid their own struggles against the poverty, discrimination, and brutality facing peoples of color" (2). Young further states that "this U.S. Third World Left created cultural, material, and ideological links to the Third World as a mode through which to contest U.S. economic, racial, and cultural arrangements" (3). It is under such conditions in the United States that the radical Filipino American organization Katipunan ng mga Demokratikong Pilipino and its cultural arm, Sining Bayan, performed its revolutionary practices.

By the time of the Vietnam War, theater was being continually invoked as a primary cultural medium through which radical politics could explore and spread ideas of social and revolutionary change. As a well-documented form of social protest, theater was a tool of political action, utilized to expose, critique, and re-envision U.S. race relations, to denounce patriarchy, to explore a "safe" space for women, and to rally against oppressive and unfair labor conditions. Groups such as El Teatro Campesino and the San Francisco Mime Troupe provided crucial sources of artistic and political inspiration for Sining Bayan. Along with these groups, Sining Bayan was part of a theater movement committed to working-class audiences and to theater as a medium of political expression.

El Teatro Campesino, specifically, provided much creative and political inspiration for Sining Bayan's anti–Martial Law theatrical productions. Many of Sining Bayan's works paralleled El Teatro Campesino's political vision. For Luis Valdez, one of the central figures in El Teatro Campesino, theater was first and foremost a tool of revolutionary thought: "We shouldn't be judged as a theater. We're really a part of a cause" (qtd. in Elam 19).[8] El Teatro Campesino put on stage the multiple concerns of migrant workers, focusing its creative efforts on the fight for better wages and better living conditions for farm workers in California.[9] El Teatro Campesino routinely began with performers who were farm workers themselves and performed in picket lines and in the fields. Their well-known *actos* are short performances, enacted in various venues, including truck beds in fields where farm workers labored. The *actos* were quick, bilingual, and designed to educate the audience about the struggle and move them toward action.[10] Ermena Vinluan, a key member of Sining Bayan, recalls El Teatro Campesino's commitment to the Farm Workers Movement, to their Mexican roots, and to California as inspirational to her collective's creative efforts. For example, in the summer of 1973, Vinluan participated in a workshop conducted by director Peter Brooks with El Teatro Campesino, focusing on theater as a ritual field of action.[11]

Like many theater groups committed to social change at the time, Sining Bayan was equally influenced by the well-known San Francisco Mime Troupe. The Mime Troupe has retained its strong identification with working-class values since its founding in 1959 by R. G. Davis. Utilizing popular entertainment forms such as mime, juggling, clowning, *commedia del arte*, and minstrelsy, the Mime Troupe works to create theater that supports radicals, both through endorsement and through friendly critique. Mime, in the style of American Buster Keaton and Englishman Charlie Chaplin, who were known for their innovative comedic acting, was an antidote to the dominance of "psychological realism" in theaters (Shank 60). The large-scale upheavals of the late 1960s drew the Mime Troupe to apply theories of socialism to emplot a working-class–centered creative vision. In 1962, they began performing in public parks with the explicit intent of making theater accessible to ordinary people. By 1970, the Mime Troupe's attempts to reach out to a working-class audience led the group to strive toward a multiracial ensemble, reflecting the composition of the audiences they were seeking to reach. Since its inception, the Mime Troupe has been cited as a pioneering force in the history of social protest theater for "reviving the tradition of performing theatre for working-class audiences in the United States" (Friedman 173).

While the struggle for racial and class justice inspired protest theater groups such as El Teatro Campesino and the Mime Troupe in the United States, Martial Law galvanized protest actions among Filipinos in the Philippines and in the diaspora. Filipino Americans labored to oust the Marcos dictatorship and to secure a truly democratic Philippine state, linking with and taking ownership of the struggle for a liberated Philippines. Activists Madge Bello and Vince Reyes acknowledged anti–Martial Law/anti-Marcos political work in the United States as "'keeping the light of resistance' aflame" by maintaining the flow of information to and from the Philippines, and to the American public, especially in the early years of Martial Law when repression in the Philippines had silenced democratic forces (74).[12] Bello and Reyes characterize the cultural aspect of the progressive U.S.-based anti–Martial Law movement as being "largely influenced by the progressive cultural current in the Philippines" (78).

The growing "cultural current in the Philippines" included theater groups such as the University of Philippines Repertory (with leader Behn Cervantes, who was later incarcerated) and the Philippine Educational Theater Association (PETA). These groups attacked the forces of corrupt government, imperialism, unjust social structures, and worker exploitation through their theatrical innovation of contemporary versions of traditional performance forms (such as the Catholic mass and *komedyas*) and adaptations of older plays.[13] Lumbera argues that, indeed, "Of the outlets for anti-dictatorship propaganda by the national democratic movement, theater proved to be the most daring and the most effective" (3). Despite strict surveillance and regulation by the Office of Civil Defense and Relations, theater became the most visible, audible, and effective tool of anti–Martial Law protest.

Of note here is that Filipinos' deployment of theater as a means of protest predates Martial Law, and harks back to the "era of Seditious Drama." Between 1902 and 1906, playwrights Juan Abad, Juan Matapang Cruz, and Aurelio Tolentino were charged under the "Sedition Act" of 1901 for writing plays that "inculcate a spirit of hatred and enmity against the American people and the Government of the United States in the Philippines."[14] These "seditious plays," performed mostly in Tagalog and staged in greater Manila, Bulacan, and Ilocos Norte, were banned for supposed incitement of anti-American sentiments and provoking riots. Those who penned these so-called seditious plays were fined and jailed. There were numerous instances in which actors were arrested and props were confiscated. In an extraordinary measure, there was one occasion when the entire audience was also arrested (Fernandez, "Introduction"). The plays bred complicity, it was argued, where the boundaries between audience and stage become porous and "sedition" the contagion that strikes all.

Like these seditious plays, Sining Bayan's theatrical performances provided a public and shared space of critique, protest, and a call for collective reimagination of Filipino self-determination. By situating the Seditious Act, which basically deemed Filipinos as foreigners in their own land (not-yet-nation), alongside Sining Bayan, I reroute a genealogy of Filipino American protest performance through a history of anti-imperialism—a genealogy that resolutely marks the Filipino performing protest as both an effect and a problem of nationalist production.

III. "Keeping the Light of Resistance": Sining Bayan's Coup de Théâtre

Sining Bayan enacted a "culture against Martial Law" insofar as their political and artistic habits on stage and in everyday life sought to build solidarity between the struggles of Filipinos against state terror and the antiracist politics of U.S. people of color. Their body of work presents an expansive landscape of anti–Martial Law politics that decentralized Martial Law as the sole and primary object from which to build a political agenda. Such a multipronged approach linked U.S. antiracist work and struggles against Marcos's repressive state, an inventive approach made both necessary and possible by Sining Bayan's diasporic location and affiliation.

Sining Bayan enacts *puro arte* as an expression of protest performance. Their political theater makes use of the power of spectacle to invite participation and collective action. Just as *puro arte* makes a big deal out of nothing, drawing attention to the labor of performance through showmanship, it also makes spectacle ordinary. For example, Sining Bayan deploys multidisciplinary staging and casting as recruiting strategies and community building tactics. Why double cast a role when more performers meant more possibilities for recruitment and more audience members in the house? This perspective shifts the terms of organizing toward the logic of castability and role assignation; yet, in this logic, casting oddly becomes an inclusive practice rather than a selective one. Sining Bayan's approach to theater as an expression of the popular extends radical politics as imaginable and enacted by the common *tao* (person).

From 1973 to 1981, Sining Bayan rendered their theater work as a vehicle to popularize their political agenda, as an organizing tool, and as an educational tool. Self-defined as a cultural arm to the radical Filipino political organization KDP, Sining Bayan drew from the popular notion of people's theater. They were directly linked with the Philippine national democratic movement, which called for "popular democracy, national sovereignty, people's welfare and economic development, national unity, and international solidarity" (Geron et al. 618). Although the group's creative process can be described as collective creation, Ermena Vinluan, now a documentary filmmaker, was the creative force behind Sining Bayan's productions.

Sining Bayan's repertoire reflected the two-pronged approach of their political agenda: supporting the struggle for a socialist alternative in the

United States and supporting the national democratic struggle in the Philippines (Geron et al.). So, for example, they mounted productions that focused on the *manongs*, the Filipino migrant workers (*Isuda ti Imuna/They Who Were First*), as well as on Filipina war brides (*Warbrides*), using oral histories of early migrants as dramaturgical sources for these productions.[15] Such plays emphasized the violence of capital on the Filipino laboring body while simultaneously staging the resilience of these early migrants. They also produced adaptations of Filipino plays and scripts to focus on the land rights struggle of Muslims and farmers in the Southern Philippines (*Mindanao*) and Filipino peasant workers (*Sakada*). The agit-prop play *Narciso and Perez* was written for KDP's campaign to free the wrongly accused nurses Filipina Narciso and Leonora Perez. This play highlights the racist bias in the health care system, the media, and the justice system in its unfair indictment of two Filipina nurses charged with murder. Sining Bayan also addressed the pressing issue of elderly housing in their play *Tagatupad* (*Those Who Must Carry On*), echoing the eviction of long-time residents of International Hotel, an iconic activist struggle in Asian American history.[16] Sining Bayan's last production was *Ti Mangyuna* (*Those Who Led the Way*), a play about the history of organizing in the Filipino labor community of Hawaii in the 1920s and 1930s. Through these productions, Sining Bayan articulated Filipino American identity formation as historically linked to the struggles of the working class—globally and among Filipinos in the United States, the Philippines, and other parts of the world. While each play presented the stark reality of physical, systemic, and epistemological violence against Filipinos in the United States and the Philippines, each production also emphasized the triumph of collective struggle against oppressive forces. Truly a rehearsal for the revolution, as theater director Augusto Boal said of "theater of the oppressed," Sining Bayan's plays presented clear criticisms, pointed to the focus of protest, enacted their proposed tactic, and affirmed who the agents of change are.

The script of the agit-prop play *Narciso and Perez* highlights Sining Bayan's use of political theater to advance a campaign and the way their dramatic narrative emphasized the possibility of radical transformation for Filipino migrant communities. *Narciso and Perez*, a play described by Ermena Vinluan in an interview with Roberta Uno, is more directly agit-prop than the other plays in Sining Bayan's repertoire, was written as part of the campaign to defend two immigrant Filipino nurses wrongly accused of murder. In 1976, Filipina Narciso and Leonora Perez faced multiple murder charges of patients at a veterans hospital in Ann Arbor, Michigan.[17] *Narciso and Perez* was performed as a way to disseminate information about their wrongful accusation and to enlist audience members in "the movement to defend

Narciso and Perez" (*Narciso and Perez* program notes). The play very point-edly focuses on structural conditions from which, in fact, the accused nurses suffered: gross racial discrimination, poor working conditions, and negligent investigation conducted by the Federal Bureau of Investigaton (FBI). The movement to defend Narciso and Perez translates as a movement to situate the accused nurses' predicament beyond the charge of multiple murders. At the end of the play, the characters on stage turn to the audience and directly ask them to "support the movement to defend Narciso and Perez." The audi-ence becomes part of the play as the action moves off-stage, directed this time by the audience's own thoughts and responses to the call to arms. In this way, the play's action forges a collective movement toward ending dis-crimination and labor exploitation (play program). Sining Bayan's emphasis on structural conditions models a political project that builds from individ-ual struggles and puts them within a larger context of the interrelationship among political, economic, social, and cultural systems.

Illustrative of the tactic of building a culture against Martial Law, Sining Bayan turns the tables to expose the corruption of the system. *Narciso and Perez* becomes a symbolic countertrial, with the FBI and the veterans hos-pital administration as the accused. By creating a journalist character, Jes-sica Marquez, and a plot that is constructed as an investigation, Sining Bayan presents an alternative account of the veterans hospital deaths. Jessica is an ambitious rookie reporter who is temporarily assigned to write about the case. It is her first "real news," a respite from her usual coverage of social events (parties, debuts, and baptisms). In addition, the radical possibili-ties of news reporting are upheld here, in contrast to the heavy censorship of Marcos's New Society. Through this character, as well as the editor of the newspaper and the nurses at the hospital, Sining Bayan models a political ideological transformation. For example, Jessica's drive to "get to the truth" is initially introduced as a rookie reporter's enthusiasm and a liberal ideal-ism about journalism principles. Yet as she learns of wage exploitation from VA hospital nurses Parker and Mulligan, and also witnesses first-hand the deteriorating state of the hospital, Jessica's political transformation becomes apparent. Her encounter with hospital administrator Lindenhaur, an elusive, dubious, and conniving bureaucrat, further strengthens her commitment to honest journalism. Jessica inspires the VA hospital nurses to share their accounts despite intimidation by the administration. When Jessica finally reports her newly found evidence to her boss, her passion and conviction break through his caution. By the end of the play, Mr. Bayani, in contrast to the corrupt Lindenhaur, has vowed to write up several editorials to expose the injustice against the accused nurses. He also commits to creating flyers and pamphlets, both of which were popular alternative materials of social protest for disseminating the fight against Narciso's and Perez's conviction.

Narciso and Perez effectively uses the conventions of melodrama and the murder mystery—archetypes of good and bad, social conflicts, big-corporation and government conspiracy, the trope of the young innocent becoming wise as an older generation is reenergized—to generate an entertaining and rousing agit-prop performance. Sining Bayan's *puro arte* aesthetics defamiliarizes popular culture, politicizing such references as part of building an anti-imperialist culture against Martial Law. For example, in *Narciso and Perez* an opening song number with snooping FBI agents is set to the tune of a 1960s American detective show, *Dragnet*. While the FBI agents were heroes in that popular television show, in the play they are not to be trusted. In a later song number, Jessica pressures hospital administrator Lindenheur with a series of questions. He begins to sing toward the audience: "Questions questions, nothing more than questions" to the tune of "Feelings." A song popularized in English by Brazilian singer/songwriter Morris Albert in 1975, which in fact was written by French composer Loulou Gasté, "Feelings" was, for a certain generation of Filipinos, dubbed as the country's second national anthem. Popular local renditions included a version by "total entertainer" Rico J. Puno.

Sining Bayan's theater recasts the role of revolutionaries to immigrant, working people. Jessica's transformation—from a career-centered professional to a journalist concerned with responsible reporting— reimagines not only who a leader is but also what a leader values. Rey Ileto's *Pasyon and Revolution* is a pathbreaking study of the *masa* (masses) in the Philippine revolutionary movement. He argues that an alternative value system exists in the *masa's* rejection of *maginoó* (gentlemen), *pinunong bayan* (local leaders), and *mayayaman* (the wealthy) and these elites' devaluing of honesty and education (14-16).[18] He suggests that in the *masa's* reading of the *Pasyon* (story of Jesus Christ), they align with those who are "timid *(kimi)*, modest *(mabini)*, gentle, sad, and lowly of behavior" and whose story is "one of defiance toward the authorities out of commitment to an ideal" (17). The humble, common, working-class figure as revolutionary is now a well-worn trope, but I invoke Ileto here to map a genealogy of Filipino American protest theater in Filipino anticolonial movements.

Narciso and Perez does not overtly/directly articulate or include gender subordination as part of the multiple repressive conditions the immigrant nurses navigate. However, gender politics is obvious in that the majority of immigrant nurses from the Philippines at that time were women. In the play, both the journalist and editor are also women. Worth remarking upon is Sining Bayan's plays' sensitivity to gender politics, although they produce gender as a class construct. In other Sining Bayan plays, women are imagined as leaders, journalists, nurses, farm workers, mothers, daughters, students, lovers, and organizers.[19] Sining Bayan's sensitivity to the *representation* of women and hypervigilance against *machismo* may be attributed to a number of things, including the fact that a woman, Ermena Vinluan, was the leading and consistent driving force in the group. Various Sining Bayan/KDP members referred to Vinluan as a "cultural czarina." Although it was a collective group, it was well known to all in the group that primary cultural organizer Vinluan held together Sining Bayan's productions. On the stage, women were a force of presence and of complexity, a source of political power and also an inspired figure of revolution. Did Sining Bayan or the KDP maintain this critical awareness of gender politics in their everyday operation, off-stage, so to speak? What may be a form of feminist politics in their complex depiction of women should not be assumed to be consistent with the "culture of the movement" itself.[20]

In building a culture against Martial Law, Sining Bayan sought to translate their vision of a revolutionary practice through their artistic/creative process. Their plays assigned the project of revolution to immigrant, working people. Characters in these plays had names, jobs, and family histories with which the target audience could easily identify. Their capacious rendering of *who* a revolutionary can be (a woman, a mother, a farmer, a nurse, etc.) also permeated other aspects of theater. Where theater is made/created and where it is presented are determining factors for social protest theater. For a theater troupe like Sining Bayan, the negotiation of space was thus crucially linked to their cultural politics, especially given their commitment to the emergent immigrant communities. Kenyan writer Ngũgĩ wa Thiong'o's theorization of performance space within postcoloniality provides one possible understanding of the spatial politics of Sining Bayan. As Ngũgĩ writes, "These questions of access and contact become very pertinent in a colonial and postcolonial state, where the dominant social stratum is often not sure of its hegemonic control. . . . In such a situation, the question whether the space should be inside a building or not may acquire a deep symbolic value and become the site of intense power struggles" (41). For Ngũgĩ, "questions of the performance space are tied to those of democracy, of civil society" (69). Like Ngũgĩ, many social protest/political theaters were critical of the exclusionary practices of theater establishments. Sining Bayan's goal was to bring theater back to the people. Space defined not only the place in which these performances were developed and performed but also who the expected audience would be. Space is more than just a "place" in which these performances were presented. Space became a three-dimensional entity, with history being yet another character in the theater of social protest. For many political theaters of this era, an understanding of the occupation and history of performance spaces was key to the evolution of their critical projects.[21]

To that end, Sining Bayan performed in community halls, college and high school campus auditoriums, and union meeting sites. Members Ermena Vinluan and Mars Estrada and KDP Executive Committee member Bruce Occena remember their first major production at Zellerbach Auditorium in Berkeley: "The auditorium was packed with Filipinos—students, parents, *lolos* and *lolas*. It was the first time that Zellerbach was presenting a show on Filipino Americans. The space was hosting a wholly different audience" (Occena, Estrada, and Vinluan). Their plays were also presented at conferences such as the Pilipino American Far West Convention, union meetings, worker-organized events, and anti–Martial Law gatherings, as well as Asian American–related events. Their plays were seen nationally and internationally, coproduced by local chapters of the KDP in cities such as Chicago, New York, Washington, DC, Seattle, Los Angeles, and Honolulu, as well as rural settings like Delano, California. They also performed in Quebec. Although they often performed in spaces not equipped to present theater work (i.e., spaces with insufficient lighting, inflexible backdrops, etc.), these were spaces where Filipinos gathered. To argue that Sining Bayan performances were "taking over" or occupying these different spaces to assert Filipino presence is perhaps less interesting than to think through the kinds of presentations their intended/expected audiences were accustomed to seeing in these spaces. These venues typically hosted fundraisers, beauty pageants, commemoration events, and national holiday celebrations such as Filipino American Friendship Day and Independence Day. There were also workers' organizing meetings and immigration-related events such as workshops and lectures to assist Filipinos through the immigration process. Elam, elaborating on Boal's notion of "rehearsal for a revolution," argues that social protest and political theater were "rehearsals" for "the resistance efforts they hoped their audience members [might] undertake in real life" (95). Sining Bayan's productions transformed these spaces into a run-through of political action that they hoped might encourage their largely Filipino American audience to perform.

Space, in this context, is thus intricately connected to the audience. Space was also a determining factor in the demographics of the audience, the subjects of the intended social transformation. Through theater, Sining Bayan reached out to their primary audience—Filipinos in the United States. Their performances were sites of community gathering, affirming a growing

Filipino/a presence in U.S. society. Many of the audience members constituted a mix of generations: some came as agricultural workers in the 1930s
and even earlier, at the turn of the century; some were recent immigrants
who came under petition by family members already settled in the United
States or through the 1965 Immigration Act; and some were second- or
third-generation Filipinos born in the United States. For many of these audience members, Sining Bayan productions provided a new representation of
the Filipino experience; they were seeing what may have been a recognizable
expression—dramatic presentation—within a new content.

Sining Bayan questioned the pure entertainment value of theater and
the hierarchy of artists in the entire creative process. The "central force
of theatrical creation," as Elam phrases it, came into question. Thus, they
approached their theater making with the same principles as their organizing: shared responsibilities. The members of Sining Bayan brainstormed,
wrote, staged, and produced collaboratively, employing the popular
method of collective creation. Collective creation challenged mainstream
theaters' creative process with its elitist notions of an artist as a single
genius. It also flattened the director-playwright-actor hierarchy deemed as
the key structure behind theatrical creation. Alternative theaters regarded
both the stories validated by these dominant stages and their way of making theater exclusionary and complacent as expressions of oppressive cultural values.[22] Collective creation is a method Sining Bayan found compatible with their politics of shared struggles against inequality and injustice
among the Filipino people. Yet, Performance Studies scholar Diana Taylor
cautions against romanticizing the process of collective creation—more
specifically, the tendency to erase differences in the kinds and amounts of
labor performed within a group.

There was not one way of creating collectively for these political theaters.
Each theater that adapted the collective creation process practiced it differently. Sining Bayan members saw themselves and their work at the center
of the political movement in which KDP was engaged. Their assignment in
KDP was to mobilize through culture, to raise consciousness, to shape the
way in which their audience saw and interpreted key campaign issues. The
KDP's National Executive Committee and the National Cultural Group
decided on topics to be dramatized by Sining Bayan. The collective writers
of the theater troupe would then hold brainstorming sessions about possible
ways to narrativize the issue from the point of view of progressive politics.
Their goal was to educate the community and present a progressive solution
to the problem at hand, whether it was the housing crisis for Filipino elders
or the wrongful accusation of two Filipina immigrant nurses in Michigan.

They pursued this goal through theatrical content as well as through their process of creation and production.

Sining Bayan made artistic decisions with the support of the National Executive Committee and the members of KDP. The cultural work was not seen as an activity added to the political organizing of KDP. In an interview, Bruce Occena, an ex-chair of the Executive Committee, noted that KDP was most invested in mobilizing theater and music to build a radical movement that would put culture at the center of political struggles. In the case of Sining Bayan, there was no distinction made between theater work and involvement in political struggles. Sining Bayan existed in service of the KDP. There was no separation between the artists and activists. Some members were assigned to Sining Bayan productions to do cultural work, while others were assigned to do lobbying work and to organize workers.

Sining Bayan's theater pieces incorporated dance/movement and music as integral components of making theater. Their multidisciplinary approach supported their core values of collectivity and shared responsibility. In casting their plays, they did not seek to find performers who could sing, dance, and act equally. As former KDP member Dean Alegado says, "Not everyone can do it all!" (interview). Consequently, the casting pool for their multidisciplinary theater pieces was much higher than if they had simply looked for performers who were trained in all of the different expressive arts. Their plays required the presence of many actors on stage; in fact, it was their goal to get as many people on stage as they possibly could. Calls for performers were also a call for political organizing and member recruitment. Using multidisciplinary theater as an organizing strategy, along with their description of the plays, Sining Bayan was able to alert the community about the current issues affecting Filipino Americans. And because they were committed to local community politics, their smaller roles in the production were filled by local community members. It was easier to attract community members to a political rally if they were somehow involved in the "skit" that was part of the evening gathering. Such acts of localization became a strategy to forge a personal link as well as to build investment.

The process of creating collectively was not necessarily easy, even though it was, at the time, seemingly ideal. In the 1977 program of *Isuda Ti Imuna*, Sining Bayan described the difficult process of creation:

> During the early stages of the work, many difficulties surfaced. There were problems of weak commitment and incorrect attitudes circulating within the company. We realized these attitudes served only to corrode the unity of the company. Once it was realized that what ISUDA exemplified was

in fact UNITY—we began to collectively and decisively forge that unity within the company. (1977 Program 4)

Despite these disagreements, the members of the Sining Bayan collective insist on a process of multiple voices and multiple perspectives. In search of a nonhierarchical creative process, the group explored a multiplicity of voices and a multiplicity of tasks, resisting the hierarchies of traditional theater. Their theater work embodied the multiple roles of popular theater in political struggles: it was a means to raise consciousness about oppressive conditions in the Philippines and to highlight the struggles of Filipinos in the United States for their immediate audience (Filipinos in the United States). Even though Sining Bayan existed as a group for only a brief period, their performance politics and practice made "culture against Martial Law" a genuine possibility, truly within reach of the common *tao* (person).

In the following section, I turn to a closer examination of contemporary stagings of *Dogeaters* as a postscript to the early anti–Martial Law labors of Sining Bayan. While Sining Bayan decentered Martial Law with its deployment of the popular and insisted on modeling radical political action in their dramatic narratives, *Dogeaters* interrogates the lasting impact of Martial Law. *Dogeaters* continues Sining Bayan's radical legacy as it makes way for a politics of performance that conjoins the communities of theater to the materialities of diasporic life.

IV. Coming Home: *Dogeaters* on the Manila Stage

In the fall of 2004, Jessica Hagedorn's award-winning novel-turned-play, *Dogeaters*, had its third full production in Los Angeles. This was six years after the play had its world premiere at La Jolla Playhouse in San Diego and three years after its New York premiere. The highly anticipated production was the inaugural event at the newly opened performance space of the community organization Search to Involve Pilipino Americans (SIPA), a longtime Los Angeles–based community organization. While the play chronicles the homecoming of one of its protagonists, Rio Gonzaga, the L.A. production also featured a poignant homecoming for its director, Jon Lawrence Rivera. A moving director's note printed in the play program articulates Rivera's familial rootedness in the play's engagement with Martial Law and the Philippines:

In 1972, my father was blacklisted when Ferdinand Marcos proclaimed martial law in the Philippines. My father was a journalist and, at that time, published a magazine called *Pace* which addressed the country's brewing dissatisfaction with the Marcos regime. My father was forced to leave the country and was able to find political asylum in Australia, where he still lives today. This was a pivotal point for our family.

It was not until three years later when we (my mother and siblings) were reunited with my father in Sydney. . . .

I have not returned to Manila since 1979—when my sister and I vacationed in the Philippines for a month on our way to the U.S. from Australia—nor have I had a desire to visit, that is, until I began working on Jessica Hagedorn's landmark play, *Dogeaters*.

. . . This play has re-awakened my yearning for the home country. The one which haunts me still because of martial law.

Through the experience of working on *Dogeaters*, Rivera confronted the difficult historical forces that caused his family's separation and exile. The play became a haunting meditation on the myriad experiences, desires, and fears produced through and against the specter of Martial Law. For Rivera, the play was, significantly, his first Filipino-related work in over twenty years of working in American theater as a theater artist and as an artistic director. For many of the Filipino actors, *Dogeaters* also showcased the long-awaited arrival of Filipino/a American theater; it was the first play in their many years of professional theatrical production in which the actors had been cast to perform Filipino characters. For the non–Filipino American actors in the show, the theater experience was equally novel as it was the only time they had been cast as Filipinos in a play about the Philippines. For example, Dana Lee, a Chinese American pioneer in Asian American theater, took on the roles of Senator Avila and "Uncle" (Joey Sand's pimp) in the play, and confessed that it was daunting to perform a Filipino character in a Filipino play. Lee, however, welcomed the challenge and noted that "it's about time" he had an opportunity to play a Filipino because Filipino actors have had to enact "everything but themselves" ("*Dogeaters*: Kirk Douglas Theater").

Dogeaters is of course not the first play (or novel, for that matter) to creatively wrestle with the enduring afterlife of Martial Law in the Philippines and in the Filipino diaspora. While the Los Angeles production was noteworthy for its engagement (materially and thematically) with Filipino American performance, the play's creative entanglements with Martial Law followed in the footsteps of a less well known but equally pioneering history of Filipino performance.

If the ghost of Martial Law haunted Rivera and his compatriots through the production of *Dogeaters*, then the social protest theater of Sining Bayan breathed life into that ghostly presence. It is this spectral intersection of the past and present within the history of Filipino American performance that most interests me. The motivating concern here is to make visible the palpable force and persistence of Martial Law in the Filipino and Filipino American theatrical imaginary. In other words, if Martial Law refers to a period of history, then what does it mean for history itself to be a ghost that haunts? To speak of history as haunting sets up a dialectical relationship among the past, the present, and those who are visited by the apparition of Martial Law. *Dogeaters* refuses any simple reparative relationship to the events of Martial Law. This work emerges more as "imaginative force[s] of what might have been" (Sharpe xii), as traces of ghostly forces past and present. While Sining Bayan productions engage the fraught experiential realities of Martial Law, *Dogeaters* confronts the way "the present is bound up in the past" (xii). In these theaters against martial law, *puro arte* emerges as a performative strategy that faces head-on a ghostly past.

Productions of *Dogeaters* perform a dual function: they return us to the terror of the Martial Law years even as they return us "home." My elaborations on *Dogeaters'* first-time staging in Manila, Philippines, foreground the temporal movements of Martial Law within the Filipino theatrical imaginary; it is a figuration of both the past and the present. A production of a play about the Philippines by a Filipina American in the early twenty-first century, in a major American regional theater and on off-Broadway stages, *Dogeaters* is a long-overdue script of a complex homecoming. The play details the liberation of memory and identification, and its staging demands a sustained decolonization of American theater. *Dogeaters'* significance in American theater lies in in the way it makes visible the corporeality of colonial subjects that the United States continues to deny. It contrasts with productions such as *Miss Saigon,* which is an exemplar of U.S. colonial nostalgia and a dramatic instantiation of the complicity of American mainstream theater with the myth of U.S. benevolence and successful democracy. In *Dogeaters*, we thus move from the protest theater of Sining Bayan to the problematics of contemporary Filipino/a performance. Here, the show goes on, albeit with a more direct nod to the workings of *puro arte*. Sining Bayan exhorted Filipino/a bodies to put on a show against oppression; *Dogeaters* draws upon Filipino/a histories of embodiment to make theater (writ large) anew. The novel *Dogeaters* has been critically analyzed as illustrative of Filipino postcolonial and neocolonial conditions, and for being a postmodern text par excellence. Many scholars of Asian American cultural critique have argued that *Dogeaters* is a "decolonizing novel," with decolonization being defined as the practice of "an on-going disruption of the colonial mode of production"

(Lowe 108). While Lisa Lowe focuses on how the novel subverts official history through the popular (gossip), Rachel Lee focuses on the novel's "female embodiment" of "postcolonial political awakening" in the figures of Daisy, the beauty-queen-turned-underground-resistance-fighter, and Rio, the *balikbayan* diasporic narrator (*The Americas of Asian American Literature*, 14).

Staging *Dogeaters* is an act of decolonizing American theater. The play adaptation maintains the decolonizing elements of the novel—fragmented narration, a "cast of thousands," and multiple plot lines. Though its time span is more centralized to 1982, the dawn of the Marcos dictatorship and the eve of the People Power Revolution, figures from distant and near pasts make appearances: Jean Mallat, a French colonial figure who authored *The Philippines: History, Geography, Customs of the Spanish Colonies in Oceania*, guests stars on a timeless entertainment program hosted by the equally, and eerily, suspended-in-time Barbara Villanueva and Nestor Noralez; her eternal excellency Madame Imelda also visits this "show of shows" (Hagedorn 17). Other encounters that stretch normative temporal frames include a scene between Filipina American *balikbayan* Rio and the ghost of Lola Narcisa as they smoke a joint in the family house garden; and a visitation in which the ghost of freshly assassinated Senator Avila visits his beauty queen-turned-captive-turned-rebel Daisy Avila just after she has been raped and tortured in a military camp led by her uncle, General Ledesma. The novel has been lauded for its creative incorporation of multigenre texts—archival newspaper articles, excerpts from President McKinley's speech about the Philippine question, popular radio jingles, and a modified version of the prayer Hail Mary. This use of multigenre texts, along with discontinuous storytelling and multiple, barely overlapping plot lines, interrupts linear narrative. It disrupts conventional modes of consumption and draws attention to both the process of production and readers' consumption of narratives.

In addition, *Dogeaters* the novel is already performative in its use of multigenre texts, shifting narrative points of view, and nonlinear, nonchronological ordering of multiple plots. The novel's approach to storytelling lends itself to theater scenes. Scene is often defined as the setting or the place on which dramatic action occurs. It is also a temporal conceit that contains/constrains the unfolding of the narrative. With *Dogeaters*, Hagedorn reimagines the novel genre, adapts this novel-renewed version for theater, and pens a demanding play including up to fifty-two characters. The play does not deploy lengthy exposition to set up the plot, the time, the place, or the characters. Though the plot lines and characters are elaborately connected, there is not one (cathartic) scene that brings them all together.

Hagedorn's theatrical adaptation stays true to the novel's multigenre sensibility, as it transforms the stage version into multiple genres of performance and defies conventional character development. Each performance within the play underscores the complex pleasures and perils of colonialism as marks on the Filipino/a body. For example, U.S. general Douglas MacArthur's famous "I shall return" phrase is spoken by General Ledesma as he climaxes from the pleasures of oral sex being performed on him by his bold star *querida* Lolita Luna. This act of fellatio is one among multiple scenes of "sex montage" in the play.[23] "I shall return," of course, was a key part of the speech given by MacArthur as he attempted to save the Philippines from Japanese invasion during World War II. As a corrupt military official ventriloquizes MacArthur's words at the very moment of sexual climax, different layers of signification unfold. "I shall return" returns not as a patriotic promise but rather as a self-gratifying proclamation by a spent patriarchal figure of empire. As we might recall, MacArthur delivered this speech after a narrow escape from the Japanese army takeover of Corregidor in an effort to shore up his masculinity as well as the image of the United States' control of the Pacific while threatened by another imperial force.

This sex act within a scene of sex acts within a theatrical performance is *puro arte* at its ironical best. Hagedorn's choice to assign "I shall return" to General Ledesma forges an identification between two military figures, one fictional and one real. Ledesma is a feared yet failed figurehead. All of his actions take place strictly in response to orders from his superiors. While he strikes terror among those below him, including his mistress, Lolita Luna, he remains a tortured man. At home, he and his wife, "Leonor the Penitent," are estranged as she has abandoned carnal pleasures for her godly devotion (17). The pleasures and perils of empire are corporealized in this subversive staging of General Ledesma *en fellatio*, uttering a statement historically designed to save face and reassert masculinity.

Having followed the various productions of *Dogeaters* and having read previews, reviews, and interviews, sat in on rehearsals, and repeatedly viewed performances, I was struck by a narrative that was attached to the U.S.-based productions. Articles and reviews of *Dogeaters* in San Diego, New York, and Los Angeles emphasized *Dogeaters* as a "return of the repressed" narrative, in which Martial Law is that which has been repressed for Filipino Americans. For many of the artists, like Jon Rivera, Martial Law was a catalyst for an entirely different life trajectory, yet one that has rarely been referenced or recognized as a central and life-altering event. Within both of these types of framing narratives, Martial Law founds the Filipino American immigrant experience. Cast within the frame of an immigrant tale, these theater productions emerge as enabling occasions that might finally release what has been deeply stifled.

I want to argue that dominant discourses around U.S.-based productions of *Dogeaters*—silence, repression, homecoming—are complexly intertwined with U.S. "imperial amnesia" (Campomanes, "New Formations") or "imperial aphasia" (Isaac) about the Philippines. Silence around Martial Law was cultivated by the regime of violence, through state-enforced censorship, denial, and coverups. Campomanes's "U.S. imperial amnesia" argues that the unrecognizability of the Philippines in American collective consciousness is symptomatic of the U.S. denial of the nation's imperial pursuits. As I sift through the ways in which Martial Law is narrated in connection to the *Dogeaters* production and Filipino American communities in the United States, I observe a conflation between the "Philippines" as repressed within the U.S. imperialist imaginary and the Martial Law as repressed within the Filipino American/diasporic imaginary.

In the Philippines, interestingly, the story takes on quite a different patina. Manila, it seems, has not forgotten Martial Law; it is present in the quotidian, where, as journalist Patricia Evangelista puts it, "the skits and stories [referencing the Martial Law] are in the everyday news, on the pages of society magazines and leftist publications, not from 25 years ago, but yesterday, 10 minutes ago, now" (Evangelista). What does *Dogeaters* mean to this "home" audience? In other words, what can *Dogeaters* mean for those who did not leave, for those who stayed? What happens when in the process of going home, *Dogeaters* becomes one of many theatrical productions about Martial Law, no longer an exceptional or once-in-a-lifetime Filipino theatrical experience as it is in the United States? The tension around Martial Law in the Philippine endures in its legacies, which are both political and cultural. Some laws may have been repealed, and criminals sent to jail, but structures built during Martial Law, such as the CCP complex, still remain resolute and standing reminders of a violent past.

Homecomings are always fraught. The one who goes back home must constantly negotiate the tension between being home as a new experience while reconciling or contending with memories of the past. In November 2007, *Dogeaters* had its first homecoming in the Philippines. As Hagedorn herself commented, Manila is after all the world of the play ("Playwright Talk"). Bobby Garcia directed this production through his theater company, Atlantis Productions, but he was not new to the play. He was the assistant director to the La Jolla Playhouse world-premiere production in San Diego, California, in 1998. Garcia was determined to direct the play, and with the 2007 production was finally able to bring it "home." As with any homecoming, the play evoked familiarity and memories, but it was also an occasion for many "first times." It was the first time the play was staged in the Philippines. It was the first play by a Filipino American playwright that Atlantis had staged. It was the first time that the play had a cast of all-Filipino actors. Previous productions in the United States were lauded for their multinational, multiethnic, multiracial ensembles. For award-winning, highly acclaimed television and film actor Gina Alajar, as Narcisa Ledesma, this was her first time performing in an English-language play (Dimaculangan). *Dogeaters* also reunited Alajar and her husband, renowned actor Michael de Mesa, who had been separated for many years. Much to the disappointment of those awaiting a reunion or an ex-lovers' feud, however, there are no scenes where their two characters interact. Though this was not the first *Dogeaters* production to have cross-gender casting, Andoy Ranay performed the character Madame Imelda in drag for the Manila production.[24] Director Bobby Garcia spoke of the diversity of actors in the production, drawing attention to the various Filipino performance industries with which the cast was associated (personal interview). The performance industries included the Cultural Center of the Philippines Theater, television and film, Atlantis (Garcia's theater company, which mainly produces English-language plays from Broadway productions), and independent artists such as Jon Santos, who is known for the impersonations of Imelda Marcos he performs in nightclubs and alternative performance venues.

    Dogeaters may be set in Manila, but the return home posed a specific challenge to the play: Was this yet another product of the Martial Law cottage industry of representations? What could a diasporic artist possibly say about this historical experience that would provide insight and resonance to those who did not leave? What relevance does the play have today? These were some of the questions that a few of the actors themselves raised when they first heard about the plans for this production.[25] Hagedorn's encouragement of the director, actors, and artistic team to interpret and reintepret the play because "they lived through it and lived after it" yielded minor changes in the published script.[26] The actors suggested deleting unnecessary translations or explanations that would be repetitive to a Philippine-based audience. In a similar dramaturgical approach, director Bobby Garcia and set designer Kalila Aguilos envisioned a set design that was a stylized representation of the rubble left behind by the Marcoses when they fled the Malacañang Palace in 1982 (personal interview). Rather than recreating the image of Manila on stage, Garcia and Aguilos chose as the visual and spatial inspiration for the Manila production the forced evacuation of the Marcoses and the reclaiming of Malacañang by the People Power Movement. Upstage center was an

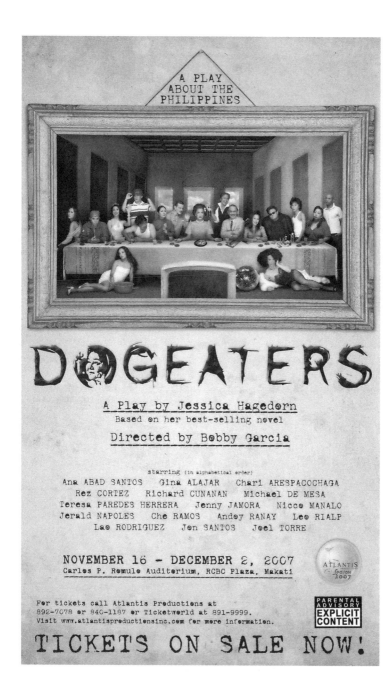

Poster for *Dogeaters*. Produced by Atlantis Productions. Directed by Bobby Garcia. Manila, Philippines, 2007. Photograph by Raymund Isaac. Graphic Design/ Art Direction by G. A. Fallarme. Permission granted by Atlantis Productions.

Last Supper. Dogeaters. Produced by Atlantis Productions. Directed by Bobby Garcia. Manila, Philippines, 2007. Photograph by Raymund Isaac. Graphic Design/Art Direction by G. A. Fallarme. Actors in image: Cheryl Ramos, Teresa Herrera, Jerald Napoles, Jenny Jamora, Joel Torre, Michael de Mesa, Gina Alajar, Rez Cortez, Andoy Ranay, Leo Rialp, Ana Abad Santos, Richard Cunanan, Chari Arespacochaga, Nico Manalo, Jonjon Santos, Paolo Rodriguez. Permission granted by Atlantis Productions.

uneven and precariously hanging portrait of Madame Imelda, an unmade bed was placed upstage left, downstage slightly to the right was an empty bench, and pieces of broken concrete were scattered on stage.[27]

Dogeaters' theatrical adaptation could not be a more perfect example of *puro arte* in its embrace of the spectacular, its joy in the performance of excess, and its facing head-on the risk of balancing between archetypes and stereotypes, mockery and homage. There were aspects to the Manila production that encapsulate *puro arte* in ways that previous productions could not have done. Indeed, the U.S. multiethnic/multiracial productions testify to the portability of this postcolonial narrative, as crafted by Hagedorn. In this case, the fungibility of the Filipino performing body emerged in previous productions with a multiracial cast that underscored, as Allan Isaac puts it, Filipinos' "racial schema that recognizes a long history of cultural and national mixing" (xxi). Yet, I want to elaborate briefly on some of the pleasures of this all-Filipino cast. One is the casting. Rez Cortez is an actor who is known for his *kontrabida* (villain) roles.[28] In *Dogeaters*, he was cast in three roles: as the über-*kontrabida* General Ledesma, as the waiter who is at the receiving end

Andoy Ranay. "Madame." In *Dogeaters,* produced by Atlantis Productions. Directed by
Bobby Garcia. Manila, Philippines, 2007. Photograph by Raymund Isaac. Graphic Design/
Art Direction by G. A. Fallarme. Permission granted by Atlantis Productions.

of a Manila *sosyal*'s (upper-class person's) tirade, and as Pedro the houseboy to nightclub owner drag queen Perlita Alacran. Assigning Cortez the servant characters of the waiter and the houseboy is a contrast to the ultimate *amo* (boss) General Ledesma, and serves to highlight these characters as alter egos. The poetry in this casting is that Cortez immortalized *kontrabida* characters like General Ledesma. The character Ledesma was in fact inspired by actors like Cortez performing as syndicate leaders, drug pushers, rapists, sleazy neighbors, kidnappers, and right hands to Mafia bosses in countless movies. Yet, in the performance of this role, Cortez did not make this self-referentiality into a show of its own. He interpreted the character's existence in the *Dogeaters* world and the relations that make up this world.

Aesthetically, what the Manila production captured more than the U.S. productions was the distinctly pleasurable sound of Filipino English, also known as "Taglish" (contraction of "Tagalog" and "English"). It is a particular sonic aesthetic that would not be possible in an ensemble whose members did not all speak or understand Filipino. The poetry of short phrases such as "*Ay naku, coup*" was not lost on the audience. "*Ay naku coup!*" is a tight little pun, like many one-liners in this play, that captures a common vernacular expression, in this case "*Ay naku*" ("*Hay nako*," "*Ay nanay ko*" are other versions of it.). Possible interpretations of the expression, which I cannot begin to translate directly, include "oh my," "oh dear," "oh well," and so on. This contraction of "*hay nanay ko*" (Oh my dear mother) is invoked on multiple occasions and can express multiple sentiments. Often, it is a sigh of exasperation—"*Ay naku ang hirap ng buhay* (Oh goodness, life is so hard). At other times, it expresses surprise, relief, joy. In this case, "*Ay naku coup!*" means "Oh my, a coup, a military takeover!" In this brief expression, the play on the sound of "*ko*" into "coup," much comes across: exhaustion, irritation, panic, fear, exasperation at, and submission to the imposition of martial rule that follows from the coup's upheaval.

On November 13, 2007, four nights before *Dogeaters*' Manila premiere, Batasang Pambansa, the Philippine Congress National Complex, was bombed. Batasang Pambansa is in Quezon City, a long way away from Makati, in Metro Manila's thick traffic. It was reportedly caused by political rival violence that killed six people and injured a few others (Ager). That night, *Dogeaters* was in tech rehearsal focusing on lighting and sound aspects of the performance. The rehearsal was at the Carlos P. Romulo Theater, in Makati's RCBC Plaza, where the production would be performed. The theater is housed in a building that is home to seven different international consulates and sits across the street from Glorietta Mall (where a deadly bomb explosion occurred less than a month before). Rio Gonzaga's final words in

the play, "Everything is different but nothing has changed," may be overdetermined. And yet they come to mind for a reason; while a play that deals
with the past decades of Philippine politics is in production, violent political scenes are played out off-stage and on the streets. Martial Law becomes
today's reference, shorthand for Philippine government corruption and violence both then and now.

Even as Sining Bayan and *Dogeaters* are clearly different theater projects,
each wrestles against and supplements the pervasive structures of Martial
Law. In this chapter, the two artistic projects come together in their shared
centrality in the emergence of Filipino American theater. Within these theater productions and practices are acts of brave theatricality and excruciat-
ing labor that dare (against all odds) to repeatedly put on a show, to be *puro
arte*. In many ways, this chapter serves as a homecoming for precisely such a
show.

4

"How in the Light of One Night Did We Come So Far?"

Working Miss Saigon

Many of the artists appearing in *Miss Saigon* have come from the Philippines. In London a special school was set up to help train young performers in the singing and dancing skills required.
—"The Original *Miss Saigon*," 2010

[T]hey were looking for specific types of girls, that were very Filipino looking. They were very specific.
—Fay Ann Lee, *Asian American Actors*, 2000

"How in the light of one night did we come so far?" is a line from a duet titled "Sun and Moon," sung by the star-crossed lovers of *Miss Saigon*, Kim and Chris. Kim sings these last words of the musical as she takes her final breath in the arms of Chris, her lover and the father of her child. "How in the light of one night did we come so far?" captures the telos (one night becoming a much longer story) and geography (the routes between the United States and Vietnam) of their love story, a plot line painfully familiar by now: One fateful night, a Vietnamese prostitute and an American G.I. meet in a Saigon brothel. They have sex, and then fall in love. They commit to spending their life together but become separated by the larger force that brought them together in the first place, the Vietnam War. The Vietnamese prostitute continues a life of struggle while hoping to rekindle her love affair with the American G.I.; the American G.I. moves on—with reservations but nonetheless moves on—to marry a white American woman.[1] Years later, the two meet again. Unbeknownst to Chris, they have a love child—Tam. The story ends with the ultimate sacrifice: Kim's death in exchange for their child's life with his American parents in the United States.

"How in the light of one night did we come so far?" equally comments on the journey the audience takes with the performers and with the story in the course of one night at the theater. The musical compels the audience to engage with what is often narrated as one of the most painful chapters of American history. A reworked version of Puccini's 1904 opera *Madama Butterfly*, *Miss Saigon* uses the Vietnam War as a backdrop for the greatest love story of all: a mother's selfless love, and the immense sacrifices she makes for her child.[2] Audience members experience the grand journey of *Miss Saigon* through Alain Boublil's and Claude-Michel Schönberg's creative collaboration, noted for its transformative use of a more narrative-driven approach to musical theater.[3] In one evening, theatergoers are awed by spectacles such as a helicopter and a pink convertible Cadillac on stage and introduced to newly discovered world-class talents.

This chapter recasts "How in the light of one night did we come so far?" as an instructive allegory for the emergence of the Filipino/a performing body in *Miss Saigon*, and on the contemporary global stage at large. Filipino/a participation in this popular musical has by now introduced to the world a cadre of talented artists worthy of the global stage. Lea Salonga, for example, garnered multiple prestigious awards and became an instant world sensation for her performance of Kim in the premiere production of *Miss Saigon* in London. Her success has been replicated, in different "one nights," by numerous Filipinas who have performed the lead role, and by other Filipino/a actors who have gained recognition and employment through their participation in the *Miss Saigon* industry. For better or worse, the significant and enduring presence of Filipinos in the *Miss Saigon* phenomenon has become a testament to the viability and sustainability of Filipino/a talent on the world stage. In what follows, however, I am interested in a different understanding of the performing Filipino/a body's global success, one that situates it within and against a complex geopolitics of labor and representation. I have deliberately chosen to move the Filipino/a body back into the familiar script of *Miss Saigon*, to establish a genealogy of performance that is profoundly marked by the historical and material stress of its own production. Even as this particular repeat(ed) presence of the Filipino/a performer worldwide endorses the triumph of colonialism/globalization, how do Filipino/a performers enact and/or exceed the forces responsible for their "overnight" success on the global stage?

The centering of the Filipino/a performing body within the history of *Miss Saigon* does not by any means displace "Vietnam" from this genealogy.

As is well documented, *Miss Saigon* has been repeatedly critiqued for its erasure of the Vietnamese in a narrative that simultaneously capitalizes on Vietnam; Vietnamese subjects rarely, if ever, factored into the casting or the making of the musical, and were never active participants in the creative process. Nevertheless, I seek to track the figuration of Vietnam as it is routed through and embodied in the Filipino/a performer. My concerns thus deviate from questions of authenticity that pit Vietnamese against Filipinos. In this chapter, I sift through histories that are conflated and collapsed in the phenomenon of Filipinos in *Miss Saigon* to sort out what the Filipino/a actor performing a Vietnamese character references. The trope of the sacrificial and dying Asian woman has become such a familiar figure within the American imperialist imaginary. How did the Filipino/a body come to bear the performative weight of such representation?

In a broader and more critical sense, the relentless casting of Filipinos in the *Miss Saigon* industry further extends this query in the Filipino/a performing body as an "archival embodiment," to use once again David Román's phrase, of U.S.-Philippine imperial relations. The proliferation and systematic funneling of Filipinos into a musical based in war-torn Vietnam clearly requires a more sustained and localized historical analysis. *Miss Saigon*'s narrative and casting practices position the Filipino/a performing body at the intersection of multiple colonial histories—U.S. empire in the Philippines, French colonial rule in Vietnam, U.S. intervention in Vietnam, and the role of the Philippines during the U.S. war in Vietnam. Just as Karen Shimakawa astutely links *Miss Saigon* productions in the late 1980s and early 1990s with the first U.S.-led war in Iraq, I am compelled to situate the Filipino/a presence in the *Miss Saigon* industry within the triangulated imperial histories of the United States, the Philippines, and Vietnam. More specifically, how do Filipino/a performing bodies in *Miss Saigon* prompt us to examine the role of the Philippines *in* the Vietnam War?

To attend to the links between U.S.-Philippine imperial relations and the presence of Filipinos in *Miss Saigon*, I turn to the work of Lynda Hart, who theorizes the female performing body as a conflation of sign and referent, and to Neferti Tadiar's exploration of the commodification of Filipinas in processes of globalization. This approach refuses the segregation of Performance and Postcolonial Studies and privileges instead the complex of labor, self, and affect in *Miss Saigon*. In so doing, I propose a shift in the conversation that surrounds *Miss Saigon*. While much scholarship on *Miss Saigon* has famously highlighted American theater's fraught history of yellowfacing, racist labor practices, and Asian female stereotypes, I begin instead by considering the historical and affective specificity of Filipino/a participation in the musical, with regard for the actors and, by extension, the Philippines. Even as one tracks the Filipino/a performing body as a "Saigonista"—a term that identifies Filipino/a performers who have been part of the show—one must also consider what this global recognition, as vexed as it may be, signifies for the Philippine nation, for the Filipino people. If the Filipino/a performing body gains international renown for its exceptional affective force (Filipino/a actors make people feel), as a participant in this global stage industrial complex, how might this emotive skill inform Filipinos' feelings toward one another?[4]

Last but not least, my analysis of *Miss Saigon* struggles to balance ideological critique with pleasure in seeing Filipinos working in a successful international production. For example, images of Lea Salonga's success in *Miss Saigon* bring back fond memories of when I was a preteen, before my family migrated to the United States. I enjoyed watching Salonga, as she sang Filipino songs and Broadway show tunes on noontime variety shows and other Philippine-based entertainment television programs. I remember being amused by her American English accent and *pilipit* (twisted), yet charmingly awkward Filipino speaking skills. I remember being drawn to her bookish aesthetic—her glasses, decorously plaited hair, and button-up shirts. After my family left for the United States, I lost track of Salonga. Hearing about her part in a famous, controversial show allowed me to return, hesitantly but still with pleasure, to my formative years as an adolescent in the Philippines.

When I finally saw a touring production of *Miss Saigon* at a southern California regional theater, I anticipated the stereotypes, the raunchy bar scenes (2008 touring productions were equipped with poles and movable cages), and the white liberal guilt that is at the core of *Miss Saigon*'s narrative. Even so, a desire for identification persisted, as I was quietly overtaken with pleasure at seeing Filipinos sing and dance in a major American musical theater on a big regional theater stage. I scanned the program for Filipino names and eagerly read the short biographies that listed their accomplishments. I felt a strange kind of affirmation upon reading variations on this kind of acknowledgment: "*Maraming salamat sa Diyos, at kay nanay, tatay, kuya, ate, at sa lahat na minamahal kong pamilya*" (I give my thanks to God, and to my mother, father, older brother, older sister, and to all the rest of my loving family.) "Look at all the Vietnamese Filipinos on stage!" my friends and I jokingly said to one another. My reactions, of course, are hardly unusual and were broadly echoed by many other Filipinos who have expressed pride in the presence of Filipinos in this musical. Indeed, I am well aware, as are many other Filipinos, that my fraught nationalist association/identification with the production is an effect of U.S. racial formation and the pull of the politics of representation. As Mari Yoshihara writes, "Orientalist performances continue to have a strong appeal not only for Western audiences but also for those represented in such productions: the performances function as a powerful political, cultural, and artistic tool for asserting their racial, national, and cultural identities" (977). My delight at seeing my *kababayans* perform so well on stage embodies precisely these kinds of identifications. After all, I was born and grew up in Olongapo City (*sa labas* [outside the U.S. naval base], not *sa loob* [inside]), which hosted the U.S. naval base, and later lived in Porterville, a desperately impoverished migrant town in the United States. This chapter resides within and against the habitus of enduring analytical and affective histories shaped in specific times and places.

I. Drama on and off Stage

Filipino/a actors in *Miss Saigon* have performed multiple roles in the musical's productions in the West End (London), on Broadway (New York), and in its worldwide tour in cities such as Toronto (Canada), Stuttgart (Germany), Luxembourg City (Luxembourg), and Sydney (Australia). Filipinos' success in *Miss Saigon* productions has marked them as actors worthy of the global stage. Lea Salonga's award-winning and green-card-deserving (through the category of "exceptional person of interest") performance as Kim is often credited with placing the Filipino/a performing body on the map of world-class theater. For example, Ralph Peña, Filipino American playwright, actor, and artistic director of the Asian American theater company Ma-yi Theater Ensemble, praised Salonga's accomplishments and popularity for raising much-needed awareness about Filipino/a talents in the theater world (Burns 3).[5] Salonga's performance also garnered multiple honors, including the Laurence Olivier Award for Best Actress in a Musical (1989), the Tony Award for Best Performance by a Leading Actress in a Musical (1991), the Drama Desk Award for Outstanding Actress in a Musical (1991), and the Theatre World Award (1991). The online Filipino literary magazine *our own voice* similarly heralded the participation of Filipinos in *Miss Saigon* and saw the production as having preceded the rise of multicultural productions in recent years. Editor Remé-Antonia Grefalda wrote,

> Salonga and the Filipinos in the original cast of *Miss Saigon* flung the doors open for Filipino performing artists in musicals before multicultural stage productions became the sound byte.

> Every Filipino actor, male and female, who has participated in the gru-
> eling daily performances of *Miss Saigon* worldwide in the last two decades,
> deserves acclaim. As performing artists, they stamped the image of the
> Filipino professional actor in the international theatre circuit—not merely
> as a generic Asian artist, but as a Filipino one. (Grefalda)

More than thirty Filipina actors were hired to perform Kim in Cameron
Mackintosh's productions alone (premiere and touring).[6] A list of other
awards bestowed on Filipina actors who played Kim includes the Helpmann
Award (Australia) for Best Female Actor in a Musical in 2007, won by Laurie
Cadevida. Aura Deva, playing Kim in the German-language production from
1994 to 1997, was astonishingly named "one of the most influential people"
in Germany.[7] Filipino/a actors have been cast in other roles in the musical:
the Eurasian pimp Engineer, the wise but hardened bar girl Gigi, numerous
ensemble parts, and even Chris's second wife, Ellen. The role of the Eurasian
Engineer, originally played by Jonathan Pryce, has gone to Filipino/a actors
such as Jon Jon Briones, Leo Tavarro Valdez, Junix Inoucian, and Raul Ara-
nas. These actors have also garnered high praise and international recognition for their performances. Ensemble players, who also served as understudies to lead and supporting roles, were eventually given the opportunity
to perform as lead characters over the course of the play's long runs, and
received numerous awards and accolades.[8]

Filipina actors toured the world as Kim, in a role imagined to embody,
for some, "the Ultimate Sacrifice . . . giving her life for her child" (Schönberg). But the musical was equally criticized for recapitulating "familiar
tropes of Asian female representation (as alternately sexually available/
willing/exotically enticing or virginal/maternal/desexualized)" (Shimakawa 33).[9] In many ways, the character Kim exemplifies the myth of Asian
women's selflessness that recurs in musical productions extolling the
benevolence and democratic ideals of U.S. empire.[10] *Miss Saigon* had a
successful ten-year run in the West End, and on Broadway, and in subse-
quent touring productions in major cities around the world. It is notable
as one of a handful of musicals with several nonwhite, specifically Asian,
lead characters. So, too, 50 percent of the actors-workers in the Broadway premiere were Asian/Asian Americans. They performed a range of
roles: Kim, Gigi, and Thuy, and as ensemble members cast in roles such as
"Vietnamese soldier," "bar man," and "bar girl." At the close of the show's
ten-year run on Broadway (with more than four thousand performances,
estimated to have been seen by thirty-three million people), producer
Cameron Mackintosh took pride in being able to "deliver on our promise

of putting on a production that has been the greatest platform for Asian talent in history" (qtd. in "Miss Saigon," 68).

Despite its resounding popularity, the show also garnered heated criticism. The initial storm about the Broadway premiere of *Miss Saigon* concerned the casting of Jonathan Pryce, a white actor, in the role of the Eurasian Engineer. Asian American artists and activists organized to denounce this choice, calling the casting process exclusionary and racist. A series of actions, referred to by writer/performance artist David Mura as "anti–*Miss Saigon* organizing," galvanized Asian American artists and communities throughout the United States (qtd. in Kondo, *About Face*, 234).[11] These multicity protests drew public attention to the long history of racist labor practices in theater and entertainment fields. More specifically, the *Miss Saigon* casting controversy exposed the history of yellowface—the practice of white actors donning an "Asian" face, mannerisms, voice and speech patterns, as well as Oriental clothing, to perform an "Asian character" in American theater.[12] National media played up the casting controversy, though at times they overshadowed the protesters' critique of Orientalist representations of Asians in *Miss Saigon*.

Reactions to the protests were varied. Playwright David Henry Hwang and scholar/writer Dorinne Kondo, for example, stridently suggest that while the casting controversy was an issue, it was "minor" because, as Kondo argued, "*Miss Saigon* restages and conveniently expiates American guilt over Vietnam" (*About Face*, 232). Kondo also further described the musical as a "'colored museum' of Asian stereotypes, including the tenacious trope of Asian women's sacrifice and death" (231).[13] In light of this observation, producer Cameron Mackintosh's view of the musical as "the greatest platform for Asian talent" captures the very problematic conditions that exist for Asian American artists in American theater. That a musical that is a "colored museum" of Asian stereotypes could indeed be the "greatest platform for Asian talent in history" underscores the fact that the institution of American theater is steeped in racism.

In highlighting the yellowface problem, the large-scale anti–Miss Saigon organizing challenged the predominance of a binary U.S. racial formation, unsettling common assumptions of American race relations as simply black and white. These counterperformances publicly demonstrated how Asian Americans were equally subject to racism, both in the theater industry and, by extension, in the society at large. One very heated protest involved the use of the Broadway production of *Miss Saigon* as a fundraising event for the Lambda Legal Defense and Education Fund (LLDEF) and New York City's Lesbian and Gay Community Services. Spearheading the protests were

Lea Salonga (Kim) and
David Platt (Tam) in
the original London
production. Photograph by
Michael Le Poer Trench ©
Cameron Mackintosh Ltd.

the Asian Lesbians of the East Coast (ALOEC) and the Gay Asian Pacific Islander Men of New York (GAPIMNY).[14] Queer Asian American activist groups criticized mainstream gay and lesbian organizations involved in the fundraising event for their endorsement of, and capitalization on, a musical production that portrays Asians in a racist light. Initially, these Asian American queer organizations urged LLDEF and the Lesbian and Gay Community Services to cancel their fundraising, but soon the organizers expanded their focus to protesting the show, reaching out to the larger Asian American community and other communities of color.[15] According to one reporter, this protest was a "catalyst in bringing together many Asian gay and straight political activists to the forefront" (qtd. in Manalansan 56).

Monique Wilson (Kim) and Robert Sena (Thuy), London 1991. Photographs by Michael Le Poer Trench © Cameron Mackintosh Ltd.

In a similar vein, the musical's 2000 Philippine premiere was a fraught homecoming. Just as *Miss Saigon* was a site of contention for Asian Americans in the United States, it also received critical scrutiny in the Philippines. Protests centered on the musical's continued reproduction of an imperialistic global economy (the abuse of the local artist pool, exorbitant ticket prices), its romanticization of the Vietnam War, and its perpetuation of stereotypical depictions of Asian women. Philippine-based artists and activists condemned the displacement of resident artists at the Cultural Center of the Philippines to accommodate the *Miss Saigon* production.[16] The musical production was also censured for participating in the "imperialist globalization of culture"; for continuing elitism in theater and perpetuating the inaccessibility of "culture" to the people; and for rehearsing the image

of the "oppressed and exploited Third World woman whose only deliver-
ance is in the feudal and patriarchal embrace of the gallant and gentle [white
American] G.I." (Concerned Artists of the Philippines 68). Other aspects of
the production that came under criticism included the modern-day feudal
relationship between the Philippine government and the Philippine elite.
For example, J. V. Ejercito, the owner of *Miss Saigon*'s local production company, Bayang Makulay Foundation in Manila, became a member of the Philippine Congress. Ejercito is the son of the former action hero, movie star,
impeached president, and 2010 presidential candidate, Joseph Estrada. At the
time of the production, Joseph Estrada was still in power in the Philippines.
Journalists and artists alike, particularly the members of the Concerned Artists of the Philippines, heavily criticized the Bayang Makulay Foundation for
its choice of leadership, implying that the large profit earnings from the *Miss
Saigon* production investment were not gained "by virtue of free enterprise,
JV Ejercito being the president's son" (qtd. in Concerned Artists of the Philippines 68). Protesters of the musical astutely mobilized language such as
"refugee" and "imperialist globalization" to highlight the romanticized and
liberal-humanist approach of exploitation in *Miss Saigon*.

The Filipino/a actor-worker's alleged exceptionalism, the very traits that
stamp his/her specificity and make the Filipino/a unique as opposed to being
"generically Asian," are of course embedded within multiple colonial peda-
gogies of the Philippines. Filipinos' near-perfect articulation of English, their
knowledge of and ease with "Western" culture and ways, all qualities that
make them enviably cosmopolitan, purportedly set them above the rest. It is
no accident that these are the very traits that the Philippine state commod-
ifies as it promotes Filipino workers in the global market.[17] Joi Barrios, in
her article "Staging/Upstaging Globalization: The Politics of Performance,"
makes explicit the commodification of Filipino performers/laborers in the
Miss Saigon production:

> *Miss Saigon* can be read as a metaphor for globalization because ultimately,
> it is not different from raw material, such as pineapple, processed by cheap
> labor in a multinational factory (Dole, Del Monte) and sold right back
> as canned dessert to a developing country with the aid of local business-
> men and politicians who espouse the liberalization of industries. In these
> developing countries, many of which are former colonies of Europe and
> the United States, these products are more appealing because the people
> have been conditioned to believe that everything the colonizer produces is
> superior to that of local products. Hence, the canned pineapple is sweeter
> and more uniformly cut than the one from the local market. (22)

Barrios situates Filipino/a performers within the circuit of global capital, alerting us to the commodification of art and culture and to the brutal materiality of performance. By thinking about *Miss Saigon* alongside the thousands of Filipino/a transmigrant entertainment workers exported overseas, I engage with performance as a skill and a form of desirable exportable labor. While *Miss Saigon* performers are welcomed back home and adored as "stars," one cannot help but wonder if the same warm welcome is extended to the entertainers, whose jobs vary from singer to dancer to comedian, in hotel bars and lounges of Japan, Hong Kong, Singapore, and South Korea, as well as cities in Europe, the Americas, and Central and East Asia.[18] Barrios's emphatic reading of Filipino/a performers as laborers, instrumentalized in the processes of global capitalism, stresses the multiple colonial legacies of the Filipino people and demystifies the celebration of the Filipino/a actor's uniqueness and exceptionalism.

Filipino/a participation in this popular musical theater poses a unique challenge to the dominant values and perspectives in scholarly and activist analyses of the musical. Scholars such as Martin Manalansan and Celine Parreñas offer alternatives to dominant critical approaches to *Miss Saigon*, many of which have focused on the musical's Orientalist narrative. Manalansan considers the production, circulation, and consumption of *Miss Saigon* from the perspective of gay Filipino transmigrants who chose not to participate in "anti–Miss Saigon mobilizations." For these gay Filipino men, protest actions condemning racist and sexist representations of Asians conflicted with their love and admiration for their idol, Lea Salonga. For Manalansan's informants, Salonga was not just a model of femininity; her success at acquiring a green card through this musical was an equal source of inspiration. The Filipino queering of *Miss Saigon*, through their drag tributes to Salonga's *byuti* and talent, opens up a space for alternative political, performative acts in the drama of *Miss Saigon*. Manalansan turns to queer fandom practices and desires to expand settled forms of nationalist identification and alliance. Gay Filipino transmigrants' dedication to Salonga, like gay audiences' worship of opera divas, thus "subverts patriarchal sexist male-female consumption" (Koestenbaum).

For Celine Parreñas Shimizu, the performance of Asian American actors in *Miss Saigon* must be read as an act of "productive perversity" (21). She analyzes the apparent "hypersexuality of racialized subjects" to imagine political possibilities beyond the bid for respectability. The fields of African American Studies and Queer and Sexuality Studies have both developed a critique of the politics of respectability in terms of its concession to mainstream values. Feminist Black Studies scholar Farrah Jasmine Griffin writes of the implication of the "politics of respectability" as it influences race politics: "[A]fter a century of being concerned with presenting positive images of black lives, we have so policed our intellectual efforts that we often find ourselves caught up in narrow representations that in no way allow for the full complexity and humanity of black people, particularly black women" (34). Parreñas Shimizu considers how the "slut, whore, easy Asian" image of Asian/Asian American women can function in a resistant politics. She asks, "Can 'bad object' representations, such as whorish Asian women, contribute to anti-racist politics?" (5).[19] Both Manalansan and Parreñas Shimizu attend to the Filipino/a performing body in *Miss Saigon* productions to demonstrate the possibility of forming resistant communities even within perceived projects of racism.

II. Labor, Self, and Representation

Filipino/a performing bodies in *Miss Saigon* do not merely represent or reenact the intimate connections among U.S. imperialism (particularly through militarization), sexuality, and gender relations. Instead, they further reconstitute this imperial history and relations through both performance and production. The emergence of Filipinos in *Miss Saigon* on first-class global stages (West End, Broadway) coincides with the emergence of Filipinas as the largest export commodity of the Philippines for the international work force. Filipinas performing Vietnamese prostitutes on stage are a throwback from an earlier image of Filipinas popularized by U.S. military men as Little Brown Fucking Machines, or LBFM. By the time *Miss Saigon* was in production in the 1990s, the LBFM image had been eclipsed by that of the domestic helper, the maid, the Filipina as the server to the world, or, as the title to Rhacel Parreñas's book reads, "servants of globalization."

The conflation of the Filipina as performer, and her character as a prostitute, or even as a body savaged by war, is not the only visual echo—think Cio Cio San, Liat, and Suzi Wong in *Madame Butterfly*, *South Pacific*, and *The World of Suzi Wong*—of theatrical and cinematic characters that have been assigned to Asian women.[20] Lynda Hart writes that "the female body on stage appears to be the 'thing itself,' incapable of mimesis, afforded not only no distance between sign and referent but, indeed, taken for the referent" (5). While Hart refers to the female body in general, her analysis is equally relevant for the phenomenon of Filipina performers in the role of prostitutes in *Miss Saigon*. What happens when the sign and referent become indistinguishable, when the sign is taken for the referent itself? A realist theatrical imaginary, as Hart and other feminist performance theorists have argued, routinely reads the female performing body as "natural." In other words, the female performer is seen less as an actor who is performing a role than as an embodiment of herself; she is simply being who she is. Feminist performance theorists lambasted early realist genres for their blinkered vision of women, whether they functioned as signs or referents or both. The task most important to me is to make visible the conditions that collapse the sign and referent.

The case of the Filipino/a performing body in *Miss Saigon* extends this concern to a larger geopolitical stage. Neferti Tadiar characterizes the Philippines as a mistress to the United States, where the mistress is a prostitute, a feminized commodification of the Philippines by the United States. Tadiar considers the historical prostitution of Filipinas as an apt paradigm of U.S.-Philippine relations, one that is exploitative and reduces the very being of Filipinas to a source of cheap labor along with the country's natural resources, properties, land, and other facilities. It is as if Filipinas can have no meaning outside of their bodies, and no circulation outside the significations of colonialism/globalization.

In the world of sexist/masculinist realist theater, Hart argues, the female body is incapable of mimesis. What is mimesis? Mimesis is a faculty, an ability denied to the female performing body. She is, as mentioned earlier, unable to not be herself—is rendered, in fact, *incapable* of acting. Mimesis becomes the key mediating factor that is made invisible in the collapse of sign and referent. If mimicry is recognized, then the difference between the acting body and its referent is distinguishable. If, as Hart suggests, the female body's detriment on stage is being "the thing itself," the task of feminist performance theory is to demystify, to lay bare the historicity of the body that has been obscured. What is the relationship of mimesis to the historicity of a performing body? As feminist performance theorists argue, mimesis asks us to turn to the history of representation, to visual echoes, rather than to presume mimicry of a discoverable "real"—the "real" Asian woman, the "real" prostitute, the "real" Vietnamese.[21] More precisely, the recognition of Filipinos on the global stage rests on and wrestles with their remarkable ability to "perform back" what they have imbibed through their colonial education. My interest in mimesis, used here interchangeably with imitation, consequently lies specifically in the material and affective labor it takes to imitate.

To attend to the literal labor of Filipina participation in *Miss Saigon*, I want to focus on the exhaustive training rituals required of these actors. Like Hart and others who have approached mimicry as a complex practice, I see imitation as an ability, a skill that requires training and also demands creativity. Acts of imitation are often reduced to mere "derivative realms of

conformity or tertiary imitation"—a notion of performance that regards performance as unthinking, devoid of an involved process (Jackson 14). From
that point of view, racialized bodies that inhabit hegemonic forms of performance can only produce forms of unoriginality or inauthenticity. While
brown performing bodies' mimicry of Western performing arts is looked
upon as reinforcing their unoriginality, their slow catch-up to modernity,
white bodies performing across cultural borders are labeled interculturalist,
postmodern, and avante garde. What would it mean, I want to ask, to recognize mimesis as a method, a practice, an act that provides the separation, the
distance between the sign and the referent? What would it mean for Filipinas
to work *Miss Saigon* through mimesis?

Harry Elam and Alice Rayner pose a question relevant to an understanding of the Filipino/a performing body in *Miss Saigon*: "Where does the costume end and the real body of the actress begin?" ("Echoes," 271). They raise
this key question in their discussion of Suzan Lori Park's *Venus*, a play dra-
matizing the life of Sarah Baartman, aka the Hottentot Venus, a sexualized
and racialized emblem of the nineteenth century. Unlike Park's play, *Miss
Saigon* is not a postmodern play that comments on the very project of representation. It does not implicate musical theater as a spectacle that reproduces
prostitution as a form of U.S.-Philippine imperial relations and the feminiza-
tion of Asia in the U.S. imaginary. In fact, the musical believes that its storytelling brings a much-needed imaginative resolution to the crisis of empire. It
relies on this catharsis, masking the relations of exploitation in this gendered
and racialized dramatization of U.S. imperialism. *Miss Saigon's* dramatization of Kim's "humanity" as a prostitute and the seductiveness of the dance,
music, and staging collapse the sign and the referent at work. The musical's
humanization of the consequence of war—prostitution, fatherless children,
broken relationships—solicits identification and sympathy with Kim, even as
she lies dead at the end of the play, her child left with Chris and his American
wife. Acknowledging Filipinas playing a role, donning a "costume," training
their bodies to perform is a critical intervention in the discourse around *Miss
Saigon*. A closer look at Filipino/a performing bodies in *Miss Saigon* makes
transparent the continuing reconstitution of the U.S.-Philippine imperial
relations.

III. Philippines-U.S.-Vietnam War

The discourse of "discovery" is often used to portray Filipino/a talents in
global productions of *Miss Saigon*, obscuring the historicity of the Filipina
performing body. While the popular musical purports to remember, to never

forget a painful history of a war touted as one in which the United States lost its innocence, the very performing bodies that enact this narrative cannot but recall a longer history of U.S. foreign interventionism. Vietnam's historicization in the American collective memory has contributed to the misrecognition of Filipino/a performers in *Miss Saigon*. Filipinas may have been performing the role of prostitutes in the musical set during the American war in Vietnam, yet what this association allows us to remember, or at least prompts us to ask about, is the role of the Philippines during this war. Here, I shift historical sightlines to highlight the part that Filipinos and the Philippines played in the U.S.-Vietnam war. The decade immediately following the American-Vietnam War marked the Philippines as a doorway to the United States, particularly for those who had been newly bestowed with American imperial graces. The Philippines harbored thousands of Southeast Asian refugees in camps where they began their transition to American culture. Philippine Executive Order 554, declared by Ferdinand Marcos in August 1979, assembled a Philippine task force on international refugee assistance and administration in cooperation with the United Nations' UN High Commission for Refugees. The Philippines, along with Indonesia and Thailand, housed the United States' refugee processing centers (built in areas that displaced the indigenous Aeta population). In 1988, Corazon Aquino instituted Philippine Executive Order 332 in an effort to reconstitute the task force. By this time, the surge of refugees had substantially dwindled and less attention was paid to the entry and exit of foreign bodies. Such historical genealogies of collaboration and conflict found the Filipino/a performing body in and through the phenomenon of *Miss Saigon;* the myth of the U.S. empire's benevolence and democratic ideals lives on through the circulation and popularity of *Miss Saigon*.

Of significance is that the U.S.-Vietnam War was also a cause for protest in the Philippines. Filipino opposition to the Vietnam War aligned the U.S. invasion of Vietnam with the long history of U.S. occupation in the Philippines, where military offensives were justified as democratic interventions. In a congressional request in 1966, Marcos called for a "combat engineer battalion" to send to South Vietnam (Lockwood par. 1). This request for military troops was a complete reversal from his campaign position the year before, when Marcos criticized the ruling president, Diosdado Macapagal, and advocated for humanitarian and medical support in Vietnam. Once in office, Marcos pledged Philippine soldiers to aid the United States in its war against Vietnam, and more specifically against the communist forces threatening to take over the divided nation. The Philippines played host to a seven-nation meeting, in which the participants signed a "Declaration of Peace," pledging to facilitate a peaceful withdrawal of troops in Vietnam within six months.[22] In joining the United States in this war, Marcos played out on the international arena his own commitment toward squelching "communist threat," realizing this commitment more locally in his declaration of Martial Law in 1972. As Neferti Tadiar has argued, Marcos's New Society "reconstruct[ed] social order to attend to demands of global capitalism" (*Fantasy Production*, 43) inasmuch as it was a dictator's move to centralize power.

The key location of the Philippines in the Pacific made the country a central strategic military post in the geopolitics of the American war in Vietnam. As is well documented, the Subic U.S. Naval Base and Clark U.S. Air Force Base were critical military sites used for ship repair, as supply bases, and for fighter-squadron installation ("Clark Air Base"). Though the United States was given free-reign use of these bases through the 1947 Mutual Agreement Act (signed by Manuel Roxas) soon after the transition from Commonwealth to Third Republic status of the Philippines, the bases reached another level of development during the Vietnam War. As Herman Tiu Laurel notes, under an "agreement between unequal nations, . . . the country found itself, being a crucial part in the web of U.S. military installations spreading throughout the globe, with the Philippines ranking as one of the lowest in terms of compensation and sovereign rights to control abuses of American military personnel" (10). American soldiers received additional training in jungle combat in the forests of Subic from its indigenous inhabitants, the Aetas, in a program called Jungle Environmental Survival Training Camp (JEST).[23] When the U.S. bases left and ports like Olongapo were developed into commercial seaports, JEST became a featured tourist adventure option. The reformed JEST program boasts of the techniques used to train the U.S. military as a main feature in its extreme sports offerings:

> So, you want to be John Rambo? Why not give yourself a little more validity with an overnight survival training class brought to you by the same indigenous people who helped train the U.S. Navy Seals and Special Forces Units how to survive in the Jungle? The United States Military troops learned many survival and warfare tactics from the indigenous Aetas people in these same forests during the Vietnam War. You can now avail yourself of these same techniques and be the talk of your town. ("Jungle Environmental Survival Training Camp")

JEST's transition from a military combat training camp to a survival-adventure tourist activity overlaps with the musical *Miss Saigon* in both projects' relationship to the history of war as a source for entertainment, tourism, and adventure. Such pleasure activities that capitalize on legacies of war can function as coping gestures of moving on, as shields against the pain of history.

It is thus no coincidence that bar scenes and campsites are backdrops to *Miss Saigon's* love story. Such locations make possible an elaborate choreography of dance routines and dramatic exchanges that in turn highlight the desperate and overdetermined failure of Chris's and Kim's union. Filipinos performed a popular human "service" during the U.S.-Vietnam War as they provided "hospitality" for the U.S. servicemen who were en route to/ from Vietnam. Filipinos also functioned as soldiers, as natural resources for on-ground military bases. They provided staff support in base retail stores (commonly known in the Philippines as PXes), banks, and restaurants and performed other blue- and white-collar jobs. The two principal host cities to the U.S. naval and air stations were Olongapo and Angeles. These cities were rest and relaxation sites lined up with "beer houses," dance clubs, massage parlors, and souvenir shops catering to the *Amerikanos*. In the 1970s, Marcos's efforts to open up the country for tourism sanctioned the rise of the sex industry, particularly prostitution. To construct his regime of Martial Law as an exception from other societies under military rule, Marcos welcomed an international presence through tourism, business, and other foreign exchanges. While the formation of sex work in Olongapo and Angeles is distinct from its growth in Manila during the Martial Law years, they were not exclusive of nor isolated from one another; those who engaged in sexual services, both patrons and workers, could move about among various cities. Night acts of various kinds developed as entertainment for U.S. soldiers, and women were employed as "hostesses" who provided companionship. These relations were often sexual, in varying degrees. Like the taxi dancers I describe in chapter 2, the women in these beer houses and clubs provided much-needed relief and respite from the business of war. Such caretaking tasks were necessary to the survival and continuation of these good wars in bad places. Filipinos in these bars performed companionship and intimacy, affective labor that became immediately sexualized in the context of war.

Such acts of labor in turn provide the context and material for the relationships and encounters represented in *Miss Saigon*. Out of wars are born such star-crossed relations, as represented in the Kim-and-Chris union in *Miss Saigon*. I want to reiterate here that this entanglement of love, war, and militarization is a recurring trope in various theatrical genres, as noted in my discussion of *Shoo-Fly Regiment* in chapter 1. Such a triangulation is central in other popular musicals and operas such as *Madame Butterfly*, *South Pacific*, *Carmen*, and so on. But unlike the overtly tainted labor of prostitution, the ill-fated Kim-and-Chris union proclaims its alleged separation from the fleeting, transactual, and purely carnal relationship between American G.I.'s and bar girls. Indeed, the very integrity of *Miss Saigon* relies on the exceptionality of the Kim-Chris union, on the "purity of love," fleeting and momentary as it may be. While I do not wish to collapse the affective labor performed by hostesses in Olongapo and/or Angeles with its dramatization in *Miss Saigon*, I do want to consider what specific kind of affective labor the Filipino/a performing body enacts in this global musical phenomenon. Filipinas who worked as hostesses and as other types of sex workers provided relief, friendship, and intimacy during wartime. They supplied an ordinariness that lay within and outside the brackets of the very conditions that created the exchange. In many ways, the Filipino/a performing body in *Miss Saigon* also assuages memories and feelings about the Vietnam War, about the continuing stress of U.S.-Philippine imperial relations. By acknowledging this laboring body, we are able to address the continuity of a longer history, across time as well as geopolitical wars. The narrative of an exemplary imperialist war, performed by actors whose connection to U.S. imperial history has been a case of "imperial amnesia" (Campomanes, "The New Empire's Forgetful and Forgotten Citizens") and "imperial aphasia" (Isaac) reproduced globally, could not stage more clearly the intersection of U.S. imperialism and globalization. Filipinos in *Miss Saigon* embody the indiscernibility of when U.S. imperialism ends and globalization begins, and so too the *continuity* between these two regimes of world domination.

IV. *Tawag Ng Tanghalan, Himig ng Bayan* (Call of the Stage, Sound of the Nation)/*Himig Ng Tanghalan, Tawag ng Bayan* (Sound of the Stage, Call of the Nation)

Musicals, among live theatrical performances, continue to be popular. Like any good melodrama, *Miss Saigon* creates its world and produces emotion through bodies, voices, music, costumes, sets, lighting, and other stage elements. The ten-year run of *Miss Saigon* on Broadway and the West End is reported to have been seen by over "33 million people" ("The Original *Miss Saigon*"). The majority of reviews of performances in New York, London, Sydney, and Toronto praise the numerous Filipinas for their powerful singing voices, placing the character of Kim within a long and heralded lineage of musical heroines.

Catherine Clément, in writing about conventions and structures of nineteenth-century melodrama and opera, introduces the notion of voice types as a way of creating a world, placing characters within that world, and conveying relationships. I am interested in the "society of voices" generated in *Miss Saigon* as it gains recognition on the global stage (19). Clément's work on voice types follows a notion of social order similar to that of melodrama. Melodrama's archetypes—the hero, the heroine, the villain, the elder—represent and perform a role in the world (the hero saves; the heroine gets rescued; the villain threatens). For Clément, musical theater casting must thus consider voice type in addition to the "overall look" of the actor for certain roles, and the resulting voices together create the "society of voices" (19).

What do we hear in the singing voices of *Miss Saigon*?[24] What does the voice of the character Kim, a mixed belt voice, a mezzo soprano, say about her and her place in the musical's "society of voices"? Belting requires that the song be delivered with intensity, with an intent to evoke strong emotions. We hear Kim reach deep in her chest voice to convey the story of how her family was destroyed, her village burned. As she begins her "tale of a Vietnam girl," the music begins softly and builds with cymbals and a diverse set of percussion sounds as the tale narrates the violence she has lived through ("This Money Is Yours"). She belts in low voice, defiant in her promise to "not look back" at her "fill of pain." Sounds shift to the softness of wind and string instruments as the song transitions to the love song "Sun and Moon." In her soft head voice, Kim turns demure once again. The duet is rendered as a tender ballad where we hear Kim's and Chris's voices blend harmoniously. And thus the actor who performs the role of Kim travels a vocal range in her emotional journey from "This Money Is Yours" to "Sun and Moon." The audience is treated to an auditory extravaganza that features the vocal strength of the actor who plays Kim. This is also a turning point in the story, as we fully hear Kim's story, told defiantly to Chris. Not just one more "Vietnam girl," Kim becomes a real person to him. Such a poignant moment of realization conveys the depth of Kim's moral strength to the audience through the vocal power of the actor.

Well-known musicologist Carolyn Abbate, whose work on opera has been influential in bringing "voice" back into studies of opera narratives, cites a male opera goer's (Paul Robinson's) critique of the overdetermination and overprivileging of the woman's death in many opera narratives. Abbate takes seriously this male operagoer's attention to the "triumph: the sounds of the women's voices" [ix]. Like Abbate and Robinson, Kim portrayer Aura Deva highlights the complexity of "the woman undone by plot yet triumphant in voice" (ix). She responds to criticisms of Kim as a meek and weak character, pointing out that over half the singing in the musical is carried by this character. According to Deva, the actor playing Kim sings nearly 65 percent of the songs. Her attention to the vocal strength as a neglected characteristic of

Kim is worth considering. By redirecting our attention from the plot to the singing, Deva offers another lens through which we can begin to understand the labor of the performing body. I also hear Deva's, Abbate's, and Robinson's arguments as an opportunity to rethink viewing, listening, and pedagogical practices. Why weigh the value of a performance in terms of the ending? Could there be something worthwhile in reading against the narrative arc? Could a turn to other performative elements provide us with a different and renewed understanding of racialization in performance? If we *listen* to the singing, will we *hear* against the stereotype of Asian women that we *see* in *Miss Saigon?* In other words, the question that remains is, How do we reconcile the "triumph" of the women's singing voices and the power of their performances with a continuing narrative of a long representational history that uncritically reproduces a colonialist script? Is a successful performance of this colonialist script necessarily a reinforcement of it?

Filipinos in *Miss Saigon* are the embodiment of a colonialist genealogy of performance training—of imperialism through education. Once again, we encounter Filipinos' splendid dancing, angelic singing, and natural acting as visible and embodied evidence of the success of colonial education. The initial cohort of Filipinos in the West End premiere production went through additional performance training in London, even though many of them had had a long career in theater, television, and Philippine cinema. A similar training site was launched in Manila in 1994. The program was primarily designed to get Filipino/a performers ready to audition for *Miss Saigon* performances worldwide. My information on the "school" (as it was also referred to) draws on my multiple conversations with Philippine theater impresario Dong Alegre, who coordinates this training program. Three former *Miss Saigon* actors, Lea Salonga, Aura Deva, and Monique Wilson, also generously shared stories about their experiences working in this musical. In our exchanges, I focused largely on their personal and professional challenges while they worked on the production. These conversations with Alegre, Salonga, Deva, and Wilson primarily inform my understanding of the training school. One of my contentions here is that providing the details of the *Miss Saigon* school allows us to more carefully understand the process of making Filipinas into world-class performers. This training program reveals part of a system by which Filipino/a actors are produced, and then fed into the global *Miss Saigon* pipeline. That such a training method works and is highly successful is evident in the multiple Tony, Helpmann, and Laurence Olivier awards garnered by Filipina actresses, as well as in their employment in other mainstream theatrical productions worldwide.[25] Indeed, those who go through this training and perform in the production see their employment in *Miss Saigon* as a foot in the door of an otherwise inaccessible industry. My critical task here is to expose the linkages between the processes of colonialism and globalization at work in the production of this musical. In doing so, I do not wish to diminish the labor and recognition of these fine actors. Rather, these stories of "success" go beyond the modalities of the personal, of talent and fine genes, or of an inherent national/racial trait to account for a system that is organized around supply and demand.

Salonga and Wilson are the Filipina actors set up as rivals for the coveted role of Kim (*The Making of Miss Saigon*). Both actors grew up in musical theater in the Philippines. Though it was *Miss Saigon* that made her known worldwide, Salonga had been famous in the Philippines and Asia prior to being selected to play the musical's lead. Her first album, titled *Small Voice*, received the country's top music awards and gained her a television show show titled *Love, Lea*. In 1988, she was part of an international public service project to "promote sexual responsibility" among teens, spearheaded by Johns Hopkins University's Population Communication Services. Her recorded duet with Menudo, a popular Puerto Rican teen boy band, titled "The Situation," instantly climbed up the sale charts. These are only a few of Salonga's already charted national and international successes before she was "discovered" by the production team of *Miss Saigon*.

Like Salonga, Wilson was an established performer in Philippine theater. Wilson began her training as a performer at Repertory Philippines. As noted in her biography, "By the time she was 17 and entering university, she had appeared in over sixty professional productions. She enrolled as a Theatre Major at the University of the Philippines, but fate soon intervened in 1988 when Cameron Mackintosh came to Manila to audition for the musical *Miss Saigon*" ("Biography"). At the age of twenty-four, Wilson founded her own theater group, New Voice Company. She also pursued further formal training and earned a degree in theater at the Central School of Speech and Drama in London. Today, Wilson continues to have a successful career performing, directing, and recording music while serving as the youngest faculty director of the M.A./M.F.A. in Acting program at the University of Essex East 15 Acting School ("Monique Wilson, Head of MA/MFA in Acting").

Before she became Aura Deva of the *Miss Saigon* German-language production, Angel Sugitan was a member of the Filipino pop band The Opera.[26] In 1989, The Opera broke up as a group, and Sugitan found herself seeking another project to sustain her creative career. One afternoon, her mother knocked on her bedroom door and told her to audition in what turned out to be the casting call for *Miss Saigon*. Sugitan, soon to become Aura Deva, was "earmarked" to perform the role of Kim for the German tour.[27] She performed the role in the German-language touring production of *Miss Saigon* from 1994 to 1997. During the three years Deva lived in Germany, she and the other Filipino/a members of the *Miss Saigon* musical performed ambassadorial roles such as having lunches with local government officials and holding benefit concerts to raise funds for various Philippine-related causes. The musical's popularity and the fame Deva gained through this production resulted in her being voted as "one of the most influential people in Germany" (Deva).

Along with twenty-five other Filipino/a performers, Deva was among the first batch of "Saigonistas"—a term Alegre uses for those who have been part of the production—to train in the *Miss Saigon* school in Manila. Having "discovered" the talents of Lea Salonga and Monique Wilson during their worldwide search for an actor to play the role of Kim, Mackintosh approached Dong Alegre, a known theater impresario in the Philippines, to move Filipino talents toward the production of *Miss Saigon*.[28] The story of this search has been recorded in the film *The Making of Miss Saigon*. In this documentary, we come to know about the quest to cast the role of Kim that brought the artistic team of Mackintosh, Boublil, and Schönberg to major cities, including New York, Los Angeles, Honolulu, and Manila. It was in Manila where the perfect Kim, and her understudy, were found. It was also in Manila that a number of ensemble members were cast. Anticipating worldwide, or at least European and American, tours, Mackintosh worked with Alegre to find Filipino/a talents and develop them into "Saigonistas." Alegre, a longtime professional theatrical and performing arts show producer, auditioned Filipino/a performers for the *Miss Saigon* school. According to Alegre, the "Saigonista" training program is designed to train performers for the musical's audition pool; those who made it to the training school were not guaranteed a part in the production itself. Training in the school is, however, part of the regimen for those who do end up being cast in the show.

From January to September 1994, Deva and twenty-five other performers who were "earmarked" for the German touring show of *Miss Saigon* trained continuously. Their preparation included voice lessons and strengthening, learning the songs and dance numbers for the musical, and mastering the basics of the German language, as the musical was performed in German in that production. For nearly seven days a week, they alternated voice and dance lessons with language training at the Goethe Institute in Manila. Deva memorized German phonetically for the rehearsals and worked with a phonetic coach in Germany.

Those performers "earmarked" or "short-listed" for training in the *Miss Saigon* school were not provided a stipend during training months. Nor did they pay for their training. The producing company of Cameron Mackintosh subsidized the cost to train these Filipino/a performers for the German production. Top voice and music teachers and choreographers were recruited, emphasizing musical theater training that focused on both singing and dancing.[29] This extensive training was designed to put students on par with or even in a more competitive position than other actors auditioning from all over the world.[30]

Voice and music lessons were crucial for these performers, who would be performing on a massive world/global stage, which demanded a range of performing skills that these Filipino actors ostensibly did not possess. Training sessions geared them toward performing five nights a week and twice a day on the weekends. For the role of Kim, however, these actors performed five days a week, while other performances employed the work of understudies. With approximately 65 percent of the singing carried by "Kim," the demand on the actor playing this part was exacting. The toll it took on Lea Salonga for her eight-shows-a-week performance in London's West End, for example, had alerted producers to the risks of such extended training and performance. Salonga credits the training required by the role of Kim as the professional challenge that dramatically altered her life. Monique Wilson, who performed the role of Gigi and was Kim alternate to Salonga in the original London production in the late 1980s, describes the physical discipline they went through during this production's run as transformative. She describes what is required to perform in a musical theater on a global stage:

> When you're doing a musical, it's like you have to sleep X number of hours for your stamina, you have to take voice lessons, go to the gym and take dance classes and aerobics. Doing a musical is like doing aerobics on stage. In fact, we do aerobics for our warm-ups. And we have no life when we're doing a show. We don't go out, we can't have a drink somewhere, nowhere where people are smoking. Extreme discipline. But if you have proper technique, the everyday rehearsals actually strengthen your voice. ("Verbatim: Monique Wilson")

Wilson, like Salonga, attributes her physical skills to her invaluable training as an actor in *Miss Saigon*: "Definitely, it has helped me develop stamina in performing since you do it everyday. It also taught me humility, because any moment anybody can take your place. There were so many people who could just step into your shoes so you really had to be humble," she explained. "And you really have to work hard because you owe it to your audience to be good each night. You can't afford to be bored with it or feel lazy. Doing *Miss Saigon* gave me a lot of courage, the wisdom, the higher standard of working and be[ing] professional" (Vanzi).

I want to emphasize that these training sessions involved physical artistic training but *did not* include a course on Western theater repertoire. Salonga, Wilson, Deva, and many, if not all, who make it in the *Miss Saigon* productions need not receive schooling in Western theater repertoire. Their educational training in theater and music already incorporated, or more specifically *constituted*, a curriculum of Western dramatic literature and musical repertoire. In a 1990 interview on the London talk show, the *Terry Wogan Show*, Salonga emphasized that she was quite familiar with American musicals. Her first performance was in the musical *The King and I* at age seven, and her first lead role was *Annie* at age nine. Similarly, Deva, who earned a degree in music at the University of the Philippines, had performed in productions such as *The King and I* at the Repertory Philippines. Here, the colonial markings on Asian/Asian American actors are undeniable, wherein the repertoire of shows upon which one builds training and a career consists of what Sheng Mei-Ma refers to as "chopsticks musicals," such as Rodgers and Hammerstein's *The King and I, South Pacific,* and *Flower Drum Song.* The *Miss Saigon* school in Manila was intended to build these performers' physical capacity rather than their theatrical knowledge because, although they were trained artists, they were not skilled in performing five to eight shows a week for months and months on end. They needed training for the kind of labor demands and conditions that did/does not exist in the Philippines. These specific labor skills are compatible with economies that can fill up 300-plus theater seats for a full week of shows that would run for months or years.

The *Miss Saigon* school in Manila thus served to train Filipina performers in the labor skills necessary for sustaining a familiar script of globalization, mass production, and the overall international gendered division of labor. The labor of these "Saigonistas" is in many ways continuous with the labor of the hundreds of Filipinas deployed daily to service various needs of the global economy. Filipino labor is the largest "export item" of the Philippines, with Filipinas constituting over 70 percent of all Filipino overseas contract workers. Various Philippine-government-sponsored and private employment agencies are set up to train workers whose destination is inevitably overseas. Overseas jobs include health care provision, domestic work, and entertainment. More specifically, thousands of Filipino/a transmigrant entertainment workers are exported to other countries such as Japan and Australia to market their wares in much the same ways as is done with other, more recognizable forms of contract labor. Alegre speaks with pride of the "Saigonistas" as Filipinos gaining acknowledgment for their talents performing a "respectable" job on a world-class stage. "Being a 'Saigonista' meant something," he says; and indeed it does. He implies that having been a part of a *Miss Saigon* production elevates one's value within the professional theater and performing arts business, as indeed it does. But Saigonistas are set apart from the rest of the overseas labor pool. Thus this training program creates a select pool of entertainers who are seen, and perhaps see themselves, as having an exclusive relationship to global stage productions. This hierarchy of labor and performing stages exemplifies Filipino/a artists' transnational labor and its uneven acceptance by the Philippine nation-state.[31]

In addition to rigorous professional training never encountered before despite previous performance training, I want to also mention here that many of the performers in *Miss Saigon* productions came into their adulthood while in the show. For example, Salonga shared that the West End was where she first set up her own checking account and took the tube to go to work (personal communication). Similarly, Joanne Almedilla recalls that being in the New York production afforded her her first apartment (Almedilla, Paz, and Salma). From the perspective of these actors, and a generation of them, working in *Miss Saigon* coincided with their ascent to adulthood. More such stories are captured in *Road to Saigon*, a production with music that featured the experience of three actors—Joan Almedilla, Jennifer Paz, and Jenni Selma—leading up to their performing the role of Kim. They shared stories about their auditions, rehearsals, and being a member of the "Kim farm" to capture what being in this production has meant for them and their careers in theater. Deborah Paredez, in writing about the phenomenon of thousands of Latinas who auditioned for the role of Selena in the movie about the Tejana singer/songwriter's life cut short, offers an observation that may resonate with the experiences of Saigonistas. "*Selenidad*," writes Paredez, "thus provided young Latinas with a cultural script and a repertoire of gestures and attitudes for enacting emergent versions of Latina subjectivity within and against the grain of representational spaces that circumscribe their lives" (128-29). Though the regard for Selena in relation to Latina femininity contrasts against the figure of Kim and the women of *Miss Saigon*, I invoke Paredez's comment to point to the intersection of fictional "scripts" and "gestures," "of representational spaces" with transitions toward a life of adulthood, independence, and work responsibilities.

V. We Know Drama

As the stage beckons, Filipino/a performers trying their luck on diverse global stages are also responding to the call of the nation. Their recognition as

Filipinos performing in global productions is a recognition of the Philippine nation; that is to say, they are embodied representations of the Philippines in the world. Their successes are proudly claimed by the nation and its people. And thus, Filipino/a performers, in addition to negotiating a separation with their assigned characters, must also parlay the projections of the nation. On May 7, 1991, the news of her nomination for a Best Actress in a Musical Tony Award was telecast nationwide in the Philippines, interrupting regular television programming to air a recorded video of Lea Salonga singing "Tagumpay Nating Lahat" (Our Success).[32] The first minute of the broadcast consists of behind-the-scene excerpts, showing Salonga and the crew working on the video of the song. It is then followed by the actual video for the song. We see Salonga walking on the streets of New York, strolling past the Shubert Theater, and frames of Broadway musical marquees including *Miss Saigon* and *Les Miserables*. As the song and the video close with the words *"Hangad ko'y tagumpay nating lahat"* (I wish for our collective triumph), Salonga stands in front of a night silhouette of the famous New York City skyline, with the Empire State Building and surrounding edifices. New York City is the fitting background as Salonga wishes for the triumph of Filipinos, for the fulfillment of her *kababayan's* (fellow Filipinos/as') dreams. This city of cities is after all where dreams, particularly of making it on the Broadway stage, are pursued every day; as the song goes, if one makes it there, one can make it anywhere. Triumph on the Broadway stage is synonymous with conquering the world stage because the U.S. mainstage is the barometer for true international stardom. Though Salonga has received England's Olivier Award, her recognition on America's premier performance stage is the ultimate form of affirmation. Salonga's success is extended to that of the nation; it is both a collective triumph and an exceptional one to be emulated by the rest of the Filipino people.

News of Salonga's nomination and win offered some relief from a series of disasters the Philippines had been experiencing. Less than a year before, in 1990, a major earthquake that shook the central Luzon/Cordillera mountain region had claimed many lives, left thousands homeless, and crippled towns and cities, including the hill station/tourist city and U.S. military post Baguio City. Later that year, the Philippines experienced its most destructive typhoon. The country was also anticipating the term limits of the U.S. Military Agreement (1947), according to which the U.S. bases were scheduled to close. As news of Salonga's nomination and win erupted, Mt. Pinatubo in Luzon had been spewing ashes, with forewarnings of earthquakes and small eruptions leading up to an unprecedented natural disaster. The volcano became active after centuries of dormancy. Its awakening devastated towns and villages, as well as making Clark Air Base nearly inoperable by the time the U.S. Senate was voting on a bill to extend the U.S. lease of the bases. This catastrophic volcanic explosion sped up the U.S. bases' impending departure date. Thus, while the search for Kim led the creative power house of Cameron Mackintosh, Boublil, and Schönburg to the Philippines and to Salonga, who would beat out two hundred hopeful actors, the United States was packing up one of its long-time strategic military sites in the Pacific. Salonga's historic 1991 win of the most prestigious theater award on the grandest stage was a welcome respite from a long list of national suffering.

Suffering or drama is something Filipinos know, as intimated by Aura Deva when asked about the absence of acting classes in the *Miss Saigon* training program. Interpreting acting as drama and drama as suffering, Deva suggests that Filipinos did not need further training in the experience of anguish, or in conveying it, because Filipinos already live it. The idiom of "drama," along with "*byuti,*" used by Filipino gay transmigrants,

> encapsulate a self-conscious notion of performance that is embedded not only in gendered phenomena but in the exigencies of everyday life, including those of kinship and family, religion, sexual desire, and economic survival. These idioms serve as a means of understanding the world, and, more importantly, assessing proper conduct and action. (Manalansan 15)

Manalansan's take on "drama," as deployed by Filipino gay transmigrants, is relevant and connected to Deva's comment about Filipinos' knowledge of drama. To say that drama is in Filipinos' everyday life is to deemphasize it. There is so much drama that it is quotidian—it is a way of life and a way of being in life.

Monique Wilson echoes Deva's reference to "drama" as she evokes Filipinos' emotionality. She elaborates on the uses of Filipinos' *ability* to access emotion, and on where Filipinos need to direct such a skill:

> *Filipinos have natural talent,* that's for sure. *We're a lot more emotional creatures, we wear our hearts on our sleeve and we can access our emotions very quick. But we lack discipline and focus,* and we also lack a process or a procedure of working, which is part of the discipline. So many of us become one-show wonders. We know we can do it just like that, but to be able to sustain it is another matter. *Dito kasi* [Because here—Philippines], some Filipino actors think 20 performances is a long run *na* [already]. What happens if you're doing a year, 8 shows a week? You need to be fresh each night, it has to be like opening night every time.

But, you see, what I teach *in London,* you're just teaching them how to access their emotions, because *they're so repressed and they're much more stoic.* But once they learn that, it becomes a technique that they can just call upon forever.

With us Pinoys, unless we train, natural talent gets burned out or defused, or it cannot get replicated each night. Discipline is where I think we're weak at. But natural talent, we're far superior in some cases to people in the West, because we're open and very giving. ("Verbatim: Monique Wilson"; emphasis added)

Both Deva and Wilson provide much to comment on and offer insights upon which to build further thoughts on the phenomenon of Filipinos in *Miss Saigon.* In their variations of "Filipinos know drama," they affirm Filipinos' distinctive and instinctive capacity not only to access emotions but also to portray them naturally. Their comments naturalize Filipinos' emotional expressivity, perhaps even reinscribe stereotypes. To characterize Filipinos as "emotional creatures" who "lack discipline" may reinforce racist colonial beliefs that portray natives as unthinking, therefore unmodern. How do we negotiate such comments about innate characteristics of Filipinos without either dismissing them as generalizations or accepting them as truth? In other words, what possible function could comments that link expression, emotion, talent, and performance have? And why must we consider this linkage? For one thing, Filipinos and their "natural talent" have opened up the global market of entertainment and other service industries such as health care and domestic labor. To be sure, this presumed national trait has been capitalized on and has been used for the purposes of disseminating Filipino performing bodies to labor for the nation.

Jose Esteban Muñoz's work on national affect is helpful here. In his essay "Feeling Brown," Muñoz offers a complex theory of normative national affect in which he names whiteness as the unnamed standard through which the performance of emotion is measured. With whiteness as the barometer, as the proper enactment of emotion, brownness is thus excessive—too loud, too bold, too much. He writes, "Rather than run from this stereotype, Latino as excess, it seems much more important to seize it and redirect it in the service of a liberationist politics" (70). Muñoz's productive redirection of stereotypes helps to read Deva's and Wilson's comments within the context of the racialization of affect. From this point of view, their statements convey their awareness of national and racialized affect. In constructing a "repressed them, emotional us" polarity between Filipinos and the students she teaches in England, Wilson rejects the inferiority of being emotional and inverts the hierarchy of racialized affect. She does not lament Filipinos' quickness to feel or to feel too much. Both Wilson and Deva suggest that being emotional is an ability, indeed a talent, that can be relied upon and honed.

I want to dwell further on the notion of Filipino emotionality and its usability. As mentioned earlier, the Philippine state has capitalized on such mythologies to broker Filipino labor, most especially in work classified as human services. I also hear from Wilson's comment that Filipinos' "natural talent" to perform, to be dramatic, is unrealized. Wilson proposes discipline as that which is missing for this asset to be fully accessed. Elsewhere, Wilson has spoken of the limits of narratives such as *Miss Saigon*, remarking that such stories cannot be the channel through which Filipino/a talents can truly emerge, be realized, and flourish. Now armed with a deeper knowledge and understanding of the relationship among power and representation, and imperialism, sexism, and racism, Wilson says she would approach *Miss Saigon* differently: "I would be more conscious of the reality of the Asian women onstage. In my time, 1989, and no offense to anyone who did the show, we were also not politicized ourselves. We thought bar girls loved what they were doing and they were just dancing to hook up with guys" ("Verbatim: Monique Wilson"). These comments provide insight into the process through which iconic images are created, embodied, and enacted on stage from the point of view of a performer. I include them here to also illustrate the ongoing process of reflection and engagement that artists undertake. Wilson's own theater group, New Voice Company, offers a space in which to redirect the Filipino/a performing body's unrealized potential. New Voice Company, based in Manila, proposes feminist perspectives and approaches to theater as a possibility for maintaining "natural talent." By establishing a theater company that is committed to a feminist politics of theater making, Wilson/New Voices understand the possibility of using this "natural" talent for drama to critique hegemonic representations as well as dominant theater practices.

Though Wilson continues to work overseas, teaching in England, her commitment to the theater company in Manila is significant. Her choice of founding a theater company, a feminist one specifically, in the Philippines defies the tendency to overdetermine the global stage as *the* point of arrival, *the* ultimate site of destination for success. Wilson admits,

> But this is what I'd like people to see: Maybe now it's time *naman* to focus on Philippine theater, to see that the very same thing you're proud of us for, which is that you exported us all for "Miss Saigon," etc., is the very

same talent and resources you have here, now. So why can't we enjoy that same kind of support? ("Verbatim: Monique Wilson")

This longing for support "at home" is especially poignant within the context of the global outsourcing of Filipino/a labor. The Philippine state continues to push for Filipinos to seek work elsewhere and for foreign destinations as the primary site of work, funneling its resources toward creating a work force that can be of service elsewhere. In directing primary efforts toward placing the Filipino/a out in the world, the Philippine state has reified the Philippine nation's and the Filipino people's imaginary as being in service of the world. What would it mean to invest in the local, to cultivate national resources, including theater and arts, to create possibilities within the bounds of the nation? I interpret Wilson's articulation of Filipino's natural talent and lack of discipline as a productive launching point for the transformative utility of the Filipino/a performing body.

VI. *Tagumpay Nating Lahat* (Our Collective Success):
World Stage Success and Filipino/a Social Relations

By recognizing Filipinos in *Miss Saigon*, I direct our attention to the proliferation of Filipino/a laboring bodies worldwide, acting, singing, and dancing on all kinds of stages, so to speak. Hundreds of Filipinos deployed daily to perform work outside the Philippines are motivated by dreams of performing, of fame, and of stardom and material needs. A 2000 news article titled "Fame Beckons: Filipinos Find *Miss Saigon* a Hard Act to Follow" lays bare the various pressures that bear upon these performing bodies as they compete for limited roles: after all, "there can only be one Lea Salonga." It also most clearly aligns the performers in *Miss Saigon* as part of the Philippines' most valued national asset—Filipino overseas workers. Maya Barredo, who was performing the role of Kim when she made the statement, shared her concern about the uncertain nature of overseas contract work, particularly in the entertainment industry: "It's not secure. We live contract by contract. And every time the next contract comes along, you are sitting there, wondering Am I or Am I not?" Beyond the recognition of talents, the glamour of the world-class stage, and the resounding applause of one good night at the theater, these jobs are limited and unsecured.

Thus far, I have focused my concern on the conditions of labor that produce the world-class Filipino/a performing body. I conclude here with comments on the hierarchies and socialities produced under these conditions. Barredo's statement itself calls attention to the supposed exceptionality of

Saigonistas. The opportunity to perform on such a distinguished stage, she says, in particular *Miss Saigon*, is "a big responsibility. Because of *Miss Saigon* the world doesn't think of Filipinos as just servants, domestic helpers, and maids" ("Fame Beckons"). In identifying Filipino/a performing bodies in *Miss Saigon* as a different breed of overseas workers, Barredo's own comments reflect some interesting tensions. Barredo critiques the stereotypes of Filipinos, typecast in service-oriented jobs in the drama of globalized labor, asserting that Filipinos employed in *Miss Saigon* are a catalyst toward a shift in worldwide perception. Her statement, echoing theater impresario Dong Alegre, is directed against the pervasive image of Filipinos as "servants, domestic helpers, and maids." She creates a distance between performers such as herself and ordinary "servants, domestic helpers, and maids."

I am more concerned at the implied hierarchy in the process of making such distinctions between artists like her and domestic helpers, health care providers, and indeed sex workers. It is a classed hierarchy and, perhaps relatedly, even a moral one. As is well understood, Marxist theories of labor and capitalism have taught us that labor as constituted in the context of capitalism is never simply about work. It is also a form of relation that creates a system of hierarchy to justify exploitation. There is a fine line between playing the role of a prostitute and doing sex work, if we recall the condemning analysis of the musical's depiction of Asian women, particularly Filipinas, as perpetuating misconceptions of hypersexuality and acting as a mere foil for white men's (read: the West's; read: the world's) subjectivity. Once again, Neferti Tadiar's notion of "a feminized commodification of the Philippines" is relevant here because it links the violence of representation, which is Barredo's primary concern, with the system of relations through which Filipinos' overseas labor has been reduced under global capitalism. Of equal significance is that the individual Saigonistas' successes are utilized by the national agenda. Hence the individual desire for a more positive representation of Filipinos—as world-class artists—must push beyond the desire for respectability. It must account for a reimagining of Filipino social relations.

Coda: Culture *Shack*

It seems only fitting that I close my discussion of *puro arte* with a focus on the world premiere staging of *Rolling the Rs*, R. Zamora Linmark's highly acclaimed novel, produced by Honolulu's Kumu Kahua Theater in November 2008. The play and its consequent production in Hawaii deftly weave together questions of race, performance, imperial relations, and Filipino subjectivity, providing continuities and interruptions to the sites on which I have discussed the Filipino performing body. The Hawaii setting of *Rolling the Rs* begs an overdetermined invocation of U.S. offshore imperial beginnings and continuing colonial practices. Like *Dogeaters*, the novel *Rolling the Rs* is a self-consciously performative text. Within the novel form, Linmark packs multiple literary and performance genres, ranging from poetry, book reports (written by a fourth grader), and reenactments of *Charlie's Angels* episodes and Donna Summer concerts to the lyrics (or poetic interpretations of lyrics) and sounds of late 1970s and early 1980s disco hits.

Linmark's multiethnic Hawaii is far from its popular depiction as an island of paradise and a haven of interethnic relations. It is complex, dark,

and volatile. Through the lives and perspectives of three Filipino fifth graders—Vicente, Edgar, and Katrina—the violence of the American dream and
the false promise of Hawaii as paradise are underscored. Their ten-year-old
voices, punctuated with a bitter and biting sarcasm, speak of betrayed attachments to "American tropics'" innocence and to Hawaii as a (failed) model
of interethnic sociality.[1] Their quick, know-it-all quips, their veiled-in-sass
confusion about and longing for intimacy as their preteen bodies experience
internal turmoil proffer up a turbulent Hawaii full of disappointments and
frustration. Amidst it all, Mrs. Takemoto's fifth grade classroom's confrontations with racism threaten catastrophic eruption:

KATRINA: You in Hawaii and a Caucasian is a Haole is a Haole is a Caucasian. And if you cannot handle the tropical heat, braddah, go back to
Antarctica.
EDGAR: . . . (*EDGAR first points his finger to NELSON.*) You, Mr. Haole
Wanna-be. (*Then points to STEPHEN.*) And you, Mr. Haolewood.
You guys think you so hot-shit, but you know what? The ground you
standing on is not the freakin' meltin' pot but one volcano. And one
day, the thing goin' erupt and you guys goin' be the first ones for burn.
(unpublished script, pp. 12-13)

Not only is multiracial cohabitation confronted in *Rolling the Rs*; divisions
within the Filipino diasporic community are also equally scrutinized. In this
work, Filipino migrants regard the promise of the American dream in Hawaii
with increased and sustained suspicion. As the *mares* (women friends) put it,

MRS CAYABYAB: *Hoy,* listen to this, *Mare.*
MRS ARAYAT: I'm all eyes and ears, *Mare.*
MRS CAYABYAB: (*Reads with pride*) Three to five thousand Filipinos have
been coming to Hawaii since the Immigration Act was amended in
1965.
MRS ARAYAT: No wonder I did not experience culture *shack* when I got here.
MRS CAYABYAB: Why would you? Coming here is like taking a bus ride from
Manila to Ilocos Norte, *ading.*
MRS ARAYAT: And getting stuck there.

The *kumares* (friends) liken the ten-hour flight to Hawaii to a "bus ride
from Manila to Ilocos Norte," alluding to the fact that a majority of Filipino
migrants in Hawaii come from Ilocos. This quick plane ride and and the
absence of "culture *shack*" signal disappointment and a sense of ironic dread.

Jason Kanda. "Farrah." Photography by Cheyne Gallarde. From Kumu Kahua's production of R. Zamora Linmark's *Rolling the Rs*, directed by Harry Wong III, Honolulu, Hawaii, 2008

Filipinos find themselves trapped (again) on a different island, with the very people they were supposed to leave behind. Their gossip further reveals class, regional, and linguistic prejudices against fellow Filipinos in the Kalihi neighborhood.

Kumu Kahua's production of *Rolling the Rs* highlights such complexities within Filipino experience in Hawaii, I want to suggest here, through an artistic engagement with the potentialities of *puro arte*. To be looked at and to command attention found the performative structure of *puro arte*. Such a structure is vividly captured in scenes where the fifth graders perform their expanding vocabulary of the English language for their teacher while simultaneously unfolding a scene of themselves to others. When the two *daldaleras* (gossips), Mrs. Cayabyab and Mrs. Arayat, comment on the spectacle of daily life in Kalihi, their remarks doubly function as instances of exposure and as tributes to their heightened sense of self-knowledge. *Puro arte's* exteriority and duality is tightly linked with the interiority of self-realization. In these scenes of self-realization and self-revelation, the characters appear both deeply flawed and deeply insightful in their views of the world. Ms. Cayabyab ponders aloud to her *Kumare* Arayat, "*Ay naku Mare.* I sometimes wonder what will we ever talk about once these Filipinos leave our sight?" and her response to her question is, "Probably some peace of mind, and a boring life."

Nothing more captures *puro arte* as a way of being in the world than Vicente's, Katrina's, and Edgar's performances of *Charlie's Angels* or their reprisal of Donna Summer's and Barbra Streisand's duet concert. These performances consume their time and emotions, as they invest hours in practicing their dance moves and in their attachments to who gets cast in certain roles. They artfully approach mimicry, use the power of being looked at, and perform to interrupt the strangulating monotony of their everyday life. Hardly conforming or tertiary, their *Charlie's Angels* is performed in various accents and languages (pidgin, Filipino English), with creative pronunciations and deliberate enhancements of the television characters. Vicente's, Katrina's, and Edgar's interpretation of *Charlie's Angels* liberates the characters—"Sabrina Duncan look butch enough for pass for one guy" (74).

With his blond wig styled in the famous feathered waves of Farrah Fawcett, the brown male body of Edgar, performed by Jason Kanda, brilliantly portrays the potential of *puro arte* to transform (and parody) the act of performance.[2] The hairpiece is not merely an insignificant prop used to approximate Farrah. The blond, wavy hair is a bodily display, signifying a desire for whiteness, beauty, and intimacy. Yet, in this staging, donning the wig is an act that produces incongruity, not seamlessness. In other words, the jarring image of a blond, wavy hairpiece on the body of a brown man portraying an excitable ten-year-old boy serves more to expose variegated mechanisms of subjection.[3] Throughout scenes of performances in *Rolling the Rs*, these brown bodies do not merely attempt to be like the white American female stars'; rather, their *Charlie's Angels* is a re-creation/recreation that liberates performance from itself. Within such re-creations/recreations, the racialized constructs of femininity as reimagined by and through Edgar, Katrina, and Vicente are not acts of uncomplicated mimicry or pathological colonial mentality.[4] Instead, their re-creation/recreation is an active and playful consumption of hegemonic standards of beauty, femininity, and masculinity that

Jason Kanda,
Maila Roncero,
MJ Gonzalvo.
"Charlie's Angels."
Photography by
Cheyne Gallarde.
From Kumu
Kahua's Produc-
tion of R. Zamora
Linmark's *Rolling
the Rs*, directed by
Harry Wong III.
Honolulu, Hawaii,
2008.

are corrupted, transformed, and pleasured through the act of performance. Their queer, postcolonial appropriation of dominant American popular culture founds the material processes that make *puro arte* literally and metaphorically a space of performance. *Puro arte* turns the notion of performance as "derivative realms of conformity or tertiary imitation" on its head.

Puro arte has allowed me to regard mimicry as a performance strategy and methodology. Within regimes of colonization and globalization, mimicry has featured as a central discursive analytic to bring to sense and make sense of Filipinos. While much has been said about mimicry and colonialism, part of my interest here is to think about Filipino acts of imitation, and those behaviors perceived as acts of imitation, within the logic of globaliza-tion. I tie the phenomenon of Filipino-performers-for-export in the "global theatrical complex," of which *Miss Saigon* is a part, to the emergence of the Filipina as global worker.[5] Through *puro arte,* I have shifted away from the perception of performance by racialized bodies as derivative, most espe-cially when they inhabit hegemonic forms of expression.[6] Filipinos' "splendid dancing" in U.S. taxi dance halls in the 1920s and 1930s brilliantly conveys how Filipinos relied on the perception of their bodies as excessive and incon-gruent with American popular dances as they reveled in others' awe of their skillful dancing.

The stakes of *puro arte* range. I began my discussion of *puro arte* with an anecdote about a young girl's struggle over control of her body against parental/adult authority. In each chapter, I wrestle with the conceptual pos-sibilities of *puro arte* as instantiated in the Filipino/a performing body under different forms and conditions of subjection. In doing so, I am less interested in creating structures of parity or coevalness. The risks for Filipino patrons dancing in taxi dance halls in Watsonville, California, in 1929 are not com-mensurate with a nine-year-old girl's struggle to assert control of her own body. Spaces of leisure such as taxi dance halls produce different sets of rela-tions and circuits of power from the social protest theater of Sining Bayan. Yet, there are clear continuities in the forms through which the Filipino/a performing body is rendered visible and intelligible within new and old imperial orders. For instance, the contact zone of the St. Louis World's Fair in 1904 and taxi dance halls in the late 1920s and early 1930s occasioned an alternative articulation of identity not only for Filipinos as imperial subjects but also for white women. Another continuity, though differentiated across temporal moments, is the enactment of nationalism by and onto the bodies of protest in Sining Bayan and the "Saigonistas."

In this book, I have staged varying scenes, locations, historical conditions, and forms that put in focus the Filipino/a performing body. In doing so, I elaborate on the notion of *puro arte,* building from the tension of the term—as pure art, as purely acting, as purely artifice—toward a lens with which to analyze the Filipino performing body. Through the analytic of *puro arte,* I suggest a link, rather than an obvious chronological relationship, among Filipino performing bodies in performance sites that (re)locate them in the St. Louis World's Fair, in taxi dance halls, on protest lines, and on world-class theater stages on the West End and Broadway. The sites I have cho-sen span more than a century, but my project considers how the structure of U.S.-Philippine colonial relations impacts *puro arte* across time and space. In each of the different chapters, *puro arte* describes, conveys sentiments and attitudes, and enacts Filipinos as subjects of and subjected to imperial rule, forced migration, repressive regime, and globalization. The singular construct "Filipino/a performing body" is not deployed here to neatly track one version of a colonial subject either conforming to or contesting one totalizing historical condition. The Filipino/a performing body's order of appearance in this book places it first on the stages of the 1904 St. Louis World's Fair—an early form of a global stage, as suggested by Coco Fusco in "The Other History of Intercultural Performance"—and the American musical theater of African American legendary creative team Bob Cole, James Weldon Johnson, and J. Rosamond Johnson. In the last chapter, it appears on world-renowned platforms such as the West End and Broadway. This ordering, however, is not meant to provide a teleological view of the Filipino/a performing body, one that interprets its earlier appearance as coerced under a totalizing scene of subjection while its later entry onto world-class venues symbolizes an achieved virtuosic modern subjecthood. No salvific progression is on offer here, where hostile beginnings give way to happy endings. With *puro arte* as my conceptual pivot, I leave open the relationship between these stages and these different scenes, to make room for contradictions, interruptions, and continuities. In this book, the Filipino/a performing body as *puro arte* is at once a force of transformative and thwarted possibilities and a call to improvisation and critical engagement. If this account of *puro arte* combines theatrics and materiality, it equally insists on the centrality of embodied difference as the critical domain on which studies of performance must be built.

NOTES

INTRODUCTION

1. *Puro arte* has served as inspiration for numerous arts projects. In 2003 I co-organized a day-long symposium with writer joel b. tan, artistic director/choreographer Alleluia Panis of KulArts, Inc., performance studies scholar Christine Balance, and theater and administrator artist Olivia Malabuyo. This gathering, held in San Francisco, facilitated a dialogue among Filipino/Asian American artists, scholars, and community-based workers and advocates. The event worked to strengthen the mutually beneficial relationship between community-based organizations and artists.

   In the mid- to late 1990s, an art gallery in Los Angeles focusing on contemporary Filipino art was also named "Puro Arte." Ruben Domingo and Napoleon Lustre were among the artists who collaborated in creating this space and curated this project. It supported emerging Filipino American visual artists and was also a hub for artists who were exploring interdisciplinary creative forms.

2. As explained by Shannon Jackson, J. L. Austin's speech act theory maintains that certain speech enacts its world-creating power in the moment of utterance. Speech-as-action has animated theater/performance studies with debates around intentionality, iteration, citation. My invocation of "world-creating power" here is much simpler. I believe that the Filipino performance acts I analyze here are attempts at alternative ways of moving, inhabiting, and even undoing the world and various histories.

3. Worth mentioning here is the well-established body of scholarship that has decisively linked performativity to the process of racial formation. See Josephine Lee's *Performing Asian America*, which analyzes the use of theater and performance discourse in theories of racialization. Martin Manalansan turns to performance and "juxtaposes" it with citizenship, to expand the notion of cultural citizenship developed in the field of anthropology (*Global Divas*, 14). These works, among others, critique the facile use of theater and performance as metaphors of racial formation, citizenship, and democracy, while the object/practices themselves remain relatively segregated.

4. Vince Rafael, in his introduction to *Discrepant Histories*, describes how the essays in the collection engage with "the conditions of possibility which make the past thinkable as simultaneously constitutive and disruptive of the present" (xiv). This critical simultaneity aptly describes the structure of the copresence of the past and the present in each chapter.

5. Lucy Burns, "Staging Anti-U.S. Imperialism: Seditious Plays in Early Twentieth Century Philippines," Association of Asian American Studies Conference, Boston, MA, 2004.

6. Critiques of occularcentrism have been robust in performance studies, and they have gained ground in Filipino Studies. Summarized simply, these critiques decenter visibility and its easy association and conflation with belonging and inclusion. They also seek to foreground somatic approaches to understanding knowledge formation that integrate other senses of perception.

CHAPTER 1

1. Alicia Arrizón has also interpreted "contact zone" as an analytical lens for the study of performances of border subjectivities. See *Queering Mestizaje: Transculturation and Performance*.

2. Robert Rydell's *All the World's a Fair* is a leading text that analyzes the phenomenon of world expositions as an imperial project. Others that have built on Rydell's work, specifically focusing on the Filipinos in the St. Louis World's Fair, include Benito Vergara Jr.'s *Displaying Filipino*, Sharra Vostral's "Imperialism on Display," and Paul Kramer's "Making Concessions: Race and Empire Revisited at the Philippine Exposition, 1901-1905." See also the special issue of *Philippines Studies* 52.4, edited by Patricia O. Afable and Cherubim A. Quizon.

    For writings on Filipinos in the *chautauqua* circuits, see Jean Vengua and Eloisa Borah.

    There are numerous works that have examined the politics of world expositions, colonialism, and human displays. The following have been most helpful and formative in my argument about Filipino performing bodies in the St. Louis World's Fair: Priya Srinivasan's "The Bodies beneath the Smoke; or, What's behind the Cigarette Poster: Unearthing Kinesthetic Connections in American Dance History" and *Africans on Stage: Studies in Ethnological Show Business*, edited by Bernth Lindfors.

3. My account of the World's Fair and the responses it generated is drawn from secondary resources ranging from newspaper accounts to other scholarly writings about the World's Fair, and movies such as *Meet Me in St. Louis*. These are all key cultural materials that illuminate the signification of the World's Fair in the American cultural imaginary.

    John Eperjesi's *The Imperialist Imaginary: Visions of Asia and the Pacific in American Culture* is a helpful text that discusses the emergence of imperialist ambitions in American visions of itself as a nation. Eperjesi convincingly argues the occupation of the Philippines as the moment of off-shore American imperialist realization.

4. On this latter point, Pao's elaboration of yellowface practice is quite helpful. In her discussion of the musical *Miss Saigon* in "The Eyes of the Storm," Pao considers the practice of yellowface as having the potential to expose how the "oriental" is produced through makeup, prosthetics, accoutrements, gestures, and sounds.

5. It is important to note here that the implications of such performances for the white actors enacting them are radically different from the implications for Filipinos, who must negotiate multiple legacies of colonialism from the subordinate position of being colonial subjects. Brenda Dixon-Gottschild has emphasized the material and psychic violence of blackface among black people, taking to task sympathetic studies of white actors performing blackface.

6. The movie version of *Meet Me in St. Louis* is based on Sally Benson's account of her small-town Missouri life at a time of great transition for the Benson family, for the town of St. Louis, and for the U.S. nation. The story follows the lives of the Smith family, a year before the fair opens; in particular, the story centers around the Smiths' two daughters of marrying age, Rose and Esther, and their quest for a proposal. The film adaptation of *Meet Me in St. Louis* highlights the parallel anticipation for sexual awakening (albeit domesticated in the form of marriage) with the anticipation of the fair's opening. Esther in particular speaks of the fair nearly as much as she desires to be with her neighbor John Truett. Played with spunk by celebrated actress Judy Garland, Esther dreams about a kiss from her neighbor-future-husband John with the same breath(lessness) that she speaks about the fair. By the end of the movie, the family has narrowly escaped moving to New York City, each of the marriageable Smith girls are betrothed, and the family gathers at the much-awaited fair's opening. In awe, members of the Smith family marvel at the lights and grandeur of the fair.

7. Original statement cited from "Teaching English to Sixty-Nine Different Tribes," *Portland Oregonian*, 17 Sept. 1905, 44.

8. For an analysis of Filipinos as "savage" in the St. Louis World's Fair, see Chris Vaughan's "Ogling the Igorots." See also Nerissa Balce's dissertation, "Savagery and Docility: Filipinos and the Language of the American Empire after 1898," for an extended examination of Filipino representation and U.S. empire.

9. On the "missing link," see Jose Fermin, who writes, "at the Pan-American Exposition held in 1901 in Buffalo, New York, the 'missing link' was Esau, a monkey that could do anything but talk." At the St. Louis Exposition, the "'missing link' was Ibag, a Negrito" (107).

10. "Filipino Baby Christened: Born at the World's Fair, President Francis Stands Godfather; Fiesta Follows," *New York Times*, 1 Aug. 1904. "Moro Chief to Wed Slave: Romance of a Philippine Girl on Reservation at the World's Fair," *New York Times*, 6 May 1904.

11. Original quotation from a June 20, 1904, anonymous correspondence, series 14, folder 1, Louisiana Purchase Exposition Company Collection, Missouri Historical Society. Cited in Sharra L. Vostral, "Imperialism on Display: The Philippine Exhibition at the 1904 World's Fair."

12. "Man Offers Dogs to Igorrotes," *Missouri Republic*, 20 April 1904.

13. N. Balce writes about the Filipina breast as "a sign of conquest" in photographs that circulated in early-twentieth-century travel books ("The Filipina's Breast," 90).

14. Among these was Senator Benjamin Tillman of South Carolina, who feared that annexation of the Philippines would lead to an influx of nonwhite immigrants, thus undermining white racial purity in America.

15. For Missouri as a determining state in the U.S. election of 1904, see http://uselectionatlas.org/RESULTS/state.php?year=1904&fips=29&f=0&off=0&elect=0&minper=0.

16. Original source is a wire sent by General Taft to Edwards, 23 June 1904, quoted in Rydell.

17. "President at Fair Spends Busy Day," *New York Times,* 27 Nov. 1904.

18. I wish to thank Lawrence Padua for sharing this unique World's Fair memorabilia with me. His play-in-progress on the Igorots of the World's Fair, "Origins Obscura: Phrenology, Physiognomy, Anthropology, and Spectacle," can be accessed at http://langeleopadua.blogspot.com/2007/02/origins-obscura-phrenology-physiognomy.html. A version of it was published in *disOrient* 9 (2001).

19. See *The Life and Work of Susan B. Anthony* by Ida Husted Harper.

20. Ward's Natural Science was an enterprise that collected specimens all over the world and sold them to museums, colleges, and other educational institutions. Sally Gregory Kohlstedt, "Henry Augustus Ward and American Museum Development," *University of Rochester Library Bulletin* 38 (1985), http://www.lib.rochester.edu/index.cfm?PAGE=4582, 12 April 2012.

21. See Kristin Hoganson on the tensions created by the "Philippine Question" for the suffrage movement, specifically the discussion of Filipinos as a "colored race." Ward was one of the early supporters of the admission of "colored clubs" in the General Federation of Women's Clubs, which splintered the federation into warring halves ("Women's Federation May Split in Social Equality," *New York Times,* 3 May 1902).

22. Though there is not much written about this commission, Eloisa Borah's essay entitled "The Other Filipinos at the 1904 World's Fair in St. Louis: The Honorary Board of Filipino Commissioners, Louisiana Purchase Exposition" provides some information on who these members were. Borah argues that the HBFC consisted of regionally, occupationally, and ideologically diverse Filipinos. She calls for a more nuanced analysis of HBFC, beyond assessments that label it "'elite,' 'mostly Visayan,' and a 'puppet commission'" (2).

23. Robert Rydell details the process of Filipino recruitment for the St. Louis World's Fair, which included the Philippine Commission's collaborations with the World's Fair officials.

24. Fuentes's choice to play the narrator in the film brings tension to the notion of "auto-ethnography." The film raises the following questions, particularly as they relate to the impossibility of a "native ethnographer": Though the search for identity and history is staged, is it less real? Is the narrative more believable because a "native" is scripting it? Or is it less reliable because objectivity is inherently inaccessible to the "native"?

25. Reid Badger and D. J. O'Connor similarly observe this. O'Connor, in *Representations of the Cuban and Philippine Insurrections on the Spanish Stage, 1887-1898*, offers the following insights: "Traditionally the theater has been important as a conduit for ideologies and propaganda because it does not require a literate audience. In effect, the theater was a vibrant part of popular culture; its importance as a place where competing ideas might be aired was not lost on potential molders of opinion during the period from 1895-1898" (xiv).

26. See Vince Rafael, Eric Reyes, Theo Gonzalves, and Sharon Delmondo for further discussion on the phenomenon of Filipino centennials. I will analyze (later in the chapter) divergent approaches to the centennial, focusing specifically on the multiple ways in which contemporary artists turn to this commemoration event to contend with the intersection of the Filipino/a American performing body and these early brownface performances.

27. Between 1900 and 1910, Cole and J. Rosamond Johnson, with frequent contributions from James Weldon Johnson, "wrote over 150 songs for more than a dozen shows, including their own shows for all-black casts *Shoo-Fly Regiment* (1906) and *The Red Moon* (1908)" (Riis 35). Cole and J. Rosamond performed duets in vaudeville as well as theater shows. A song from a "white-oriented" musical, *The Little Duchess*, "The Maiden with Dreamy Eyes," sung by Anna Held, is noted to be the Johnson brothers' and Cole's biggest hit (Bernard Peterson, 216). Though their musical theater work garnered professional and financial success, they were still seen as working within white theater establishments. They also received criticism for being complicit in perpetuating stereotypical images of African American people and ways of life. *The Shoo-Fly Regiment* is thus a break from the predominant productions with African Americans of this time, and most certainly for this musical team.

28. Patrick Joseph, in his article titled "From: Minstrel and Medicine Shows; Creating a Market for the Blues," writes, "In 1908, the *Shoo-Fly Regiment*, with Cole and Johnson, played the Crawford Theatre in Wichita and 'scored a tremendous hit before an audience that filled every seat,' according to a *Wichita Eagle* review. The newspaper pronounced the show 'the best production ever given by a colored organization in this city'" (3).

29. I have been fortunate to come across a number of scholars at UCLA who are also exploring the intersection of black and Filipino performing bodies. They include Carolina San Juan, Mark Villegas, and Lorenzo Perillo.

30. The collection *AfroAsian Encounter* is worth mentioning here, for its varied examination of Afro-Asian relations through cultural contact.

31. Bob Cole and the Johnson brothers, three of the most successful artists of their time, were the composers and lyricists of the African American anthem "Lift Every Voice." Seniors documents Cole's close relationship to Booker T. Washington and the latter's possible direct involvement with *The Shoo-Fly Regiment*.

32. I am grateful to David Krasner for sharing his insights on the work of Cole and the Johnson brothers. Our email exchanges in January 2009 were central to generating the line of inquiry I pursue here.

33. These include three shows— *In Dahomey, Abysinnia,* and a musical revue titled *Oriental America*—produced by John Isham. Actors who performed in *The Shoo-Fly Regiment* were also involved in these earlier musical productions.

34. For more on African American soldiers and the Philippine-American War, see Scot Ngozi-Brown's "African-American Soldiers and Filipinos: Racial Imperialism, Jim Crow, and Social Relations."

35. Marian Hannah Winter writes,

    The *Herald Correspondent* also gives an interesting version of the origin of the famous *Shoo-Fly* song and dance: "Shoo-Fly is said to have come originally from the Isthmuss of Panama, where the Negroes sang 'Shoo-Fly' and 'Don't Bodder Me' antiphonally while at their work. A Negro from there, Helon Johnson, took it first to California and taught the song to Billy Birch. Dick Carroll and others also had versions of it which they performed. (233)

36. Winter observes that *The Shoo-Fly Regiment,* and other forms of "Negro entertainment" in the latter part of 1890s and the first decade of the twentieth century, "have a close relationship to the minstrel show stereotype. . . . But the music and dances were unfettered by past conventions, and the raw elements of twentieth-century popular music acquired a style which would supersede the schottisches, waltzes, and cotillions of the nineteenth" (240-41).

37. KulArts, Inc., took the lead, with Yerba Buena Center for the Arts serving as a presenting partner and providing generous rental subsidies.

38. Even as such a variegated history cannot be neatly compiled and documented in book form, Theo Gonzalves's *Stage Presence* is a wonderful collection of essays, interviews, and artist statements that attempts to chronicle such wide efforts. Artists included are Panis, Manalo, Ubungen, all members of the consortium. Others are Jessica Hagedorn, Ralph Peña, Joel Jacinto, Danongan Kalanduyan, Eleanor Academia, Gabe Baltazar Jr., and Remé Grefalda.

39. Philippine centennial commemorations were dual state declarations. The year 2006 has been noted as the one hundredth year of Filipino migration to Hawaii by Philippine Presidential Proclamation 954. In the United States, the centennial was ratified by Senate Resolution 333, sponsored by Hawaii Representative Daniel Akaka.

40. See Alicía Arrízon's *Queering Mestizaje* for an analysis of Otalvaro-Hormillosa's work.

CHAPTER 2

1. Cressey dedicates an entire chapter to the Filipino patron, while a second chapter focuses on several "types" of patrons. Cressey's typological study also includes the different categories of dancers and dance halls. Varied spellings of

"taxi dance halls" are used in the available scholarship on the subject. Throughout this chapter, I use the term "dance hall" as two words. When I quote other sources, I maintain their spelling of the word.

2. The McIntosh suit was the most fashionable and expensive American men's suit in the early decades of the twentieth century. Linda Maram, in her study of Filipino American masculinity in Los Angeles, notes, "Dressing up in the latest style was always important to Filipinos, in part because a snazzy ensemble transformed brown bodies from overworked, exploited laborers to symbols of sensuality, style, and pleasure" (138). Maram proposes that Filipinos challenged the customized, ready-to-wear, mass-manufactured clothing because it had to be "tailored and refashioned to fit the shorter brown body" (139–40).

3. Original source: Associated Filipino Press (Los Angeles), 24 April 1938, 8.

4. There are accounts that compete with this rendition of the Filipinos as perfect gentlemen in the taxi dance halls. Clyde Vedder, in his 1947 dissertation, records an observation of "dancing that was thoroughly immoral": "Couples dance or whirl about the floor with their bodies pressed tightly together, shaking, moving, and rotating their lower portions to rouse their sex impulses. Some even engage in 'biting' one another on the lobes of the ears and upon the neck" (183). These competing narratives could be attributed to the different historical periods of the projects. Although there may only be a difference of a few years, the years leading up to and following the passing of the Tydings-McDuffie Act may provide some insights into these competing narratives.

5. In his formative study on American taxi dance halls, Cressey notes the Filipino patrons' dexterity on the dance floor and their familiarity with the music and the latest dance steps. Such "Filipinos Occidental ways," more specifically American ways, Cressey says, have "contributed" to Filipino life in the Philippines. He adds, however, that unlike his fellow "Orientals," "the Filipinos . . . assimilated all too rapidly" (149).

6. There is, of course, a related but slightly different genealogy of the term "exception," explored most notably in the work of scholars such as Giorgio Agamben. I continue with this discussion in chapter 3.

7. As noted by Richard Meynell, "the brown menace" was used to describe Filipino men during the time of the anti-Filipino movement ("Remembering the Watsonville Riots"). He notes the use of this term to refer to Filipinos by Judge Rohrbach's resolution, printed in *The Pajaronian*, and Senator Hiram Johnson's Filipino Exclusion Bill to the U.S. Senate, cited in the *San Francisco Chronicle*.

8. I draw from David Román's formulation of "archival embodiment" as he argues for the constitutive role of dance in pre- and post-Stonewall queer life ("Dance Liberation").

9. Filipino immigration was largely facilitated by labor demands from the agricultural, canning, and fishery industries that wanted to replace other "Oriental" laboring bodies—specifically Japanese and Chinese workers. Many scholars have argued for the link between Chinese and Japanese exclusion and the

recruitment of Filipino labor. See Bruno Lasker (1969), Carey McWilliams (1964), and Dorothy Fujita-Rony (2003). See also texts on Asian American history such as Sucheng Chan's *Asian Americans: An Interpretive History* (1991) and Ronald Takaki's *Strangers from a Different Shore: A History of Asian Americans* (1989). There is an exception to the restricted number of Filipino immigrants allowed into the United States in the case of Filipino workers who were allowed to enter Hawaii to work on the Hawaiian plantations. The Hawaiian sugar planters lobbied for additional numbers of Filipinos as plantation workers whenever they needed more workers. However, Filipinos in Hawaii were not permitted to proceed to the continental United States, except under "limited circumstances" (Lasker 3). It was not until 1946 that the quota was increased to one hundred individuals per year and Filipinos were eligible for citizenship status.

10. Burgess is an instrumental figure in the formation of the American School of Sociology in Chicago.

11. Randy McBee's *Dance Hall Days* is a study of European working-class immigrant communities' heterosocial and homosocial practices in taxi dance halls. McBee argues that the dance hall was a site for negotiations of shifting gender identities between immigrant European men and women. This work makes central the role of dance halls in working-class immigrant communities' leisure time but underplays issues of race and racism.

12. It is important to note, however, that Parreñas mindfully differentiates the signification of dance and dancing for the taxi dancers.

13. Maram similarly argues that taxi dance halls were a site through which state authorities policed youth of color.

14. McBee notes,

The use of violence or intimidation often produced the results for which these men [white men] may have been looking. A week after the gang fight at the Plaza Dancing School, no Filipino men were present, while the controversy attracted an unusually large number of "American" men either fascinated by the prospect of seeing Filipino men dance with the "white" women or eager to take part in the possible melee and help defend white "American manhood." (146)

15. Jules Tygiel comments that most of what is now Los Angeles took its form in the 1920s (2).

16. The second floor eventually became the Main Street Gym. A rich resource for historical cinemas in Los Angeles is the Cinema Treasures Website, founded by Patrick Crowley and Ross Melnick: http://www.cinematreasures.org. It is devoted to movie theater preservation and awareness.

17. *Metropolis in the Making* is an impressive collection of essays that provides a varied, insightful glimpse at Los Angeles in its most formative years. The collection is attentive to the majority of migrants in those early years—Mexicans who

were dislocated from the Mexican Revolution and African Americans from the South.

18. Cressey's discussion of segregation is based on a list of "types": establishments that catered primarily to Filipino clients; establishments that "serve[d] those who [were] antagonized by the presence of Orientals"; and establishments that permitted sensual dancing (220).

19. This riot gained international attention when Fermin Tobera, a young farm worker, was killed. The Philippine government held a national funeral for Tobera. Filipino state officials criticized the killing and violence as racist attacks against Filipinos. For an excellent account of the popular and scholarly interpretations of the riot and its possible causes, see Howard Dewitt and Manuel Buaken. See also Emory Bogardus for another report of the events leading up to and the riot.

20. For an intricate and meticulous tracking of the category "nationals" in relation to Filipino status, see Rick Baldoz's *The Third Asiatic Invasion: Empire and Migration in Filipino America, 1898-1946.*

21. See Julian Go and Anne Foster. On U.S. cultural imperialism in the Philippines, see Luis Francia and Angel Shaw (2002).

22. Other works have specifically linked the American colonial project in the Philippines and the Filipino/a body. These works include Choy's *Empire of Care* and Anderson. Both works engage the body through discussion of health care, regulation, and U.S. empire. Related discussions of imperialism and the U.S. colonial subject's embodiment include Rafael on the implementation of the census during the American colonial period; Salman on Filipinos, slavery, and U.S. expansion; and Vergara on photography as surveillance during the U.S. acquisition of the Philippines.

23. Of course, repressive state apparatuses (RSAs) and ideological state apparatuses (ISAs) are not mutually exclusive. See Althusser.

24. See the works of Bruno Lasker, Emory Bogardus, Howard Dewitt, Brett Melendy, Mae Ngai, John Park, and Ron Takaki.

25. The appearance of Filipinos in the taxi dance halls is an early instance where Filipinos became visible to the larger American society. The hip hop video/song "Bebot" by Filipino American artist Apl De Ap of the Black Eyed Peas pays homage to this history. The "Bebot Generation I" video interprets the joy, camaraderie, Filipino male desirability, and good dancing skills of Filipinos in taxi dance halls. See http://dipdive.com/member/XtiveN/media/26591. The video sets the narrative of *manongs* in the taxi dance hall in Stockton, California, partly to support the campaign for making Little Manila in Stockton a recognized historic site. It also reroutes the genealogy of Filipinos in hip hop to this historical social space.

26. Laura Kang redirects the politics of visibility toward a wider possibility of analysis and interpretation. She does so by situating "Asian America" as a construct, as an epistemological project emerging from academia, as activism, and as state sponsored.

CHAPTER 3

1. In 2006, together with Dr. Barbara Gaerlan, I co-organized a symposium commemorating the anti-imperialist work of Daniel Boone-Schirmer and the U.S. Anti–Martial Law movement at UCLA. Dr. Stephen Shalom was one of the speakers. It is his presentation, *"America's Next Top Model? The Philippines and the American Empire,"* that I make a reference to here. Shalom argues against ex–U.S. president George Bush's citation of the Philippines as "a shining democracy in the [Asian] region" in a speech made during a visit to the Philippine Congress in October 2003. In this speech, Bush draws a direct parallel between the U.S. occupation of the Philippines in the early twentieth century and his/the United States' war against Iraq in the early twenty-first century.

2. One of the many Philippine examples to illustrate Agamben's point about security measures implemented during crisis that become the state of affairs is the government's ongoing war against Moros in the Southern Philippines. This war dates back to early twentieth century, partly justifying U.S. occupation of the Philippines. Relatedly, the Philippine government has sanctioned violence against its own people with an undeclared, ongoing war against pro-national democratic activists. These efforts have sustained U.S.-Philippine state relations, enabling the continuing reliance of the Philippine government on U.S. military presence in the country. It sustains U.S.-Philippine alliance to curtail dissenting forces and Islamic forces not just in the Philippines, but in Southeast Asia at large.

3. Among scholarly writings on Philippine political theater are Maria Josephine Barrios's unpublished master's thesis "Tungo sa Estetika ng Dulaang Panlansangan" and Doreen Fernandez's *Palabas*.

4. As I have argued elsewhere, the Filipino anti–martial Law activism was a transnational movement informed specifically by international politics that underscored liberation from class struggles. See my dissertation, "Community Acts." Augusto Espiritu's essay titled "Journeys of Discovery and Difference: Transnational Politics and the Union of Democratic Filipinos" provides an excellent depiction of the KDP's transnational politics as sources of "cooperation and tension" (44).

5. For an analysis of how the Marcoses built lasting cultural institutions, see Pearlie Baluyut's dissertation titled "Institutions and Icons of Patronage: Arts and Culture in the Philippines during the Marcos Years, 1965-1986."

6. See Gerard Lico's *Edifice Complex: Power, Myth, and Marcos State Architecture* for an analysis that links architecture, space, and the Marcoses' regime. Lico specifically discusses the construction of this CCP Complex in chapter 3.

7. This land was in fact returned to the Ibaloi families because they were coerced to sell it during the Martial Law (Cabreza).

8. Original text from "New Grapes" in *Newsweek*, 31 July 1967, 79.

9. Although popularly perceived as a cause predominantly affecting and organized by California's Chicano community, the farm workers' strike, later to be organized as the United Farm Worker's Union, could not have happened without the

earlier organizing and campaigning work by Filipino farm workers and activists such as Larry Itliong and Philip Vera Cruz. See Glenn Omatsu's article "In Memoriam Philip Vera Cruz" and E. San Juan's "From National Allegory to the Realization of a Joyful Subject."

10. Yolanda Broyles-Gonzales links El Teatro Campesino's aesthetics to traditional Mexican performance traditions such as *la carpa* (tent shows) and the comedics of popular artist Cantinflas (10).

11. Another example of Valdez's and El Teatro Campesino's influence on Filipino American theater artists at the time is a play staged by Filipino Americans in Seattle. In 1998, at the first Asian American theater conference in Seattle, Washington, Filipino American artist Stan Asis shared that in the mid-1970s, he and fellow artists adapted a version of Valdez's *Los Vendidos*. This is a popular satirical *acto* that takes stereotypes of the Mexican migrant worker as lazy, white-identified, underhanded, and even overeager revolutionary, only to turn them all on their heads. *Los Vendidos'* focus on migrant farm workers could be easily adapted to narrate the plight of Filipino migrant workers.

12. Several groups emerged. One was the National Committee for the Restoration of Civil Liberties in the Philippines (NCRCLP), which later became the Anti–Martial Law Coalition and morphed once more into the Coalition against the Marcos Dictatorship/Philippine Solidarity Network (CAMD/PSN). Other groups include the Movement of Free Philippines (MFP) and the KDP. Writings on the U.S.-based Anti–Martial Law Movement include Barbara Gaerlan's "The Movement in the United States to Oppose Martial Law in the Philippines, 1972-1991: An Overview" and *The Philippines Reader,* edited by D. Boone Schirmer and Stephen Shalom. For more on the KDP, see Helen Toribio's essays and Estella Habal's *San Francisco's I-Hotel.*

13. For example, the much-cited production *Pagsambang Gabi*/Midnight Mass tackled head-on, using the structure of Catholic Mass, the conditions of Martial Law in its darkest hour, describing the killing of freedom and democracy, wanton violations of human rights and loss of human dignity, government corruption, and the insatiable greed of those who are in power. Playwright Boni Ilagan had just been released from incarceration (for charges of dissent against the government) when he wrote this play (Fernandez).

14. The Sedition Act Executive Summary reads,

Enacted on 4 November 1901 by the Philippine Commission, Act No. 292 defines the crimes of treason, insurrection, and sedition against the authority of the American colonial government in the Philippines. The Act prohibits any form of propaganda for Philippine independence, and the utterance and writing of seditious words or speeches against the United States. It prescribes harsh punishments for committing such crimes. (Philippine Commission, Law against Treason, Sedition, Etc. (Act No. 292), Manila, Philippines, 1901)

Juan Abad's plays written and produced at this time include *Tanikalang Ginto* (Golden Chains) and *Isang Punlo ng Kaaway* (The Enemy's Bullet). Other writers and their plays are Juan Matapang Cruz's *Hindi Pa Aco Patay* (I Am Not Dead Yet) and Aurelio Tolentino's *Kahapon, Ngayon at Bukas* (Yesterday, Today, and Tomorrow). These plays were staged in various areas of Luzon. See Amelia LaPeña-Bonifacio's *"Seditious" Tagalog Playwrights: Early American Occupation* and chapter 1 in Vince Rafael's *White Love* for critical analyses of "seditious plays."

15. *"Manong"* literally means "older brother" in Filipino. In Filipino American history, the term *"manongs"* has been used to refer to the generation of male migrant workers who came to the United States in the mid-1920s.

16. The International Hotel in San Francisco's Manilatown housed a majority of aging *manongs* and Chinese American workers. The fight against corporate takeover of downtown San Francisco and the diminishing of affordable housing as a result of this created a multigenerational and multiracial coalition. For more on the I-Hotel anti-eviction movement, specifically the Filipino American participation in this effort, see Estella Habal's *San Francisco's International Hotel: Mobilizing the Filipino American Community in the Anti-Eviction Movement.*

17. See Catherine Ceniza Choy, "Trial and Error: Crime and Punishment in America's 'Wound Culture,'" in *Empire of Care.*

18. Ileto's *Pasyon and Revolution* suggests a reinterpretation of the common people's consumption of the *Pasyon*, the text narrating the life of Jesus Christ used in public readings during Holy Week. For Ileto, the *Pasyon* provided "lowland Philippine society with a language for articulating its own values, ideals, and even hopes of liberation" (12). He underscores the significance of such alternative sources of social change "in a society without freedom of speech and legitimate channels of protest" (16).

19. Much has been said about gender as a blind spot for other social protest theaters such as El Teatro Campesino and the Black Revolutionary Theater. Elam himself comments on the limits of masculinist practices in the culture of these social protest theaters: "During this period, Valdez's and Baraka's theatrical strategies and social protest ideologies were decidedly male-centric, heterosexist, and patriarchal. In their organizational hierarchies and performance work El Teatro and the BRT reflected the philosophies of male hegemony and female subjugation, which were a significant element of Chicano and black cultural nationalism in the 1960s and 1970s" (4).

For more discussion on the politics of gender, specifically the tension around the masculinist culture of political theater, see Yolanda Broyles-Gonzales's "Towards a Re-Vision of Chicano Theatre History: The Women of El Teatro Campesino" and Garcia, Gutierrez, and Nuñez, eds., *Teatro Chicana: A Collective Memoir and Selected Plays.* For a perspective on gay activists in the Filipino American movement, see Gil Mangaoang's "From the 1970s to the 1990s: Perspective of a Gay Filipino American Activist" in *Asian American Sexualities.*

20. The politics of gender and sexuality within the AMLM is yet to be fully analyzed. When I attended the KDP's twenty-fifth reunion in Oakland, California

in 1999, there was a table of women activists who initiated a conversation about the specific demands of the movement on women. The demands they spoke of included the way the movement had a say in relationships, partnerships, and locations. Conversations with activists like Ermina Vinluan introduced me to terms such as "ideological vacillation," which questioned the commitment of KDP members. For more on the participation of women in the Anti–Martial Law Movement in the United States, see Catherine Ceniza Choy, "Towards Trans-Pacific Social Justice: Women and Protest in Filipino American History"; Rose Ibañez, "Growing Up in America as a Young Filipina American during the Anti–Martial Law and Student Movement in the United States"; and Estella Habal, "How I Became a Revolutionary."

21. See Rick Bonus's *Locating Filipino America* for a discussion of how Filipino American communities have contested and negotiated public spaces in the United States, thereby politicizing identity as the "power to define selves and gain access to resources" (4).

22. El Teatro Campesino developed a distinct performance style, what is now known widely as "*actos*." The Bread and Puppet Theater based in Boston utilized giant puppets, influenced by popular Latin American theater techniques.

23. For an analysis of the 1998 La Jolla Playhouse staging of this scene, see Victor Bascara's *Model-Minority Imperialism*.

24. A college production of *Dogeaters* at the all-women's college, Smith College in Northampton, Massachusetts, directed by Krystal Banzon, was performed by an all-female cast.

25. Actors Gina Alajar, Jon Santos, and Lao Rodriguez shared variations of these questions during different moments in the rehearsal process and in informal conversations.

26. This citation is from a comment made by Hagedorn during rehearsals in Manila (November 2007).

27. Many of the previews and reviews of the Manila production hardly paid attention to the story of Martial Law in *Dogeaters*. They focused on Hagedorn as a *balikbayan* and on the stellar cast. Substantial reviews rehearsed familiar comments that were noted about the novel, which is inevitable for a play based on the novel. Patrick Henson's review in the *Manila Bulletin* took issue with the play's characters, which he found to be stereotypical and shallow depictions of Filipinos. He identified this as a symptom of someone who has stayed away too long. Another review hailed *Dogeaters* as a wake-up call to Filipino people who were apathetic toward the corrupt system of government.

28. For an article that pays homage to "cruel, brutal, devious, macho *kontrabidas*," including Cortez, see Nerisa Almo's "Bad Guys of Philippine Showbiz."

CHAPTER 4

1. In some productions where the role of Ellen is given to an Asian actor, it is explained that Chris, in his inability to get over Kim, seeks for a replacement

in the love of another Asian woman. This casting choice does not replace the racialized desire driving the love story of the musical. It also does not displace or subvert the role of women (Asian and white) as a foil for American white masculinity and the tension around his mixed-race progeny.

2. *Madame Butterfly* was a short story penned by John Luther Long and published in 1898. Puccini's opera is based on Long's and American playwright David Belasco's collaborative play adaptation of *Madame Butterfly*, which was staged in New York in 1900. Pierre Loti's 1887 "novel of Japanese manners," *Madame Chrysanthéme*, precedes Long's short story. Eve Oishi, in her introduction to the reprinting of *Miss Nume of Japan* by Onoto Watanna/Winnefred Eaton, details the legal battle between Long and Watanna/Eaton regarding the issue of authorship of *Madame Butterfly*.

3. Boublil and Schönberg emphasize the following in their approach to musicals: their narratives "deal with individual stories set in a historical context at a moment of crisis and handle themes that are at once universal and personal to every audience," and offer cohesion and "emotional clarity with stories that carry the audience along with them" (Vermette x). As Vermette argues, "Lyrics are not intended to dazzle with wit and cleverness" and are written "not to convey attention to [themselves] but to convey in a natural way the thoughts and emotions of the characters." Additionally, their scores are "marked by musical sincerity and are full of variety and vitality, with soaring often heart-rendering melodies" (xi).

4. I wish to thank Martin Manalansan for offering the phrase "global stage industrial complex." I invoke it here as I appreciate the phrase's link to formulations such as prison industrial complex and academic industrial complex. This phrase exposes the intricate and intimate connections of world stage, entertainment, capital, consumption, labor, and the state. More importantly, it exposes an exploitative process that produces uneven relations of power and the violent practice of creating a subordinate underclass, all in the pursuit of profit. Mike Davis has been cited as the first to introduce the term "prison industrial complex." My understanding of the social meaning of prison is informed by Angela Davis's work on the subject.

5. New York–based Ma-yi Theater Ensemble started as a Filipino/Filipino American theater company. In 2000, they expanded to being an all–Asian American theater.

6. Filipina performers who have played such roles represent a long and significant chapter in theatrical history: Joanne Almedilla (Broadway 1995), Karen Alvarez (U.S. tour 2002-2003), Joanna Ampil (Broadway 1993, Sydney, UK tour 1995), Maya Barredo (London 1995), Emy Baysic (Broadway 1995), Annette Calud (Broadway 1993), Cezarah Campos (Sydney 1995, London, Manila), Ima Castro (Manila, Asian tour), Melinda Chua (first U.S. national tour 1995, Stuttgart, Broadway), Leah de los Santos (Stuttgart), Jenine Desiderio (London), Aura Deva (Stuttgart), Ma-Anne Dionisio (Toronto, Sydney, London), Rona Figueroa

(Broadway 1993), Leila Florentino (Broadway 1999), Caselyn Francisco (Stuttgart, the Netherlands), Jennifer Hubilla (U.S. tour 2002-2003), Jennie Kwan (Chicago, first U.S. national tour 1992), Annjanette Laborte (Stuttgart), Cornilla Luna (Toronto 1993), Deedee Lyn Magno (second U.S. national tour 1995, Broadway, Asian tour), Roanne Monte (London), Michelle Nigalan (second U.S. national tour, Germany, Luxemburg), Christina Paras (first and second U.S. national tours, Stuttgart), Jennifer Paz (first U.S. national tour 1992, U.S. tour 2004), Hazel Ann Raymundo (first U.S. national tour), Kristine Remigio (second U.S. national tour), Jamie Rivera (London), Ruby Rosales (Stuttgart), Riva Salazar (London), Roxanne Taga (Broadway, Paper Mill), Miriam Valmores (Sydney), Monique Wilson (London) (R. San Juan "The *Miss Saigon Page*").

7. This is noted in Deva's curriculum vitae. In addition to the recognition, "a new breed of Orchid (micranthum 'Bubble Gum' x delenatii) was named after her" ("Aura Deva: Curriculum Vitae").

8. For example, in a West End premiere production, Lea Salonga played one of the lead roles. Ensemble member and Kim understudy Monique Wilson took over the role after Salonga finished her run. Also, those who perform in supporting or ensemble roles take on the lead in touring productions. Rona Figueroa, for instance, was an ensemble member and a Kim understudy for the 1992 Chicago run, and then went on to play Kim on Broadway in 1993.

9. Scholars who have analyzed representations of Asian women in musicals and operas include Angela Pao, Dorinne Kondo, Teresa de Lauretis, Mari Yoshihara, Rennie Christoper, and Celine Parreñas-Shimizu.

10. See *South Pacific*, *The King and I*, and, as discussed in chapter 1, *The Shoo-Fly Regiment*.

11. Original source: *City Pages,* 9 Feb. 1994.

12. See Sean Metzger, Krystyn Moon, and Josephine Lee for discussions of yellowface and the racialization, or more specifically the Orientalizing, of Asian/Americans in the American theatrical imaginary.

13. The term "colored museum" here is borrowed from George Wolfe's play on stereotypes and caricatures of African Americans.

14. See Yoko Yoshikawa's "The Heat Is on *Miss Saigon* Coalition: Organizing across Race and Sexuality."

15. Other arguments that complicate this casting debate include Velina Hasu Houston's point about the character being biracial. Another point to ponder is the hiring of Lea Salonga, an Asian actor, as the lead in the role of Kim, as opposed to an Asian American. The Actor's Equity demanded that the role of the "engineer" be recast with an Asian American actor. Why did the tensions between nationals and U.S.-born Asians around employment and educational opportunities not surface?

16. A protest statement titled "Miss Saigon: A Musical (Foul) Play" was published as a letter to the editor of *CyberDyaryo*. The artists-protesters, Concerned Artists of the Philippines, who collectively penned this letter, drew a parallel

between the "tragic-idyll tale of Kim, the Vietnamese refugee" and the forcing out of the local artists. The artists-protesters likened the expulsion of local artists to forced evacuation of refugees (Raul Reyes 68). I quote Juliet Po, the secretary general of the Concerned Artists of the Philippines (CAP), who provides the following critique in the protest letter: "Meanwhile, local resident artist companies, local producers and artists are deprived of their regular venue and rehearsal spaces. On the first weekend of October, Mackintosh's *Miss Saigon* is showing at the CCP's Main Theater (1,800 seating capacity) while original Filipino musicale 'fire water woman,' which was previously assigned there, is relegated to the Little Theater (410 seats)" (Concerned Artists of the Philippines 68). This letter of protest was published in the same special issue of *Filipinas* magazine focusing on *Miss Saigon* as Raul Reyes's article. It also circulated in cyberspace through a number of Filipino-focused listservs.

17. I wish to thank Robyn Rodriguez for her insightful comments about the production and marketing of Filipino workers as exceptional by the Philippine state, which helped me arrive at this observation. See *Migrants for Export* for Rodriguez's analysis of the labor-brokering state.

18. The risks of sexual abuse and violence for Filipina entertainers are documented in a report by Aurora Javate de Dios, "*Japayuki-san*: Filipinas at Risk," in *Filipino Women Overseas Contract Workers: At What Cost?* edited by Mary Ruby Palma-Beltran and de Dios. "*Japayuki-san*" is a derogatory term "used to describe Filipinas and other Asian women entertainers working in Japan. The term is derived from *karayuki-san*, or China-bound Japanese prostitutes who serviced the sexual needs of Japanese soldiers prior to and during the Second World War all over Asia" (Tolentino, "Bodies," 59). According to Philippine Overseas Employment Administration (POEA) statistics of workers deployed under the category of "Professional and Technical Related Workers" dated 1993-2008, Japan consistently hired the most Filipinos to work as dancers, choreographers, singers, and musicians. In 2001, when the Broadway run ended and the Mackintosh worldwide tour began, POEA recorded over 70,600 performing artists. The majority of hires were deployed to Japan; the numbers of workers to other countries do not come anywhere close to the number of those who have gone to do performance-related work in Japan. These POEA records do not include those who are sea-based deployed workers.

19. An earlier text, Viet Nguyen's *Race and Resistance*, elaborates on the notion of Asian Americans as "bad subjects," but their badness is in opposition to and against dominant discourse. While Parreñas Shimizu, in *Hypersexuality of Race*, recuperates "bad objects"—"whorish Asian women"—for their political possibility, Nguyen's "bad subjects" construct exposes the "mutual interdependency" of such binarisms. Thus Nguyen holds suspect the very attachment to such binary constructs.

20. Angela Pao suggests that the creation and casting logic of the character Kim follows the internal "verisimilitude" of the theatrical world ("The Eyes of

the Storm," 24). The commitment therefore is not to the "real" Vietnamese prostitute but to the "maternal lineage," starting with Cio Cio San of *Madame Butterfly* (25).

21. See Elin Diamond's *Unmaking Mimesis* and Jill Dolan's *The Feminist Spectator as Critic*.

22. Participants in this meeting included South Vietnam, U.S. South Korea, Thailand, Australia, and New Zealand. President Johnson described the meeting as one to "show friendship for Asian countries rather than accomplish substantive policy gains" (qtd. in Gibbons 40).

23. JEST hired Aetas to impart survival and combat skills to the U.S. Navy Seals and Special Forces in preparation for the terrain of battle in Vietnam. One of the tourist packages includes a multi-activity offer that contains guided tours by the Aetas and a glimpse of their way of life through cooking demonstrations and traditional dances ("Mini Survival Adventure").

24. The sound of *Miss Saigon* is obviously more than its songs and the singing voices of the actors. The overall sound concept of the musical highlights the theme of clashing worlds. Its score features instruments identified with musical traditions of Asia. Moments of synchronicity are featured in songs such as "Sun and Moon" and "The Last Night of the World," in which flute and xylophone sounds associated with Asia and female (=Kim) are in tune with the saxophone, which is meant to correlate with the United States and male (=Chris).

25. Other Asian American performers narrate the same story about their participation in major Broadway and regional productions such as *Miss Saigon* and other major musical productions about Asia/Asian Americans (for example, *South Pacific, The King and I, Pacific Overtures, Flower Drum Song,* and occasional new works such as *Bombay Dreams*). In addition to a certain kind of cachet for working in these shows, many actors were able to acquire their equity card, providing them additional work privileges—higher pay, health insurance, etc.

26. All references to Aura Deva are from a personal conversation held in Santa Monica, CA, Friday, January 25, 2008.

27. It is not entirely clear what making it to the *Miss Saigon* school meant and what its relationship to the actual productions might be. What is clear about vague terms such as "earmarked" and "shortlist" is that making it to the training school does not guarantee a role in any of the productions. As recently as 2005, Alegre was still running the training school, emphasizing that the competition is not just with other Filipino/a actors but with actors from all over the world (Tiffee).

28. References to Dong Alegre throughout this chapter are drawn from our conversation held in November 2007, Manila, Philippines. I wish to thank director/producer Bobby Garcia, who initiated contact with Mr. Alegre as well as with Miss Salonga.

29. Vocal/music teachers include professionals in the Philippines with multiple degrees and certificates from institutions such as the University of the

Philippines, University of Illinois, Idyllwild Arts Academy, and the School of Music at Salzburg, Austria.

30. Although I do not have information on the percentage of performers who train with the Manila *Miss Saigon* school, I do know that creating a touring company for such a production costs less than auditioning and training in specific production sites. Bringing in "hired" labor costs less than local hirings, parallel to migrant labor. With shows scheduled for multiple sites, the cost of a touring artistic team is considerably less than that of producing the same show in each specific site.

31. In her essay "Domestic Debates: Women's Migration, Gender, and the State in the Philippines," Robyn Rodriguez begins to elaborate on shame (*hiya*) as a motivating factor for the Philippine state's policy reform regulating overseas contract workers, as well NGOs supporting migrant laborers.

32. I would like to acknowledge writer R. Zamora Linmark, who shared his memory of this special announcement.

CODA

1. Allan Isaac uses "American tropics" to refer to U.S. unincorporated territories, which include Hawaii, the Philippines, and Puerto Rico. He also proffers "American tropics" as a concept to highlight possibilities of alternative politics, affiliations, and affinities imagined through shared and connected histories of U.S. imperialisms. He mobilizes newly mapped geographies that emerge from U.S. imperialism toward alternative kinships among spaces that fall under the category of unincorporated territories.

2. Other moments of subversions of "white love," used here to refer to Filipinos' love for whiteness and all things American (not quite used in the ways that Vicente Rafael coined the phrase as referring to the conjoining of ambivalence and benevolence in U.S. imperialist acts), is captured in Malia Lagaso's performance of Vicki Stubing. Lagaso brilliantly enacts fantasy sequences as the iconic character Vicki Stubing of the popular television show *The Love Boat*. Lagaso's bodily and facial expressions teeter between embodying Vicki Stubing in the fantasy world of Edgar and enacting an ironic commentary on the iconic television character.

3. Christine Balance's writing on child stars and the figure of the child in Filipino American performance further explores these wonderful tensions in the Kumu Kahua Theater's production of *Rolling the Rs*.

4. Dylan Rodriguez, in his introduction to *Suspended Apocalypse*, provides a critique of Filipino American discourse's use of "colonial mentality." For Rodriguez, "colonial mentality" is a "reifying notion of collective historical trauma" collapsed into "pathologies of 'identity' and a banal rhetoric of pluralism and diversity" (34).

5. Purnima Mankekar's work on Indian call centers most clearly lays bare imitation within the logic of globalization. Locating her study in an ethnography of

call centers as well as analyses of filmic representations of the industry of call centers, she underscores the role of imitation in response to global capital labor demands.

6. Racialized bodies performing acts that are not conventionally assigned to them are deemed as unoriginal and plagiaristic. Similar nonconventional performances by white, modern, cosmopolitan bodies are deemed as cultural border crossings, explorations of interculturalism, postmodernity, and avant-garde.

BIBLIOGRAPHY

SINING BAYAN COLLECTIVE: UNPUBLISHED SCRIPTS

Excerpts from the following scripts are available in *Cultural Activism and the KDP's Sining Bayan*. Compiled with introduction by Ermena Vinluan. Reprinted by Special Permission for the F.I.N.D.S. Conference, March 1999, Harvard University. These scripts are also archived at the Uno Collection of Plays by Asian American Women in the W. E. B. Du Bois Library at the University of Massachusetts at Amherst.

Isuda Ti Imuna
Mindanao
Narciso and Perez
Narciso and Perez Program Notes
Tagatupad/Those Who Must Carry On
Ti Mangyuna/Those Who Led
Warbrides

SOURCES CITED

Abbate, Carolyn. *Unsung Voices: Opera and Musical Narrative in the Nineteenth Century*. Princeton, NJ: Princeton University Press, 1996.

Ade, George. *Sultan of Sulu*. New York: R. H. Russell, 1903. Digitized by Google.

Afable, Patricia O., and Cherubim A. Quizon. "Introduction: Rethinking Display of Filipinos at St. Louis: Embracing Heartbreak and Irony." *Philippine Studies* 52.4 (2004): 439-44.

Agamben, Giorgio. *State of Exception*. Translated by Kevin Attell. Chicago: University of Chicago Press, 2005.

Ager, Maila. "List of Dead and Injured in Congress Blast." *Inquirer.net*. 14 Nov. 2007. http://www.inquirer.net/specialreports/congressblast/view.php?db=1&article=20071114-100760. 10 June 2010.

Alegado, Dean. Interview. Honolulu, HI. June 2002.

———. "The Legacy and Challenge of *Ti Mangyuna*." Reprinted in *Cultural Activism and the KDP's Sining Bayan*. Compiled with an introduction by Ermena Vinluan. F.I.N.D.S. Conference. 1999. Cambridge, MA: Harvard University. Unpaginated.

Alegre, Dong. Personal Conversation. Makati, Metro Manila, Philippines. November 2007.

Almedilla, Joan, Jennifer Paz, Jenni Salma. *Road to Saigon*. Developed with and directed by John Lawrence Rivera. Produced by East West Players. 13 May–13 June 2010.

Almo, Nerisa. "Bad Guys of Philippine Showbiz." *Philippine Entertainment Portal*. 19 Sept. 2007. Web. 15 June 2011.

Althusser, Louis. "Ideology and Ideological State Apparatus (Notes towards an Investigation)." *Mapping Ideology*. Ed. Slavoj Zizek. New York: Verso, 1994. 100-140.

Anderson, Warwick. *Colonial Pathologies: American Tropical Medicine, Race, and Hygiene in the Philippines*. Durham, NC: Duke University Press, 2006.

Angelo, Emily. "I Cover Chinatown." 1930. Reprinted in *our own voice* literary ezine. September 2001. Web. 6 Sept. 2010.

Arrizón, Alicia. *Queering Mestizaje: Transculturation and Performance*. Ann Arbor: University of Michigan Press, 2007.

Asis, Stan. Panel Address. First Convening of Asian American Theaters. Seattle, WA. May 1999.

Aspillera, Paraluman S., rev. by Yolanda Canseco Hernandez. *Basic Tagalog for Foreigners and Non-Tagalogs*. Tokyo: Tuttle, 2007.

Atienza, Glecy. *Mukhang Maarte*. Manila, Philippines: UST Publishing Press, 2003.

"Aura Deva Curriculum Vitae." Aura Deva: Actress, Singer, Composer. auradeva.com. 20 May 2012.

Austin, J. L. *How to Do Things with Words*. Oxford: Clarendon, 1962.

Bacho, Peter. *Dark Blue Suit and Other Stories*. Seattle: University of Washington Press, 1997.

Badger, Reid. *A Life in Ragtime: A Biography of James Reese Europe*. New York: Oxford University Press, 1995.

Balce, Nerissa S. "The Filipina's Breast: Savagery, Docility, and the Erotics of the American Empire." *Social Text* 24 (Summer 2006): 89-110.

———. "Filipino Bodies, Lynching, and the Language of Empire." In *Positively No Filipinos Allowed*. Eds. Edgardo V. Gutierrez, Ricardo V. Gutierrez, and Antonio T. Tiongson Jr. Philadelphia: Temple University Press, 2006. 43-60.

———. "Savagery and Docility: Filipinos and the Language of the American Empire after 1898." Diss. University of California, Berkeley, 2002.

Baldoz, Rick. *The Third Asiatic Invasion: Empire and Migration in Filipino America, 1898-1946*. New York: New York University Press, 2011.

Baluyut, Pearlie Rose Salaveria. *Institutions and Icons of Patronage: Arts and Culture in the Philippines during the Marcos Years, 1965-1986*. Diss. University of California, Los Angeles, 2004.

Barrios, Joi. "Staging/Upstaging Globalization: The Politics of Performance in Southeast Asia." *Body Politics: Essays on Cultural Representations of Women's Bodies*. Ed. Odine de Guzman. Quezon City, Philippines: UP Center for Women's Studies, 2002. 19-36.

Barrios, Maria Josephine. "The Taumbayan as Epic Hero, the Audience as Community." In *Radical Street Performance: An International Anthology*. Ed. Jan Cohen Cruz. London: Routledge, 1998. 255-61.

———. "Tungo sa Estetika ng Dulaang Panlansangan." Master's thesis, De La Salle University, Manila, Philippines, 1994.

Bascara, Victor. *Model-Minority Imperialism*. Minneapolis: University of Minnesota Press, 2006.

Bello, Madge, and Vince Reyes. "Filipino Americans and the Marcos Overthrow: The Transformation of Political Consciousness." *Amerasia Journal* 13 (1986-1987): 73-83.

Bello, Walden, Herbert Docena, Marissa de Guzman, and Marylou Malig. *The Anti-Development State: The Political Economy of Permanent Crisis in the Philippines.* New York: Palgrave, 2004.

Berlant, Lauren. "Introduction: Compassion (and Withholding)." *Compassion: The Culture and Politics of an Emotion*. New York: Routledge, 2004. 1-14.

Bhabha, Homi. "Of Mimicry and Man: The Ambivalence of Colonial Discourse." *The Location of Culture*. New York: Routledge, 1994. 85-92.

Boal, Augusto. *Theatre of the Oppressed*. New York: Theater Communications Group, 1985.

Bogardus, Emory. "Anti-Filipino Race Riots: A Report Made to the Ingram Institute of Social Science, of San Diego, 1930." *Anti-Filipino Movements in California: A History, Bibliography, and Study Guide*. Ed. Howard Dewitt. San Francisco: R&R Research, 1976. 89-118.

Bontoc Eulogy. Dir. Marlon Fuentes. Cinema Guild. 1995. Film.

Bonus, Rick. *Locating Filipino America: Ethnicity and the Cultural Politics of Space.* Philadelphia: Temple University Press, 2000.

Borah, Eloisa Gomez. *Early Images of Filipinos in America: External Collection*. Copyright 2007-2011. http://personal.anderson.ucla.edu/eloisa.borah/EarlyImages.htm.

———. "The Other Filipinos at the 1904 World's Fair in St. Louis: The Honorary Board of Filipino Commissioners, Louisiana Purchase Exposition." Filipino American National Historical Society, 10th National Conference, 21-25 July 2004, University of Missouri, St. Louis, Missouri.

Breitbart, Eric. *A World on Display: Photographs from the St. Louis World Fair, 1904.* Albuquerque: University of New Mexico Press, 1997.

Briggs, Laura. "Notes on Activism and Epistemologies: Problems for Transnationalisms." *Social Text* 26.4 (Winter 2008): 79-95.

Brooks, Daphne A. *Bodies in Dissent: Spectacular Performances of Race and Freedom, 1850-1910*. Durham, NC: Duke University Press, 2006.

Brooks, Peter. "Body and Voice in Melodrama and Opera." *Siren Songs: Representations of Gender and Sexuality in Opera*. Princeton, NJ: Princeton University Press, 2000. 119-126.

Browning, Barbara. *Infectious Rhythms: Metaphors of Contagion and the Spread of African Culture*. New York: Routledge, 1998.

Broyles-Gonzales, Yolanda. *El Teatro Campesino: Theater in the Chicano Movement.* Austin: University of Texas Press, 1994.

———. "Towards a Re-Vision of Chicano Theatre History: The Women of El Teatro Campesino." *Making a Spectacle: Feminist Essays on Contemporary Women's Theater.* Ed. Lynda Hart. Ann Arbor: University of Michigan Press, 1989. 209-38.

Buaken, Manuel. *I Have Lived with the American People*. Caldwell, ID: Caxton Printers, 1948.

Buangan, Antonio. "The Suyoc People Who Went to St. Louis 100 Years Ago: The Search for My Ancestors." *Philippine Studies* 21.4 (2004): 474-98.

Burgess, Ernest. Introduction to *Taxi-Dance Hall: A Sociological Study in Commercialized Recreation and City Life*, by Paul Cressey. Chicago: University of Chicago Press, 1932.

Burns, Lucy Mae San Pablo. "Community Acts: Locating Pilipino-American Theater and Performance." Diss. University of Massachussetts, Amherst, 2004, http://scholarworks.umass.edu/dissertations/AAI31182.

———. "Ralph Peña." *Notes for a New WORLD,* Spring 1996, 3.

Butler, Judith. *Excitable Speech: A Politics of the Performative*. New York: Routledge, 1997.

Cabreza, Vincent. "P.7M to Pay Ibaloi Marcos Victors Set Aside." *Philippine Daily Inquirer,* 11 Aug. 2009.

Campomanes, Oscar. "New Formations of Asian American Studies and the Question of U.S. Imperialism." *positions: east asia cultures critique* 5.2 (1997): 523–50.

———. "The New Empire's Forgetful and Forgotten Citizens: Unrepresentability and Unassimilability in Filipino-American Postcolonialities." *Hitting Critical Mass* 2.2 (Spring 1995): 145-200.

———. "Filipinos in the United States and Their Literature of Exile." *Reading the Literatures of Asian America*. Eds. Shirley Geok-lin Lim and Amy Ling. Philadelphia: Temple University Press, 1992. 49-78.

Cannell, Fenella. "The Power of Appearances: Beauty, Mimicry, and Transformation in Bicol." *Discrepant Histories: Translocal Essays on Filipino Cultures*. Ed. Vicente L. Rafael. Philadelphia: Temple University Press, 1995. 223-58.

Cariaga, Catalina. "A Dime." *Liwanag* 2. San Francisco: Sulu, 1993. 91.

Catapusan, Benicio, Jr.. "The Social Adjustment of Filipinos in the United States." Diss. University of Southern California, 1940.

———. "The Filipino Occupational and Recreational Activities in Los Angeles." Master's thesis, University of Southern California, 1934.

Chan, Sucheng. *Asian Americans: An Interpretive History*. New York: Twayne, 1991.

Choy, Catherine Ceniza. "Towards Trans-Pacific Social Justice: Women and Protest in Filipino American History." *Journal of Asian American Studies* 8.3 (2005): 293-307.

———. *Empire of Care: Nursing and Migration in Filipino American History*. Durham, NC: Duke University Press, 2003.

———. "Salvaging the Savage." *Screaming Monkeys: Critiques of Asian American Images*. Ed. Evelina Galang et al. Chicago: Coffee House Press, 2003. 35-49.

Christopher, Renny. *The Viet Nam War/The American War: Images and Representations in Europe*. Boston: University of Massachusetts Press, 1995.

Chuh, Kandice. *Imagine Otherwise: On Asian Americanist Critique*. Durham, NC: Duke University Press, 2003.

"Clark Air Base." *Encyclopedia Britannica Online*. 2009. http://www.britannica.com/EBchecked/topic/119983/Clark-Air-Base. 2 June 2009.

Clement, Catherine. "Through Voices, History." In *Siren Songs: Representations of Gender and Sexuality in Opera*. Ed Mary Ann Smart. Princeton, NJ: Princeton University Press, 2000. 17-28.

Cole, Bob, J. Rosamund Johnson, and James Weldon Johnson. *The Shoo-Fly Regiment*. Originally performed in 1906, starring Cole, Johnson, and Johnson.

Concerned Artists of the Philippines. "*Miss Saigon*: A Musical (Foul) Play." *Filipinas Magazine*, December 2000, 68.

Cressey, Paul. *Taxi-Dance Hall: A Sociological Study in Commercialized Recreation and City Life*. Chicago: University of Chicago Press, 1932.

Crowley, Patrick, and Ross Melnick, eds. Home Page. *Cinema Treasures: Discover. Preserve. Protect*. N.d. www.cinematreasures.org. 7 Sept. 2010.

Davis, Mike. "Hell Factories in the Field: A Prison-Industrial Complex." *The Nation*, Feb. 20, 1995.

De la Cruz, Enrique, Pearlie Rose S. Baluyut, and Rico J. Reyes, eds. *Confrontations, Crossings, and Convergence: Photographs of the Philippines and the United States, 1898-1998*. Los Angeles: UCLA Asian American Studies Center Press, UCLA Southwest Asian Program, 1998.

De la Moreau, Jeanne. "Confessions of a Taxi Dancer: As Told to Bart Wheeler." *Los Angeles Times*, 2 Aug. 1931.

De Lauretis, Teresa. "Popular Culture, Private and Public Fantasies: Femininity and Fetishism in David Cronenberg's *M. Butterfly*." *Signs* 24.2 (Winter 1999): 303-34.

Delmondo, Sharon. *The Star-Entangled Banner: One Hundred Years of America in the Philippines*. Piscataway, NJ: Rutgers University Press, 2004.

Desmond, Jane. *Meaning in Motion: New Cultural Studies of Dance*. Durham, NC: Duke University Press, 1997.

Deva, Aura. Personal communication. Santa Monica, CA. 25 Jan. 2008.

Dewitt, Howard. *Anti-Filipino Movements in California: A History, Bibliography, and Study Guide*. San Francisco: R&E Research, 1976.

Diamond, Elin. *Unmaking Mimesis: Essays on Feminism and Theater*. New York: Routledge, 1997.

Dimaculangan, Jocelyn. "Gina Alajar and Michael de Mesa Share Stage in *Dogeaters*." *PEP: Philippine Entertainment Portal*. 17 Oct. 2007. http://www.pep.ph/guide/guide/1206/gina-alajar-and-michael-de-mesa-share-stage-in-dogeaters. 25 Aug. 2010.

Dino, Amado. "The Filipino Situation in America." *Philippine Review* 1.10 (1931): 8.

Dixon-Gottschild, Brenda. *The Black Dancing Body: A Geography from Coon to Cool*. New York: Palgrave McMillan, 2003.

Dolan, Jill. *The Feminist Spectator as Critic*. Ann Arbor: University of Michigan Press, 1991.

A Dollar a Day, Ten Cents a Dance: A Historic Portrait of Filipino Farmworkers in America. Dir. Geoffrey Dunn and Mark Schwartz. Gold Mountain Productions. 1984. Film.

Elam, Harry J. *Taking It to the Streets: The Social Protest Theater of Luis Valdez and Amiri Baraka.* Ann Arbor: University of Michigan Press, 1997.

Elam, Harry, and Alice Rayner. "Echoes from the Black (W)hole: An Examination of the America Play by Suzan Lori Parks." In *Performing America: Cultural Nationalism in American Theater.* Eds. Jeffrey D. Mason and J. Ellen Gainor. Ann Arbor: University of Michigan Press, 1999. 178-92.

———. "Body Parts: Between Story and Spectacle in Venus by Suzan-Lori Parks." In *Staging Resistance: Essays on Political Theater.* Eds. Jeanne Marie Colleran and Jenny Spencer. Ann Arbor: University of Michigan Press, 1998.

"El Centro: Dancers Held in Shooting; Shot in the Back and Stabbed through the Stomach." *Los Angeles Times,* 17 March 1930.

Engels, Friedrich. *Socialism: Utopian and Scientific.* 1880. Atlanta, GA: Pathfinder Press, 2011.

Eperjesi, John. *The Imperialist Imaginary: Visions of Asia and the Pacific in American Culture.* Lebanon, NH: University Press of New England, 2005.

Espiritu, Augusto. "Journeys of Discovery and Difference: Transnational Politics and the Union of Democratic Filipinos." *Transnational Political Behavior and Asian Americans.* Eds Pei-te Lien and Christian Collett. Philadelphia: Temple University Press, 2009. 38-55.

Evangelista, Patricia. "Inquirer Opinion/Columns: Rebel without a Clue; Dogeaters," *Philippine Inquirer.* 25 Nov. 2007. http://opinion.inquirer.net/inquireropinion/columns/view/20071125-102930/Dogeaters. 16 April 2012.

Evangelista, Susan. "Filipinos in America: Literature as History." *Philippine Studies* 36 (1988): 36-53.

"Fame Beckons: Filipinos Find Miss Saigon a Hard Act to Follow." *Asiaweek.com.* 30 Nov. 2000. http://www-cgi.cnn.com/ASIANOW/asiaweek/96/0614/feat2.html. 1 March 2008.

Fermin, Jose D. *1904 World's Fair: The Filipino Experience.* West Conshohocken, PA: Infinity Publishing, 2004.

Fernandez, Doreen. *Palabas: Essays on Philippine Theater History.* Quezon City, Philippines: Ateneo de Manila University Press, 1996.

———. "Introduction: In the Context of Political History and Dramatic Tradition." In *The Filipino Drama.* Ed. Arthur Stanley Riggs. Manila, Philippines: The Intramuros Administration, 1981. xi-xx.

"Filipino Baby Christened: Born at the World's Fair, President Francis Stands Godfather; Fiesta Follows." *New York Times,* 1 Aug. 1904.

"The Filipino Is the State's Next Problem." *Watsonville Evening Pajaronian,* 30 Oct. 1929.

"Filipino Race Clashes Laid to Red Agitators." *Los Angeles Times,* 10 March 1930, A6.

"Filipinos Apt on Stage, Soon Will Be Exporting Stars, Says Manila Theatrical Man." *New York Times,* 13 Aug. 1922, 15.

"Filipinos Say It's Time for Native Government." *New York Times,* 17 June 1904.

Fish, Stanley. "The Best 10 American Movies." *New York Times,* 4 Jan. 2009. Web. 1 Sept. 2010.

Foley, Melinda Corazon. *Coconut Masquerade*. Performed as part of POMO Festival. 2002. Performance.

Foucault, Michel. "Nietzcshe, Genealogy, History." In *Aesthetics, Method, and Epistemology*. Ed. James D. Faubion. New York: New Press, 1998. 369-89.

Francia, Luis, ed. *Brown River, White Ocean: An Anthology of Twentieth-Century Philippine Literature in English*. New Brunswick, NJ: Rutgers University Press, 1993.

Francia, Luis, and Angel Shaw, eds. *Vestiges of War*. New York: New York University Press, 2002.

Francisco, Luzviminda. "The First Vietnam: The Philippine American War, 1899-1902." In *The Philippines: End of an Illusion*. Ed. Association for Radical East Asian Studies (AREAS). London: AREAS, 1973.

Friedman, Daniel. "Contemporary Theatre for Working-Class Audiences in the United States." In *Theatre for Working-Class Audiences in the United States, 1830-1980*. Eds. Bruce A. McConachie and Daniel Friedman. Westport, CT: Greenwood Press, 1985. 197-248.

Fujita-Rony, Dorothy. *American Workers, Colonial Power*. Berkeley: University of California Press, 2003.

Fusco, Coco. "The Other History of Intercultural Performance." *TDR* 38.1 (1994): 147-67.

Gaerlan, Barbara. "The Movement in the United States to Oppose Martial Law in the Philippines, 1972-1991: An Overview." *Pilipinas* 33 (Fall 1999): 75-98.

García, Cynthia Marie. "Global Salsa: The Politics of Latinidad in Los Angeles Nightclubs." Diss. University of California, Los Angeles, 2005.

Garcia, Laura E., Sandra M. Gutierrez, and Felicitas Nuñez, eds. *Teatro Chicana: A Collective Memoir and Selected Plays*. Austin: University of Texas Press, 2008.

Geron, Kim, Enrique de la Cruz, Leland Saito, and Jaideep Singh. "Asian Americans' Social Movement and Interest Groups." *PS: Political Science and Politics* 34.3 (2001): 618-24.

Gibbons, William Conrad. *The U.S. Government and the Vietnam War: Executive and Legislative Roles and Relationships*. Princeton, NJ: Princeton University Press, 1995.

Go, Julian, and Anne Foster, eds. *American Colonial State in the Philippines: Global Perspectives*. Durham, NC: Duke University Press, 2003.

Gonzales, Marina Feleo. *A Song for Manong*. Produced by Life on the Water Company, San Francisco. 1987. Performance.

Gonzalves, Theo. *Stage Presence: Conversations with Filipino American Performing Artists*. San Francisco: Meritage Press, 2007.

———. *Taxi Dancing. Liwanag 2*. San Francisco: Sulu, 1993. 84-90. Play.

Grefalda, Reme-Antonia. "From the Editor's Laptop." *our own voice* literary ezine. 19 July 2002. http://www.ourownvoice.com/laptop/editor2002-2.shtml. 17 Feb. 2004.

Griffin, Farah Jasmine. "Black Feminists and Du Bois: Respectability, Protection, and Beyond." *Annals of the American Academy of Political and Social Science* 568 (March 2000): 28-40.

Guidote, Cecilia. *Theater for the Nation: A Prospectus for the National Theater of the Philippines*. Manila, Philippines: De La Salle University Press, 2003.

Habal, Estella. *San Francisco's International Hotel: Mobilizing the Filipino American Community in the Anti-Eviction Movement.* Philadelphia: Temple University Press, 2008.

———. "How I Became a Revolutionary." In *Legacy to Liberation: Politics and Culture of Revolutionary Asian/Pacific America.* Ed. Fred Ho. San Francisco: Big Red Media, 2000. 197-210.

Hagedorn, Jessica. "Playwright Talk and Book Signing." Makati City, Philippines. 17 Nov. 2007.

———. *Dogeaters: A Play about the Philippines.* New York: Theatre Communications Group, 2003.

Hart, Lynda. Introduction to *Acting Out: Feminist Performances*, eds. Lynda Hart and Peggy Phelan. Ann Arbor: University of Michigan Press, 1993. 1-12.

Hartman, Saidiya. *Scenes of Subjection: Terror, Slavery, and Self-Making in Nineteenth-Century America.* New York: Oxford University Press, 1997.

Hasu Houston, Velina. "The Fallout over 'Miss Saigon': It's Time to Overcome the Legacy of Racism in Theater." *Los Angeles Times.* 13 Aug. 1990. http://articles.latimes.com/1990-08-13/entertainment/ca-387_1_miss-saigon. June 9, 2012.

Hayner, Norman S. "Social Factors in Oriental Crime." *American Journal of Sociology* 43.6 (1938): 908–19.

Hoganson, Kristin L. *Fighting for American Manhood: How Gender Politics Provoked the Spanish-American and Philippine-American Wars.* New Haven, CT: Yale University Press, 2000.

Hunt, Chester L., and Richard W. Coller. "Intermarriage and Cultural Change: A Study of Philippine-American Marriages." *Social Forces* 35.3 (1957): 223–30.

Husted Harper, Ida. *The Life and Work of Susan B. Anthony.* Vol. 2. Indianapolis: Hollenbeck Press, 1908.

Ibañez, Rose. "Growing Up in America as a Young Filipina American during the Anti-Martial Law and Student Movement in the United States." In *Asian Americans: The Movement and the Moment.* Eds. Steve Louie and Glenn K. Omatsu. Los Angeles: UCLA Asian American Studies Center Press, 2001.

Ileto, Rey. *Pasyon and Revolution: Popular Movements in the Philippines, 1840-1910.* Quezon City, Philippines: Ateneo de Manila University Press, 1979.

Isaac, Allan Punzalan. *American Tropics: Articulating Filipino America.* Minneapolis: University of Minnesota Press, 2006.

Jackson, Shannon. *Professing Performance: Theatre in the Academy from Philology to Performativity.* Cambridge: Cambridge University Press, 2004.

Javate de Dios, Aurora. "Japayuki-san: Filipinas at Risk." In *Filipino Women Overseas Contract Workers: At What Cost?* Eds. Mary Ruby Palma-Beltran and Aurora Javate de Dios. Ann Arbor: University of Michigan Press, 1992.

Jenks, Albert Ernest. *The Bontoc Igorot.* Department of the Interior: Ethnological Survey Publications Volume 1. Manila, Philippines: Bureau of Public Printing, 1905.

Joseph, Melany. "Another World in Progress: A Progressive Think-Tank in Brazil Opens the Door to Artists." *American Theatre* 22.5 (May–June 2005): 54-58.

Joseph, Patrick. "From: Minstrel and Medicine Shows; Creating a Market for the Blues." *Overland Review* 32.1/2 (2005).

"Jungle Environmental Survival Training Camp." *Clark Subic Marketing.* Copyright 2007-2009. www.clarksubicmarketing.com/sports_leisure/subic_bay_jest_camp. htm. 28 May 2009.

Kang, Laura. *Compositional Subjects: Enfiguring Asian/American Women.* Durham, NC: Duke University Press, 2002.

Kikuchi, Robert. E-mail interview. June 2002.

Koestenbaum, Wayne. *The Queen's Throat: Opera, Homosexuality, and the Mystery of Desire.* Cambridge, MA: Da Capo Press, 1993.

Kondo, Dorinne. "How Do You Make Social Change?" *Theater* 31.3 (2001): 62-94.

———. *About Face: Performing Race in Fashion and Theater.* New York: Routledge, 1997.

Kramer, Paul. "Making Concessions: Race and Empire Revisited at the Philippine Exposition, 1901-1905." *Radical History Review* 73 (1999): 75-114.

Krasner, David. *A Beautiful Pageant: African American Theatre, Drama, and Performance in the Harlem Renaissance, 1910-1927.* New York: Palgrave McMillan, 2002.

LaPeña-Bonifacio, Amelia. *"Seditious" Tagalog Playwrights: Early American Occupation.* Manila: Zarzuela Foundation of the Philippines, 1972.

Lasker, Bruno. *Filipino Immigration.* New York: Arno Press, 1969.

Laurel, Herman Tiu. *The Olongapo Colonial Experience: History, Politics, and Memories.* Quezon City, Manila, Philippines: Independent Media, 2003.

Lee, Dana. *Dogeaters.* Kirk Douglas Theater Production. Los Angeles. Play program. February 2007.

Lee, Fay Ann. "Fay Ann Lee." In *Asian American Actors: Oral Histories from Stage, Screen, and Television.* Joann Faung Jean Lee. Jefferson, NC: McFarland, 2000. 68-79.

Lee, Josephine. *The Japan of Pure Invention: Gilbert and Sullivan's The Mikado.* Minneapolis: University of Minnesota Press, 2010.

———. "Between Immigration and Hyphenation: The Problems of Theorizing Asian American Theater." *Journal of Dramatic Theory and Criticism* 13.1 (Fall 1998): 45-69.

———. *Performing Asian American: Race and Ethnicity in the Contemporary Stage.* Philadelphia: Temple University Press, 1997.

Lee, Rachel. *The Americas of Asian American Literature: Gendered Fictions of Nation and Transnation.* Princeton, NJ: Princeton University Press, 1999.

Leip, David. "1904 Presidential General Election Results: Missouri." *Atlas of U.S. Presidential Elections.* N.d. Web. 1 Sept. 2010.

Lenin, V. I. "Theses on the National Question." *Marxists Internet Archive.* Originally published *Lenin Miscellany III*, 1925. http://www.marx.org/archive/lenin/works/1913/jun/30.htm. 28 Jan. 2012.

Lico, Gerard. *Edifice Complex: Power, Myth, and Marcos State Architecture.* Quezon City, Philippines: Ateneo de Manila Press, 2003.

Lindfors, Bernth. *Africans on Stage: Studies in Ethnological Show Business.* Bloomington: Indiana State University Press, 1999.

Linmark, R. Zamora. Personal communication. Quezon City, Manila, Philippines. 25 May 2009.

———. Rolling the Rs: The Play. Unpublished Manuscript.

Lionet, Francois, and Shumei Shih, eds. *Minor Transnationalism*. Durham, NC: Duke University Press, 2005.

Lockwood, Kathleen. "The Philippines: Allies during the Vietnam War." Originally published in *Vietnam Magazine,* June 1999. Published in www.history.net 12 June 2006. http://www.historynet.com/the-philippines-allies-during-the-vietnam-war. htm. 1 May 2010.

Lowe, Lisa. *Immigrant Acts: On Asian American Cultural Politics*. Durham, NC: Duke University Press, 1996.

Lumbera, Ben. "Terror and Culture under Marcos's New Society." *Multiply*. 23 July 2007. http://andrescebu.multiply.com/journal/item/19/Terror_And_Culture_ Under_Marcos_New_Society. 28 Jan. 2012.

Ma, Sheng-Mei. *East-West Montage: Reflections on Asian Bodies in Diaspora*. Honolulu: University of Hawaii Press, 2007.

The Making of Miss Saigon. New York: A&E Television Networks, 1989. Video.

Mallat, Jean. *The Philippines: History, Geography, Customs of the Spanish Colonies in Oceania*. Translated by Pura Santillan-Castrence in collaboration with Lina S. Castrence (1864). Manila, Philippines: National Historical Institute, 1994.

Malpede, John. "How Do You Make Social Change?" *Theater* 31.3 (2001): 62-94.

"Man Offers Dogs to Igorrotes." *Missouri Republic,* 20 April 1904.

Manalansan, Martin M. *Global Divas: Filipino Gay Men in the Diaspora*. Durham, NC: Duke University Press, 2003.

Mangaoang, Gil. "From the 1970s to the 1990s: Perspective of a Gay Filipino American Activist." *Asian American Sexualities: Dimensions of the Gay and Lesbian Experience*. New York: Routledge, 1996. 101-12.

Maram, Linda España. *Creating Masculinity in Los Angeles' Little Manila: Working-Class Filipinos and Popular Culture, 1920s-1950s*. New York: Columbia University Press, 2006.

Marcos, Ferdinand. *Revolution from the Center: How the Philippines Is Using the Martial Law to Build a New Society*. Hong Kong: Raya Books, 1978.

———. *Notes on the New Society*. Manila, Philippines: Marcos Foundation, 1973.

Mates, Julian. *America's Musical Stage: Two Hundred Years of Musical Theatre*. Wesport, CT: Greenwood, 1987.

McBee, Randy. *Dance Hall Days: Intimacy and Leisure among Working-Class Immigrants in the United States*. New York: New York University Press, 2000.

McKelvey, Blake, ed. *Henry A. Ward: Museum Builder to America*. Rochester, NY: Rochester Historical Society, 1948.

McWilliams, Carey. *Brothers under the Skin*. Boston: Little, Brown, 1964.

Meckel, Mary. *A Sociological Analysis of California Taxi-Dancer: The Hidden Halls*. Lewiston, NY: Edwin Mellen Press, 1995.

———. "Filipinos in the United States." *Pacific Historical Review* 43.4 (1974): 520–47.

Meet Me in St. Louis. Dir. Vincente Minelli. MGM. 1944. Film.

Melendy, Brett. "Filipinos in the United States." *Pacific Historical Review* (1974): 520-47.

———. *Oriental Americans.* New York: Twayne, 1972.

Metzger, Sean. "Charles Parsloe's Chinese Fetish: An Example of Yellowface Performance in Nineteenth-Century American Melodrama." *Theatre Journal* 56.4 (Dec. 2004): 627–51.

Meynell, Richard. "Remembering the Watsonville Riots." Excerpted from "Little Brown Brothers, Little White Girls: The Anti-Filipino Hysteria of 1930 and the Watsonville Riots." *Passports* 22 (1998). Reprinted online at http://www.modelminority.com/joomla/index.php?option=com_content&view=article&id=271:remembering-the-watsonville-riots-&catid=40:history&Itemid=56, 1 March 2009.

"Midsummer Listings." *New York Times,* 4 Aug. 1907.

Miguel, Muriel. Comment on a Panel. Intersection Conference. New WORLD Theater. Amherst, MA. Oct. 1998.

Mijares, Primitivo. *The Conjugal Dictatorship of Ferdinand and Imelda Marcos.* New York: Union Square Publications, 1976.

Millado, Chris. *PeregriNasyon.* Honolulu: Center for Philippine Studies, University of Hawaii at Manoa, n.d.

"Mini Survival Adventure in Subic Bay Jungles." *Seahorse Tours and Souveniers.* N.d. http://www.seahorsetours.com/tour/minisurvival.html. 5 June 2009.

"Monique Wilson Has Mixed Feelings about *Miss Saigon.*" *Philippine Headline News Online.* 24 May 2004. www.newsflash.org/2000/05/sb/sb001232.htm. 17 Feb. 2010.

"Monique Wilson, Head of MA/MFA in Acting." East 15 Acting School. 2008. http://east15.ac.uk/profile-monique.asp. 29 May 2012.

Montes, Veronica. "Bernie Aragon Jr. Looks for Love." *our own voice* literary ezine. N.p. Sept. 2005. Web. 6 Sept. 2010.

Moon, Krystyn R. *Yellowface: Creating the Chinese in American Popular Music and Performance, 1850s-1920s.* New Brunswick, NJ: Rutgers University Press, 2005.

"Moro Chief to Wed Slave: Romance of a Philippine Girl on Reservation at the World's Fair." *New York Times,* 6 May 1904.

Mullen, Bill. *Afro-Orientalism.* Minneapolis: University of Minnesota Press, 2004.

Muñoz, Jose. "Feeling Brown: Ethnicity and Affect in Ricardo Bracho's The Sweetest Hangover (and Other STDs)." *Theatre Journal* 52.1 (2000): 67-79.

Neal, Larry. "The Black Arts Movement." In *A Sourcebook of African-American Performance: Plays, People, Movement.* Ed. Annemarie Bean. New York: Routledge, 1999. 55-67.

Ngai, Mae. *Impossible Subjects.* Princeton, NJ: Princeton University Press, 2004.

Ngozi-Brown, Scot. "African-American Soldiers and Filipinos: Racial Imperialism, Jim Crow, and Social Relations." *Journal of Negro History* 82.1 (1997): 42-53.

Nguyen, Viet Thanh. *Race and Resistance: Literature and Politics in Asian America.* New York: Oxford University Press, 2002.

Nuguid, Nati. "The Ways of the New Society." *Toward a New Society: Essays on Aspects of Philippine Development.* Manila, Philippines: National Media Production Center, 1974.

Occena, Bruce, Mars Estrada, and Ermena Vinluan. Interview. Oakland Hills, CA. Dec. 2002.

O'Connor, D. J. *Representations of the Philippine and Cuban Insurrections on the Spanish Stage, 1887-1898.* Tempe, AZ: Bilingual Review Press, 2001.

O'Connor, Patrick Joseph. "From Minstrel and Medicine Shows: Creating a Market for the Blues." *Overland Review* 32.1 (2005).

Omatsu, Glenn. "In Memoriam Philip Vera Cruz." *Amerasia Journal* 20 (1994): iii-v.

Omi, Michael, and Howard Winant. *Racial Formation in the United States: From the 1960s to the 1990s.* New York: Routledge, 1994.

"The Original *Miss Saigon*: Facts and Figures." *Miss Saigon UK Tour, 2004-2005.* N.d. http://www.miss-saigon.com/factsandfigures/index.htm. 5 March 2010.

Otálvaro-Hormillosa, Gigi. *Cosmic Blood.* Performed as part of POMO Festival. 2002. Performance.

———. *Inverted Minstrel.* Produced by Devil Bunny in Bondage Productions. 2001. Multimedia Performance.

Otálvaro-Hormillosa, Gigi, and Heather Cox Carducci. *Dimensions of IS: A Spectacular Future.* Produced by (a)eromestiza and SpaceSuperStar. 2006. Multimedia Performance.

Padua, Laurence Angeleo. "Origins Obscura: Phrenology, Physiognomy, Anthropology, and Spectacle (An Excerpt from the Play)." Originally published in *disOrient* 9 (2001). Reprinted in *Hinge.* 9 Feb. 2007. http://langeleopadua.blogspot.com/2007/02/origins-obscura-phrenology-physiognomy.html. 26 Aug. 2010.

"Pajaro Valley Riots Quelled." *Los Angeles Times*, 25 Jan. 1930, 4.

Panis, Alleluia. Dir. *Heroes.* Alleluia Panis Dance Theater. SomArts Cultural Center, San Francisco. 30 May 2003. Performance.

Panunzio, Constantine. "Intermarriage in Los Angeles, 1924–1933." *American Journal of Sociology* 47.5 (1942): 690–701.

Pao, Angela C. "False Accents: Embodied Dialectics and the Characterization of Ethnicity and Nationality." *Theatre Topics* 14.1 (2004): 353-72.

———. "The Eyes of the Storm: Gender, Genre, and Cross-Casting in *Miss Saigon.*" *Text and Performance Quarterly* 12.1 (1992): 21-39.

Paredez, Deborah. *Selenidad: Selena, Latinos, and the Performance of Memory.* Durham, NC: Duke University Press, 2009.

Park, John. *Elusive Citizenship: Immigration, Asian Americans, and the Paradox of Civil Rights.* New York: New York University Press, 2004.

Parreñas, Rhacel. *Servants of Globalization: Women, Migration, and Domestic Work.* Stanford, CA: Stanford University Press, 2001.

———. "'White Trash' Meets the 'Brown Monkeys': The Politics of Interracial Gender Alliances between White Working-Class Women and Filipino Migrant Laborers in the Taxi-Dance Halls of the '20s and '30s." *Amerasia Journal* 24.2 (1998): 115–34.

Parrenas Shimizu, Celine. *The Hypersexuality of Race: Performing Asian/American on Screen and Scene.* Durham, NC: Duke University Press, 2007.

Perez-Torrez, Rafael. *Mestizaje: Critical Uses of Race in Chicano Culture.* Minneapolis: University of Minneapolis Press, 2006.

Peterson, Bernard L. *A Century of Musicals in Black and White: An Encyclopedia of Musical Stage Works by, about, or involving African Americans.* Westport, CT: Greenwood Press, 1993.

Phelan, Peggy. *Unmarked: The Politics of Performance.* New York: Routledge, 1993.

Philippine Commission. Law against Treason, Sedition, Etc. (Act No. 292). Manila, Philippines: 1901.

Pollock, Della. "Introduction: Making History Go." *Exceptional Spaces: Essays in Performance and History.* Chapel Hill: University of North Carolina Press, 1998. 1-46.

Post Modern American Pilipino Performance Project (POMO). N.d. http://www.kularts.org/contemporary.php. 20 June 2010.

Pratt, Mary Louise. *Imperial Eyes: Travel Writing and Transculturation.* New York: Routledge, 1995.

"President at Fair Spends Busy Day." *New York Times,* 27 Nov. 1904.

"Proclamation 1081." September 21, 1972. The LAWPHiL Project. http://www.lawphil.net/executive/proc/proc_1081_1972.html. 28 Jan. 2012.

Quizon, Cherubim A. "Two Yankee Women at the St. Louis Fair: The Metcalf Sisters and Their Bagobo Sojourn in Mindanao." *Philippine Studies* 52.4 (2004): 527–55.

Rafael, Vincente. *White Love and Other Events in Filipino History.* Durham, NC: Duke University Press, 2000.

———. "Introduction: "Writing Outside: On the Question of Location." *Discrepant Histories: Translocal Essays on Filipino Cultures.* Philadelphia: Temple University Press, 1995.

Reed, T. V. *The Art of Protest: Culture and Activism from the Civil Rights Movement to the Streets of Seattle.* Ann Arbor: University of Michigan Press, 2005.

Reyes, Eric. "Secret Nostalgias: Visual Representations of Filipino Americans." Panel presentation. Association of Asian American Studies. New York City. 6 April 2007.

Reyes, Raul. "Miss Saigon but Not Forgotten." *Filipinas,* December 2000. 62-68.

Riggs, Arthur Stanley. "Chapter One." *Filipino Drama.* Manila, Philippines: Intramuros Administration, 1904.

Riis, Thomas Lawrence. *Just before Jazz: Black Musical Theater in New York, 1890-1915.* Washington, DC: Smithsonian Institution Press, 1989.

Roach, Joseph. *Cities of the Dead: Circum-Atlantic Performance.* New York: Columbia University Press, 1996.

Robles, Al. "Taxi Dance." *Liwanag* 2. San Francisco: Sulu, 1993. 142.

Rodriguez, Dylan. *Suspended Apocalypse: White Supremacy, Genocide, and the Filipino Condition.* Minneapolis: University of Minnesota Press, 2010.

Rodriguez, Robyn. "Domestic Debates: Women's Migration, Gender, and the State in the Philippines." *Scholar and Feminist Online* 6.3 (Summer 2008). http://www.barnard.columbia.edu/sfonline/immigration/rrodriguez_01.htm. 5 March 2010.

Román, Davíd. *Performance in America: Contemporary U.S. Culture and the Perform-ing Arts.* Durham, NC: Duke University Press, 2005.

———. "Dance Liberation." *Theatre Journal* 55.3 (2003): vii-xxiv.

Rouse, John. "Comment: Special Issue; Historicizing Bodies." *Theatre Journal* 49.4 (Dec. 1997): iv-v.

Rydell, Robert W. *All the World's a Fair: Visions of Empire at American International Expositions.* Chicago: University of Chicago Press, 1984.

Salanga, Alfredo Navarro, Lilia Quindoza Santiago, Reuel Molina Aguila, and Her-minio S. Beltran Jr. *Kamao: Panitikan ng Protesta, 1970-1986, Dula.* Manila, Philip-pines: Center for Literature Cultural Center of the Philippines, 1987.

Salman, Michael. *The Embarrassment of Slavery: Controversies over Bondage and Nationalism in the American Colonial Philippines.* Berkeley: University of California Press, 2001.

Salonga, Lea. Personal communication. Makati, Metro Manila, Philippines. Nov. 2007.

———. Interviewed in *Terry Wogan Show.* 1989. Youtube: http://www.youtube.com/watch?v=Tolmg-iCZsg. 1 March 2008.

San Juan, Epifanio, Jr. "One Hundred Years of Producing and Reproducing the Fili-pino." *Amerasia Journal: Essays into American Empire in the Philippines; Part I. Pre Legacies, Heroes, Identity* 24.2 (1998): 1–33.

———. "From National Allegory to the Realization of a Joyful Subject." *Amerasia Jour-nal* 21.3 (Winter 1995-1996): 137-53.

San Juan, Ron. "The *Miss Saigon* Page." Updated 1 March 2006. http://www.rsjdfg.com/MSPage. 29 May 2012.

Schirmer, D. Boone, and Stephen Shalom, eds. *The Philippines Reader: A History of Colo-nialism, Neocolonialism, Dictatorship, and Resistance.* Boston: South End Press, 1987.

Schönberg, Claude-Michel. "This Photograph Was for Alain and I the Start of Every-thing." *Miss Saigon.com.* N.d. http://www.miss-saigon.com/theshow/inspirations.htm. 24 Feb. 2008.

Sell, Mike. "The Black Arts Movement: Performance, Neo-Orality, and the Destruc-tion of the 'White Thing.'" In *African American Performance and Theater History: A Critical Reader.* Eds. Harry J. Elam Jr. and David Krasner. Oxford: Oxford Univer-sity Press, 2001. 56-80.

Seniors, Paula Marie. *Beyond "Lift Every Voice and Sing": The Culture of Uplift, Identity, and Politics in Black Musical Theater.* Columbus: Ohio State University Press, 2009.

Shah, Nayan. *Contagious Divide: Epidemics and Race in San Francisco's Chinatown.* Berkeley: University of California Press, 2001.

Shalom, Stephen, and Daniel Boone Schirmer, eds. *The Philippines Reader: A History of Colonialism, Neocolonialism, Dictatorship, and Resistance.* Boston: South End Press, 1987.

Shank, Theodore. *Beyond the Boundaries: American Alternative Theatre.* Ann Arbor: University of Michigan Press, 2002.

Sharpe, Jenny. *Ghosts of Slavery: A Literary Archaeology of Black Women's Lives.* Min-neapolis: University of Minnesota Press, 2003.

Shimakawa, Karen. *National Abjection: The Asian American Body Onstage*. Durham, NC: Duke University Press, 2002.

"Shoo Fly, Don't Bother Me!" *Wikipedia*. Last modified 12 Dec. 2011. http://en.wikipedia.org/wiki/Shoo_Fly,_Don%27t_Bother_Me. 18 June 2010.

Sitton, Tom, and William Deverall, eds. *Metropolis in the Making: Los Angeles in the 1920s*. Berkeley: University of California Press, 2001.

Solomon, Alisa. "Porto Alegre Postcard." *The Nation*, 21 March 2005, 18.

———. "Up Front: Change the World; It Needs It." *Theater* 35.3 (2005): 3-5.

Srinivasan, Priya. *Sweating Saris: Indian Dance as Transnational Labor*. Philadelphia: Temple University Press, 2011.

———. "The Bodies beneath the Smoke; or, What's Behind the Cigarette Poster: Unearthing Kinesthetic Connections in American Dance History." *Discourses in Dance* 4.1 (2007): 7-48.

Tadiar, Neferti. *Fantasy Production: Sexual Economies and Other Philippine Consequences for the New World Order*. Quezon City, Philippines: Ateneo De Manila University Press, 2004.

———. "Filipinas 'Living in a Time of War.'" In *Body Politics: Essays on Cultural Representations of Women's Bodies*. Ed. Odine de Guzman. Quezon City, Manila: University of the Philippines Center for Women's Studies, 2002. 1-18.

Takaki, Ronald. 1989. *Strangers from a Different Shore: A History of Asian Americans*. Boston: Little, Brown, 1989.

Talusan, Mary. "Music, Race, and Imperialism: The Philippine Constabulary Band at the 1904 St. Louis World Fair." *Philippine Studies* 52.4 (2004): 499-526.

tan, joel b. "Ignacio—in 2 parts." In *Monster: Poems*. 2002.

"Taxi Dancers Start Filipinos on Wrong Foot." *Los Angeles Times*, 2 Feb. 1920. A1.

Taylor, Diana. *The Archive and the Repertoire: Performing Cultural Memory in the Americas*. Durham, NC: Duke University Press, 2003.

"Teaching English to Sixty-Nine Different Tribes." *Portland Oregonian*, 17 Sept. 1905. 44.

Thiong'o, Ngugi wa. "The Language of African Theatre." In *Radical Street Performance: An International Anthology*. Ed. Jan Cohen Cruz. London: Routledge, 1998. 238-44.

———. *Penpoints, Gunpoints, and Dreams: Towards a Critical Theory of the Arts and the State in Africa*. Oxford: Clarendon, 1998.

———. *Decolonising the Mind: The Politics of Language in African Literature*. Portsmouth, NH: Heinemann, 1986.

Tiffee. "In Love with Jesus." *Multiply.com*. http://tiffee.multiply.com/journal/item/9. http://tiffee.multiply.com/journal/item/9. 24 Feb. 2009.

Tiongson, Nicanor, Jr., ed. *Makiisa: The Philippine Experience: Proceedings and Anthology of Essays, Poems, Songs, Skits, and Plays of the MAKIISA 1, People's Culture Festival*. Manila: Philippine Educational Theater Association in cooperation with People's Resource Collection, Philippine Assistance for Rural and Urban Development, 1984.

Tolentino, Roland. "Transvestites and Transgressions: Panggagaya in Philippine Gay Cinema." *Journal of Homosexuality* 39.3/4 (2000): 325-37.

———. "Bodies, Letters, Catalogs: Filipinas in Transnational Space." *Social Text* 48 (Autumn 1996): 49-76.

Toribio, Helen. "Dare to Struggle: The KDP and Filipino American Politics." In *Legacy to Liberation: Politics and Culture of Revolutionary Asian Pacific America*. Ed. Fred Ho with Carolyn Antonio, Diane Fujino, and Steve Yip. San Francisco: AK Press and Big Red Media, 2000. 31-46.

———. "We Are Revolution: A Reflective History of the Union of Democratic Pilipinos." *Amerasia* 24.2 (1998): 155-77.

Tygiel, Jules. "Metropolis in the Making." In *Metropolis in the Making: Los Angeles in the 1920s*. Eds. Tom Sitton and William Deverell. Berkeley: University of California Press, 2001. 1-10.

Tyner, James. "Constructions of Filipina Migrant Entertainers." *Gender, Place, and Culture: A Journal of Feminist Geography* 3.1 (1996): 77-93.

———. "The Gendering of Philippine International Labor Migration." *Professional Geographer* 48.4 (Nov. 1996): 405-16.

Vanderkooi, Ronald. Preface to *Taxi-Dance Hall: A Sociological Study in Commercialized Recreation and City Life*, by Paul Cressey. Chicago: University of Chicago Press, 1969. i-xxv.

Van Erven, Eugene. *Playful Revolution: Theatre and Liberation in Asia*. Bloomington: Indiana University Press, 1992.

Vanzi, Sol Jose. "Monique Wilson Has Mixed Feelings about *Miss Saigon*." *Philippine Headline News Online*. 24 May 2000. http://www.newsflash.org/2000/05/sb/sb00122.htm. 14 Feb 2008.

Vaughan, Christopher A. "Ogling Igorots: The Politics and Commerce of Exhibiting Cultural Otherness." In *Freakery: Cultural Spectacles of the Extraodinary Body*. Ed. Rosemarie Garland Thompson. New York: New York University Press, 1996. 219–33.

Vedder, Clyde. "An Analysis of the Taxi-Dance Hall as a Social Institution, with Special Reference to Los Angeles and Detroit." Diss. University of Southern California, 1947.

Vengua, Jean. "Filipinos in the Midwestern Chautauqua Circuit." *our own voice* literary ezine. July 2004. Web. 13 Aug. 2010.

"Verbatim: Monique Wilson." *Gibbs Cadiz Blogspot*. 6 Nov. 2006. www.gibbscadiz.blogspot.com/2006/11/verbatim-monique-wilson.html. 14 Feb. 2008.

Vergara, Benito, Jr. *Displaying Filipinos: Photography and Colonialism in Early-Twentieth- Century Philippines*. Quezon City, Manila: University of Philippines Press, 1996.

Vermette, Margaret. *The Musical World of Boublil and Schönberg: The Creators of Les Miserables, Miss Saigon, Martin Guerre, and The Pirate Queen*." New York: Applause Theatre and Cinema Books, 2007.

Viesca, Victor. "With Style: Filipino Americans and the Making of Urban Culture." *our own voice* literary ezine. Jan. 2003. Web. 6 Sept. 2010.

Vinluan, Ermena. "Travels of a Cultural Gypsy." In *Cultural Activism and the KDP's Sining Bayan: Memoirs, Historical and Critical Articles*. Collected for F.I.N.D.S. Conference. Cambridge, MA: Harvard University, 1999. Unpaginated.

———. Interview with Roberta Uno. New York, NY. June 1996.

Vostral, Sharra. "Imperialism on Display: The Philippine Exhibition at the 1904 World's Fair." *Gateway Heritage, Magazine of the Missouri Historical Society* 13.4 (1993): 18-31.

Ward, Lydia Avery Coonley. *An Evening Trip to the St. Louis Fair*. N.p., 1904.

"Which Way to the Philippines?" *New York Times*, 17 July 1904.

W.I.C. "Marriage: Miscegenation." *California Law Review* 22.1 (1933): 116-17.

Williams, Raymond. *Keywords: A Vocabulary of Culture and Society*. New York: Oxford University Press, 1985.

Wilson, Monique. "Biography." http://www.moniquewilson.com/bio1.php. 29 May 2012.

Winter, Marian Hannah. "Juba and American Minstrelsy." In *The Minstrel Mask: Readings in Nineteenth-Century Blackface Minstrelsy*. Eds. Annemarie Bean, James V. Hatch, and Brooks McNamara. Hanover, NH: Wesleyan University Press, 1996. 223-41.

Wolfe, George C. *The Colored Museum*. New York: Grove, 1988.

"XVth Amendment." Harp Week. 12 March 1870. http://harpweek.com/09Cartoon/BrowseByDateCartoon.asp?Month=March&Date=12. 14 June 2010. Cartoon.

Yew, Chay. "A Beautiful Country. " *Hyphenated American: Four Plays*. New York: Groove Press, 2002. 167-275.

Yoshihara, Mari. "The Flight of the Japanese Butterfly: Orientalism, Nationalism, and Performances of Japanese Womanhood." *American Quarterly* 56.4 (Dec. 2004): 975-1001.

Yoshikawa, Yoko. "The Heat Is on *Miss Saigon* Coalition: Organizing across Race and Sexuality." In *The State of Asian America: Activism and Resistance in the 1990s*. Ed. Karin Aquilar-San Juan. Cambridge, MA: South End Press, 1994. 275-94.

Young, Cynthia. *Soul Power: Culture, Radicalism, and the Making of a U.S. Third World Left*. Durham, NC: Duke University Press, 2006.

Zero 3. Performed as part of *POMO* Festival 2002. Performance.

INDEX

ABOUT THE AUTHOR

Lucy Mae San Pablo Burns is an associate professor of Asian American Studies at the University of California Los Angeles. She is also a dramaturg.